Free Fall

SHERRY HOSTLER

WAGGLING
WOO

Cover design by Jessica Bell

Published by Waggling Woo/Sherry Hostler

www.sherryhostler.com

ISBN: 978 1 7396832 2 1

DEDICATION

G'Day me ol cobber. Good on ya mate for passing on your bonzer skills. It's been hard yakka, and I've been flat out like a lizard drinking, but it's all no drama. Grab a sambo and a stubby from the esky and I hope you're stoked. Fair dinkum

Translation:

For my wonderful Dad to whom I will always be thankful for passing on his creative genes. It's been hard work writing this book, but now it's finally finished. I truly hope you enjoy it.

ONE

A seven o'clock start in the conference room of a drab hotel was the epitome of everything that was crap in my life right now.

My alarm had gone off at home at six in the morning, and if I hadn't left my work clothes out the night before, I would have been sorely tempted to just head off into the dark, rainy morning still wearing my dressing gown and slippers. At least I didn't have to worry about waking Alex up as I stumbled around the bedroom. He was away on yet another glamorous work trip to who knows where.

I've never been a morning person, and weeks ago when my boss had strongly suggested that I might like to go along to the local small business networking group as a representative of *Pasternacki & Co, Solicitors*, I had tried my hardest to talk him out of it. I was a lowly PA; wouldn't it be better to send a solicitor? Someone who actually knew what they were talking about? Who'd drum up business more ably for the firm?

Unfortunately, he was having none of it and try as I might, he'd just raised an eyebrow and told me to sign up before striding back to his office and closing his door behind him. I was the cheapest option for the weekly event as I didn't have billable hours to waste. The discussion was over - as was the open-door policy.

And so, I now found myself ensconced in a bland hotel meeting room, as I did every Tuesday morning, with several other cheaply suited individuals, all wearing curling name badges along with an air of tired acceptance of their fate. The only slightly redeeming feature was a long table dressed in a starched white tablecloth, bearing what claimed to be breakfast.

My stomach rumbled, so I surreptitiously wandered over and selected a lukewarm bacon bap and an equally lukewarm glass of orange juice. Even the lure of breakfast was a letdown.

After a good five minutes of chewing and regretfully swallowing, followed by twenty minutes of uncomfortable conversation with various accountants and electricians, we were shepherded towards some seating which had been laid out, ready for the main event. Ten short rows of bright blue fabric-covered chairs all faced forwards to a lonely-looking flip chart and a balding man who was dressed entirely in beige.

No doubt he was really passionate about his topic, but he was no David Attenborough, and bearing in mind the early hour and my lack of attention span when it came to anything involving numbers, it didn't bode well for me being able to stay awake for the entire session. All in all, it was a blessing that the chairs were so uncomfortable, as it meant I had to keep shifting position before I could drift off.

At least I'd managed to secure a seat towards the back of the room behind a tall man, so our speaker couldn't see when my eyes did eventually start to droop after an in-depth break down of turnover versus profit. I'll just close my eyes for a bit, I thought. Just for five minutes.

A sharp poke on my left arm made me realise that maybe I actually had lost consciousness for a little while, and I turned, startled, to the man seated next to me, who had a look of amusement on his face.

"You were snoring," he stage-whispered at me.

I whipped my head around at the rest of the audience, none of whom seemed to be in the least disturbed by any unwitting noises that I might have made. I turned back to my neighbour who was now silently laughing, his shoulders shaking while no sound came from his mouth whatsoever.

"Oh my God! I was *not* snoring!" I mouthed at him. He carried on chortling under his breath, and I had no choice but to join in. "You git!"

I hadn't seen him at the networking group on the previous occasions that I'd dragged myself along. He was undoubtedly one of the handfuls of visitors that ventured along every so often to see if the group would be beneficial to join. Although of course, there were a lot of members who rarely even made it to the early morning breakfast meetings at all, choosing instead to stay in the sanctity of their beds. I didn't really blame them, as the food wasn't worth getting up for and the small talk was often exactly that…small.

I would definitely have remembered this guy though. He was around my age, maybe a little bit older, perhaps forty-ish. Tousled brown hair with a fair amount of grey peppering. Actually, on closer inspection, it was more grey with a peppering of brown. But it was nice, and it suited him, as did the designer reading glasses that he pushed up his nose when he bent over his notepad to write something down.

Yes, yes…I knew I was married, for what it was worth lately, but it didn't hurt to look, did it? A bit of harmless window shopping. This particular shop window did make me consider what my own reflection might be, though, and it kind of made me wish that I'd made a bit more effort in getting dressed that morning. In fact, *any* effort would have been good.

After another twenty minutes of mind-numbing accounting rhetoric, during which time I mentally picked out the outfit from my wardrobe that I *should* have worn this morning, and taking lots of furtive glances to my left, the group was blessed with a ten-minute comfort break so that we could either dose up on coffee at the back of the room or make a bid for freedom through the toilet window.

Leaving my coat on the back of my chair, I shuffled over to the caffeine station along the back wall of the room with the rest of the pack, where we battled with pots of coffee and those stupid flimsy wooden sticks that you get given to stir hot drinks with.

"God forbid they should trust us with spoons," came a voice from over my shoulder, as my wooden stick buckled like an over-dunked rich tea biscuit. I knew it was him before I even turned round.

Laughing, I replied, "Well at least I can use these to prop my eyes open."

He grinned at me, one side of his mouth lifting slightly higher than the other, giving him a wry laconic look. "I'm Saul," he told me, holding out his cardboard coffee cup. "Cheers!"

"Cheers!" We clinked. "I'm Ellie."

"So, Ellie, what's a nice girl like you doing sleeping in a place like this?"

"Hmmm. Well, I wasn't actually given a choice. I'm here at the behest of my boss." I swallowed some rapidly cooling coffee. "How about you?"

He gazed down at his cup. "Oh, well, I'm here to practice my meditation technique. There's nothing more calming than listening to the soothing muttering of words and numbers to allow one to drift into a place of Nirvana."

I can thoroughly recommend never to try and snort coffee. It hurts, and it doesn't look attractive, but unfortunately, it's the byproduct of someone making you laugh, mid-sip. Luckily for me, Saul had chosen that moment to close his eyes and give me an '*Om*' for emphasis. I swallowed the coffee and gave my nose a quick swipe with the back of my hand. Good God, I was like the love child of Bridget Jones and Stan Laurel.

Saul clicked his fingers in front of his face. "And I'm back in the room. What did I miss?"

"Absolutely nothing," I told him, my nostrils reeking of Nescafe.

From behind me came a sharp clapping of hands followed by an instruction from our esteemed leader to reclaim our seats. The second half of the show was about to start.

"Here." Saul handed me two wooden stirrers. "Just in case."

I giggled girlishly. Well, as girlishly as you can as a tired thirty-seven-year-old. I swatted at him with the stirrers, while he ducked out of reach.

Back in our seats, I settled in to accept my fate of sixty more minutes of hell, albeit this time with a compadre to suffer alongside me. I'd noticed that he wasn't wearing a wedding ring, which meant that either he wasn't married, or he was just one of those men who 'didn't like jewellery' - in other words, they wanted other women to think they were single.

I had also clocked the fact that he was wearing what looked like a decent suit. Not that I recognised things like that. Suits to me are pretty much like cars...grey ones, blue ones, black ones...This was a dark grey one and it fitted him well, as did the shirt underneath, I noticed, when he took his jacket off.

I knew it was morally wrong, but I had to fill my mind with something to stay awake. The lecture certainly wasn't going to do it and I had been spending so much time on my own lately that it was fun to have someone to giggle with. My best friend Helen wasn't around anymore after moving away to be with Christine; and Alex…well, these days he was what you would call 'married to the job'.

I wasn't even sure what his job was anymore. It had morphed so many times over the last few months. All I knew was that it was with a big multinational bicycle manufacturer that had offices all over the world. Offices that he frequently got to visit. Without me.

He never used to travel for work when we first met. In fact, he helped out in a bicycle shop down the road from my flat and was the only man I had ever known who didn't look like a complete fool in a bike helmet. It was lucky, bearing in mind he was a professional mountain biker. Sadly, the same could not be said for me, but fortunately, he'd managed to look past that flaw, or maybe he just never even saw it.

I twisted the pendant which graced my neck round and round on its chain as I remembered the first time I'd visited that shop eight years ago to buy a cycle bell as a stocking filler for a friend. By the time Alex and I finally got together, I had bought myself a bike, helmet, pump, lock, hi-vis jacket, shoes and a second bell, most of which now lay under a fine sheen of dust in the garage. The things we do for love, eh?

These days, though, we had become more like housemates than husband and wife. Somehow it had become safer to pretend nothing bad was happening. I was sad and he was sad, but it was easier to be sad apart than together.

And here we were, Alex in some country or other promoting a great new product for the big corporate conglomerate he worked for, and me in some soulless hotel meeting room amongst a group of strangers who couldn't give a damn if I was there or not. Other than one, it seemed. The only one who had shown an interest in me as an individual as opposed to the slightly grumpy face of *Pasternacki & Co*.

I realised I hadn't asked who Saul worked for and took a sneaky peak at the lapel of his jacket as he leaned forward to put his coffee cup on the garish carpet between his feet. One of the rules of the group was that we all had to wear a sticker which announced to all and sundry who we were and what company we worked for. Helpful, when you couldn't remember someone’s name, but it did mean you had to keep taking sideways glances at their chest which at best, was awkward, or at worst, could land you a sexual harassment charge.

He wore the obligatory sticker, but all it offered was the word ‘Visitor’. Oh well. I’d probably never see him again anyway if he had any sense.

By the time the onerous session came to an end, I had been monopolised by Melanie who was sitting on the other side of me. She ran a small marketing company and needed some advice about how to get one of her clients to pay up. Advice which I couldn't offer whatsoever due to my status within my firm. That, and the fact that I worked in the conveyancing department.

Rudely staring over her shoulder, I could see Saul manoeuvering himself towards the exit without even a second glance in my direction. Stupidly, I felt disappointed. God alone knows why. I was married! Happily married. OK, that was a lie. I used to be happily married and now I was just co-existing. It had been nice to get some attention for a change. A moment of pretending I was someone else. Someone worth being with.

"Cute, isn't he?" Melanie had followed my line of sight.

"What? Oh, him. I hadn't noticed."

TWO

The following week, I took a little more care over my outfit for the networking group. It had nothing to do with the fact that Saul might be there again. I was obligated to make a good impression on behalf of *Pasternacki & Co*. At least that's what I told myself.

Alex was home for once, although I hadn't seen anything of him. His flight had got in late the night before, so I was in bed long before he got home, cuddled up to Mr Jones, my regular nighttime companion. Poor old Mr Jones. Always slightly aloof in his nature, our five-year-old Maine Coon cat had taken on the unwanted mantle of being the main man in my life since Alex had started travelling more. He tolerated my affections with a great deal of huffiness, but I was convinced he secretly loved it really.

I'd heard Alex come in at about midnight, but I knew that as it was so late, he'd make himself a cup of tea and then go to bed in the spare room. He was nothing if not thoughtful. I briefly considered getting up and putting the kettle on for the both of us, but I couldn't stand the idea of forced conversation in the early hours of the morning. Instead, I rolled over, finding the cool side of my pillow, and listened to his predictable movements downstairs. The kettle boiling, the click of the teaspoon in the mug, and the TV being turned on quietly to watch some sport.

When my alarm went off, I was alone in bed. Even Mr Jones had left my side, whether for a night of carousing or to find Alex I didn't know. Little traitor.

I had purposely set my alarm to give me an extra half an hour to get ready this morning. It was about time that I started taking more care of my appearance. Just because Alex never looked at me that way anymore, didn't mean that I couldn't make an effort for myself.

And so, I dressed myself in my smartest work suit with a blouse showing just a suggestion of cleavage. 'Office cleavage', if you will. My well-worn ballet pumps had been left in the bottom of the wardrobe and instead I had dug out a pair of heels from the back to torture myself with. They pinched the hell out of my toes, but sod it, they looked amazing. So long as I didn't have to walk too far.

I'd washed my hair the night before so for once it didn't have to be scraped back with a hairband, and I had even dug out my liquid eyeliner, painting a slick above my lash line. This was a new me.

It had absolutely nothing to do with Saul. Nothing. The fact that someone had bothered to speak to me at a networking meeting about anything other than getting recommendations for their business or quizzing me about how to solve minor disputes was not worth this much effort.

Oh, who was I kidding? The fact that someone had actually *seen* me for a change had lifted my spirits. Someone had taken the time to joke with me and flirt with me a little and it had made me feel on top of the world. *That* was the reason why I was making more of an effort to shine. I wished I'd put some plasters in my bag for the blisters that were already forming on my heels, though.

One of the first through the doors to the conference room for a change, I didn't even bother with my usual bacon bap. I didn't want to run the risk of the light dusting of flour from the bread falling down the lapel of my suit, or any wayward pieces of rind lodging between my teeth. Instead, I helped myself to a strong coffee and perched my bottom on the back of one of the chairs, which eased the pressure that my high heels were already putting on my toes.

Slowly, the room started filling up with the usual suspects, but there was no sight of Saul. Not that it mattered. Not that it made any difference whatsoever. I was there as the face of *Pasternacki & Co* and that was it.

I briefly wondered if Alex was up yet. He often worked at home the day after he got back from a trip. I used to love those days, and I'd sometimes even take the day off work myself so that we could spend a bit more time together, but they'd just become more and more awkward lately. I felt a frown deepen on my forehead as I wondered whether he sometimes felt like an intruder in his own home. Increasingly, he would tuck himself away in the spare room with his laptop, only coming out to make tea or food when necessary. But if he was at home more, he wouldn't have to feel like that, would he?

"Hi Ellie, how's it going?"

With a sharp inhale, I turned around to see Dom, one of several shiny-suited insurance brokers in the group at my shoulder.

"Hey, you're looking really well." He seemed a little taken aback.

"Cheers, Dom. I thought I'd make a bit of an effort for a change."

"Good for you. How's work?"

Oh God, the first of many bouts of small talk was underway. “Yeah, great. The usual. Filing, typing, answering the phone. Just generally one big party.”

“Oh. Uh-huh, yes. Sure. Any big cases on the go?”

Seriously, did any of these people here know me at all? “No, Dom, I’m just a PA. Occasionally I get to make tea though…it’s a riot.”

“Yep, uh huh. I bet it is. Thought any more about getting some life insurance?”

“Um…not at the moment, I’m afraid.”

I needn’t even have answered as he was already looking past me to see who else he could speak to in the hope of boosting his sales figures for the month. I was a dead loss, with or without makeup and heels.

Half an hour and three more brain-numbing conversations later it was time to sit down and listen to the speaker. If I’d thought last week’s session was an antidote to insomnia, this one was even worse. Whoever thought it was a good idea to put an IT accounts manager in front of a room full of tired, bored people really needed a good talking to. I positioned myself in a chair towards the back of the room, as usual, and took one last look around the group to see if my saviour from the week before was anywhere to be seen, but it looked like he was going to be a no-show.

And why the hell would he turn up? He was only a visitor, the group was possibly the most boring, depressing thing on the earth to be a part of, and I was just some sad, lonely idiot to pass the time with. A sad, lonely idiot who had about as much allure as an old sock at this time of day, and who was married. Oh yeah…married.

With a deep sigh, I gave myself a mental kicking for being so stupid.

At least I could use the time to reflect on how bloody foolish I’d been in getting all trussed up to impress some

bloke I didn't even know. I had Alex at home, for God's sake. Maybe if I spent more time dressing to impress *him* then he wouldn't go away so often.

But then we'd tried that, hadn't we? We'd been down the stockings and suspenders route. I still cringed internally each time I thought about how I'd tried to emulate Julia Roberts in *Pretty Woman* and failed dismally. I'd drunk a glass of wine for Dutch courage before he was due home from one of his trips and then positioned myself in what I thought was an alluring manner on the sofa in nothing but one of his ties and a pair of stilettos.

"Wow, you look great," he'd said, seeming a little nonplussed as he put his briefcase down, and then gave me a peck on the cheek. "Is it OK if we do this a bit later, though? I'm totally wiped out."

I'd wanted to shout at him that no, it most definitely was not OK, but instead, I'd muttered that it was fine while reaching for some cushions to cover up my embarrassment. Even now, I could feel the memory heating my cheeks and I closed my eyes in shame.

After what felt like an interminable length of time, we were finally blessed with a comfort break, and I decided that there was no point in sticking around to listen to any more computer-related drivel. Under the pretence of popping to the toilet, I grabbed my coat and walked quickly down the long, ugly carpeted hallway back to reception and into the fresh morning air outside.

Fresh, other than the man having a long drag on a vape before exhaling a bloom of strangely scented smoke around him, and me. I walked through it like a contestant on Stars in Their Eyes, the vapour making me cough.

"Oh, sorry." The man turned, waving the fumes away.

"Saul!"

"Oh, hey. It's…Ellie, isn't it?"

I cursed myself for letting his name trip from my lips so easily when he'd obviously taken a moment to place me. I nodded.

"Had enough already this morning?" He grinned his lopsided smile at me which made me feel a little like one of those Victorian ladies who needed to reach for smelling salts when their knees went weak. "Or are you sleepwalking?" He *had* remembered me, and the joke instantly made me feel special.

"What are you doing out here?" I asked him. "Are you working up the courage to come in?"

"Yeah. Scary lot you networkers." He took another drag on his vape, this time blowing the smoke in the other direction, where the wind efficiently whisked it away. "The traffic was bloody awful this morning, so I just thought I'd wait until the break before coming in. Have I missed much?"

"Not unless you've got a major yearning to hear about computer maintenance." I grimaced.

He laughed, and it felt good. I couldn't remember the last time Alex had laughed at something I'd said. Actually, I couldn't remember the last time he'd laughed at all.

"Hmm." Saul squinted at me against the low-lying sun which had bravely sliced through the drizzly skies. "Why don't we do something controversial and bunk off ? Fancy a coffee?" My stomach fluttered with excitement. "That's if you've got time, of course. Maybe you're heading back to work?"

I glanced at my watch. I had just over an hour before I was expected back, and with the office only a ten-minute drive away, I had nothing to lose. "Why not?"

THREE

The coffee shop was cosy after the bitter early March air, and the windowpanes which faced the pavement outside had completely fogged up. A small corner of the glass had been partially cleared by a small child who sat, bored, painting hearts and houses on the foggy windowpane while her mother chatted to her friends about school gate gossip. I envied them a little and gave the girl a wave when she looked over. She ignored me, as did her mother who, I noticed, watched Saul making his way over to our table. I couldn't blame her.

He placed a tray in front of me with two frothy cups of cappuccino on it. "I got you a blueberry muffin too, but you can swap it for my chocolate one if you'd prefer."

I wasn't sure I'd be able to eat either of them, as my stomach fluttered with the novelty of having someone pay me attention, especially someone who looked like Saul did.

"So, what do you do at…*Pasternacki & Co*?"

Saul's eyes had flickered down to my chest, making me realise that I was still wearing my name badge from the morning meeting. God, how embarrassing. I hurriedly peeled it off, folded it over, and placed it in my coat pocket which hung on the back of my chair.

"Oh, you know, top lawyer."

One of Saul's eyebrows raised as he took a sip of his coffee. I was always impressed by people who could make their brows move independently of each other. "Really?"

"No, not really. I'm just a PA. That's my professional title. My actual role is 'dogs' body'."

"Ah, right." He put his cup down on its saucer and ran his hand through his hair, which had flopped over one eye. He looked at me sternly. "You should never do that, you know."

"What?"

"Put yourself down like that. Never say you're *just* anything. I'm sure you're bloody brilliant at what you do."

I picked at a bit of muffin, letting Saul's words sink in properly. He was right. I undervalued myself and the work that I did way too often, and it had become a habit. One that no-one else had tried to put a stop to, even Alex. To have someone point out that I was more worthy than I thought, made me feel validated.

"Point taken. What about you? I don't even know what you do."

"Ah, now that really is dull. I'm a mortgage advisor. I could tell you more, but I know what your attention span is like when it comes to talking about finance, and I don't seem to have any wooden sticks on hand to prop your eyes open. I'd much rather hear about you, anyway."

I couldn't tell if he was flirting or just being nice, but I found myself holding his gaze longer than I was used to and making an extra effort to be light and funny as I told him about some of our more interesting cases at work.

"And what about home?" he asked as I took time out to spoon some of the froth from the top of my cup into my mouth, not wanting to risk a foamy moustache. "Happily married?" He nodded towards my wedding ring. "Loads of ankle biters swarming around your legs?"

Isn't it funny how you reach a certain age, and everyone assumes you have children? I'd always thought I'd have children by this age, too, but after Alex's accident that was all put on the back burner. He'd assured me that it wasn't off the table completely, but by the same token, it wasn't really something that we spoke about much anymore. I wished someone would tell my ovaries to pipe down though as they didn't seem to have received the memo.

"I'm married," I admitted, spreading out the fingers on my left hand and noting the light glinting off my engagement ring before I tucked my hand out of sight beneath the table. I hated myself for the negative tone in my voice. I used to want to sing from the rooftops about being married, and not only that, but to the actual man of my dreams. Tall, blonde, slightly lanky but perfectly formed Alex. He was perfect. I just wished I knew what'd happened to him.

"Ah, so not *happily* married then?"

Saul's gaze was so steady that I found it hard to look away from it. In stark contrast, Alex could barely bring himself to look up when I walked into a room these days, so this kind of focus was both unusual and kind of mesmerising.

"Not so much lately," I whispered, quickly taking a sip of coffee, and using the oversized cup to cover my face.

"That's a shame." Saul's eyes were still on me as I lowered my cup. "You deserve to be happy. Hell, we all do." He grinned that lopsided smile again. Slightly self-deprecating.

"Are you not happy?" I asked him.

"Let's put it this way, I think we have a lot in common." He ran his hand through his hair again, before briefly closing his eyes, and stroking his neat beard. His hand stayed there, chin resting on its back, and I realised we were mirroring each other's positions.

"I guess life doesn't always pan out the way you expect it to, does it?" I asked.

"That's for sure. But I'm a firm believer that everything happens for a reason. Good or bad." He dropped his hand back onto the table. "And at the risk of sounding like a total cliché, we should make the most of the good things that come along."

I nodded. Clichés existed for a reason.

"Excuse me, are you done with that?" A waitress had materialised at the side of our table, gesturing towards our cups which were showing nothing more than coffee-coloured tidemarks around their rims. She was undoubtedly trying to move us along as I noted a small queue had formed at the serving counter.

"Thanks, yes we are." I pushed my crockery towards her.

"Hey, you haven't eaten your muffin," Saul pointed out as he scrunched up his wrapper and put it inside his empty cup. "Remember what we were saying about making the most of good things that come along?" He winked, making me laugh, and before the waitress could whisk the tray away, I grabbed it back from the plate.

"Starting now," I told him.

FOUR

Alex was fast asleep on the sofa when I got home from work, his snores competing with a background of sports commentary from the TV. I thought briefly about waking him, but decided to leave him to it, pulling the door closed behind me. Maybe I'd run myself a bath with that nice bubble bath that I'd bought last week.

I kicked off my shoes which were now absolutely killing my feet just as I'd suspected they would, and scooped Mr Jones up for a quick cuddle, bringing him with me as I made my way upstairs.

I pushed the bedroom door open and, if I didn't know better, I would have thought that we'd been burgled. Alex's scuffed leather travel bag lay open on top of the crisp white duvet and his dirty clothes were strewn all over the place.

"Oh, for God's sake," I huffed, putting Mr Jones down on the bed, where he immediately clambered inside the bag and curled up for a nap. "Seriously?" I asked him, scooping up Alex's clothes and chucking them in the laundry basket, noticing as I did so a smear of what looked like oil or grease on his decent pink shirt. God knows how that had got there but it was no doubt bicycle-related, and it would unquestionably be me trying to get the stain out when I did the washing.

Leaving the other man in my life snoozing on the bed, I went into the bathroom, poured a generous dollop of bubble bath into the tub, and turned on the taps. I decided that I should treat myself to a glass of wine to go with it and I padded back down the stairs and into the kitchen where Alex had also managed to leave his mark, like a dog scenting its territory. The remains of his lunch were left on the worktop. Crusts of bread and dried slices of tomato abandoned on the wooden chopping board along with an empty packet of crisps and a couple of teabags thrown into the sink. God, it wound me up so much. I couldn't understand why he wouldn't just walk the extra few steps to the bin.

I fished out the cold, wet teabags and put them and the rest of his leftovers in the bin before yanking open the fridge to find the wine. Thank God that was still where I'd left it. I poured myself a large glass and stomped back up the stairs to check on my bath. I couldn't care less if I woke him up now.

I knew that I shouldn't be feeling like this. I should be glad that he was home as I hadn't seen him for the best part of a week. But instead of wanting to curl up in his arms on the sofa, I just felt like he was intruding on my personal space. He was away so much now that I'd become used to living my own way and when he *was* home, I had started to resent it.

I ran my hands through the glistening bubbles in the bath and inhaled the aroma of jasmine which now filled the room. I needed this. A bath, wine, and some flickering candles to give me a bit of balance.

Maybe I'd give Helen a call later, too. That would make me feel a bit better. It always helped to have a good catch-up with my oldest friend in the world. I supposed I should really ask her how things were going with Christine. It had been about three months now since Helen had moved up to Birmingham to be with her. I knew it wasn't *that* far from Buckinghamshire, but it was far enough that we hardly got to see each other anymore. I missed her so much.

I sighed, clearing a patch on the fogged-up bathroom mirror so that I could see to take off my makeup. Remembering the little girl in the cafe earlier, I drew a heart shape underneath with my finger, and then traced an 'S' on the inside, smiling to myself. God, I was acting like a twelve-year-old with a crush. Stupid idiot. I couldn't help it though, and it wasn't like it was hurting anyone.

I rubbed the drawing away with my hand and leaned forward over the sink to wipe off my makeup. As I did so, my necklace swung forward from the confines of my top and the little pendant in the shape of a sycamore seed glinted under the halogen lights. I turned the charm around and around, twisting the delicate chain that it hung from, before pinching the chain at the top and releasing the charm, watching it spin round and round, just like the real thing, falling to earth from its tree.

I loved my necklace more than anything in the world, probably even more than my wedding ring. I knew that most people would frown at that, but it was a reminder of one of my happiest moments with my husband, and the twirling of that little golden sycamore seed took me back to that time whenever I spun it.

We'd only been together for about a year, and Alex had taken me on a killer bike ride, throughout which I'd moaned about the chill in the Autumn air, and the tightness of my cycle helmet. I hadn't wanted to go, but he'd been insistent.

"Come on," he'd cajoled. "It's a beautiful day!"

I’d huffed, and rolled over in bed, my head still a little tender after the wine we’d drunk the night before. “It’s too early.”

“It’s ten o’clock! Come on lazy bones. I promise you’ll love it.”

I’d dragged myself up and out on his insistence, and after the first gruelling thirty minutes, I’d had to agree that I was starting to enjoy myself, even though I wasn’t going to let Alex know.

We’d ended up at a beautiful woodland clearing where we stopped to rest under an impressive tree, its leaves swaying in the breeze, golden against the blue of the sky. Alex had unfurled a chequered blanket from his backpack, spreading it out on the grass, and the pair of us had collapsed on top of it.

“I don’t suppose you brought a drink, did you?” I was gasping for some water.

“It’s in my bag.” He’d poked me and grinned. “While you’re up.”

“Cheeky sod.” I’d swiped at him before turning and reaching over to his backpack which was just behind us at the base of the tree.

I had unzipped the top, expecting to find a big bottle of water to ease my thirst, and instead seen the glint of gold metal foil. Reaching in, I’d found a bottle of champagne and two plastic flutes. “Alex!” I’d laughed out loud, turning to face him. “What are you playing a—”

My boyfriend was on one knee, holding out a diamond ring to me. “Will you marry me, Ellie?”

I felt as though my heart would burst. I’d never expected to be so happy. “Oh my God, yes!” I’d dropped to my knees in front of him, with the champagne bottle still clenched in my grip. Alex had taken my other hand and pushed the perfectly flawless diamond onto my ring finger before taking my face in his hands and kissing me.

It was beautiful, that kiss, with the sun on my face, the scent of autumn in the air, and the breeze spiralling the sycamore seeds down from the tree around us like confetti. It could've been a scene from a movie.

On the morning of our wedding, he'd given me the sycamore seed necklace. We'd not seen each other that morning, of course, as that would've been bad luck; but he'd left it where I would find it. The thoughtfulness of the gift and the knowledge that he knew me so well had made me cry, as it did once again now as I held the tiny charm in my hand. I couldn't understand what had gone wrong.

With some regret, I removed the chain from my neck, letting it coil on the bathroom shelf. I then quickly undressed before sliding into the bath water and taking a large sip of wine. The cold liquid was at odds with the warmth of the bath, but it immediately made me feel a little better.

Maybe I should try to cut Alex a bit more slack. After all, he was undoubtedly knackered from travelling. But the logical devil on my shoulder argued back that it wouldn't hurt him to tidy up after himself or to actually try to be awake for me once I got home. Surely it wasn't too much to ask? It proved once again that he just didn't care anymore.

I took another sip of the crisp liquid, trying to shut out the inciting whispers before I revelled in my self-serving thoughts too much. I didn't want us to be like this, and I was sure Alex didn't either. The problem was that he was away all the time, and he worked such long hours that we'd just forgotten how to connect. He was busy, I was busy. We needed time out together. Perhaps I'd suggest a bike ride this weekend. It had been so long since we'd done one together. Like everything else about our relationship, Alex seemed to have lost his enthusiasm for those, too.

A knock on the bathroom door brought me out of my reverie. “Are you in the bath Ellie?”

“Yes. It’s OK, you can come in.” I’d sat up quickly, pulling my knees to my chest, aware that we were no longer at ease with each other’s nakedness.

The door opened and my husband’s tall frame edged its way into the room. I needn’t have bothered trying to cover my body as his eyes stayed fixed on the far wall, obviously not wanting to intrude on my privacy. Or maybe he just didn’t want to look at me anymore.

“Sorry about the mess everywhere,” he mumbled.

“It’s fine.”

“I should’ve tidied up, but I was just so knackered.”

“Really. It’s fine. Why don’t you grab a beer, and put the oven on? I’ll be down in a minute, and we can have some dinner together. You could tell me about your trip, and we could make some plans for this weekend if you like?”

Alex rubbed at his face, still staring away from me. “Yeah, sure. I’ll see you downstairs.” He started edging backwards then paused. His eyes flickered briefly in my direction. “Um, I did tell you about my next trip, didn’t I?”

“Yesss.” I drew out the word, resisting the urge to roll my eyes at the same time in case he saw. “It’s Friday next week, right?”

“Ahh.” I saw his Adam’s apple bob up and down as he swallowed.

“What?”

“It’s *this* Friday.”

FIVE

"What the—? Alex!"

It was too late. He'd retreated from the room, pulling the door closed behind him and leaving me to thrash my way out of my soft bubbled cocoon back into the cold reality that was our life. I hurriedly brushed off the remnants of soap that clung to my skin and wrapped my towelling robe around me.

Yanking the door open, I ran downstairs, all soothing thoughts of long-ago sunny days stomped on like Autumn leaves underfoot. I found Alex in the kitchen levering open a bottle of beer, with Mr Jones winding his way around his legs, leaving a trail of pale grey fur on the black material of Alex's jogging bottoms.

"Alex, you told me you were leaving for the convention *next* week!"

He looked up, startled. "Jesus, Ellie, I thought you were still in the bath." He held his hand to his heart.

Like he still has one, I thought meanly.

"You can't just drop a bombshell like that on me and bugger off."

He had the good grace at least to lower his head. "I'm sorry, Ellie. I know it's shit but there's nothing I can do about it. One of our clients in New York wanted to meet us before the convention starts so my boss brought the dates forward. I thought I told you."

"Oh, for God's sake, you're like their puppet. Every time they click their fingers you go running. What if we had plans? What if—"

"It's not my fault. It's my job. You know that. There's always been travel involved ever since I started."

"Not like this, though. It's crazy, Alex. You'll only be home for two days and then you'll be gone again. It's not fair." I cringed at my words which made me sound like a petulant teenager. I moved past him and plonked myself down on one of the high stools by the small breakfast bar, needing to lift my bare feet off the cold tiled floor. I wished I'd brought my wine down with me as I had a feeling that I might need it.

"I know." He picked at the label on his beer bottle, avoiding my eyes yet again. "It won't be forever, though."

"You say that, but it's already been too long. I know your accident changed your life irreparably, but it's changed mine, too!"

I watched my husband's shoulders slump and I felt guilty straight away. We didn't talk much about what had happened as he found it too distressing, but I was starting to wonder if maybe we should, instead of just bumbling along and pretending nothing had happened. After all, it really *was* life changing.

Being a professional bike rider had meant that Alex used to do lots of stunts for actors who didn't want to risk their own health and safety doing silly things when there were other people who were daft enough to do them instead. It wasn't even a big stunt that changed our lives forever, just some tricks on rails which Alex had done a thousand times before. It only took one bit of bad judgement, and it was his spine hitting the rail instead of the tyres.

Thankfully, he was one of the lucky ones and, while the accident brought about debilitating issues that we both had to deal with, he at least managed to escape a life of paralysis. Six months of hospital treatment and serious advice from a back specialist meant that he would never do another bike stunt again, though. His whole career and passion over, just like that.

It changed him. Of course, it did. And it meant that he had to get a regular job like the rest of us mere mortals. Unfortunately, though, his regular job meant that I hardly got to see him anymore.

"I'm sorry, Ellie." The words tripped far too familiarly from his tongue. It wasn't that he didn't mean them, but I was sick to death of hearing them. They didn't make anything better.

I gazed up to the ceiling for some inspiration, found none, and looked back at Alex. "I *know* you're sorry. I don't want you to be sorry for the accident because it wasn't your fault."

"But you're right, aren't you? Everything *did* change that day." He finally lifted his eyes, giving me a glimpse of regret. "It's because of the stupid accident that you can't have what you want. We both lost out. *I* can't do the job that I love, and I can't give *you* the family that you crave."

"We don't know that!"

Alex laughed bitterly. "Yes, we do." He knocked back a swig of beer before resting it on the counter and leaning against it.

"The doctor said it was unlikely, not impossible." I wanted to reach out to him, but his arms were folded tightly across his chest, his posture warding off any advance.

"Yes, Ellie. I remember it clearly. He still thought it was unlikely enough to suggest I froze my sperm though, didn't he? Just in case." A hint of steel had crept into Alex's tone.

I knew that he was hating every second of this conversation, but we had to have it. I hardened my resolve.

"Anyway, it's not like we get the opportunity to find out, is it?" I bated him further. "You're never here, and when you are it's like you're not interested in me anymore. You're just itching to get away again."

"Don't be bloody stupid." He glared at me.

"I'm *not* being stupid. You don't touch me; you barely even look at me. It's as though…" I didn't want to say the words out loud. It wasn't the first time that I'd wondered if there was anyone else. Some beautiful twenty-something at one of the overseas offices who'd caught his eye. I'd never thought Alex was that kind of man when I married him, but who knew, really? Time changes people and they say we never really know anyone, don't they?

"What Ellie? It's as though, what?"

I lifted my wet hair from my shoulders, conscious that it was dripping water down my back and soaking my robe. The movement allowed me some time to phrase things properly before ploughing in with accusations. "It's as though you don't want to be here."

He looked at me then, properly, and for a millisecond the glimmer of pain behind his eyes made me catch my breath. And then it was gone, back to dulled acceptance. "Of course, I do."

"Stay, then," I wheedled ridiculously, and he looked at me like a tolerant parent who was at the end of his tether. "At least hold me."

He waited for a beat but eventually wrapped my frame inside his arms so that I could lay my head on his chest. I could hear his heart beating, proving that he did indeed have one, after all.

"Do you still love me?" I couldn't help myself.

Ba-dum replied his heart. *Ba-dum*.

"Of course, I do."

Ba-dum.

"Then don't go."

Ba-dum. Ba-dum.

"I wouldn't if I didn't have to, but I don't have any choice."

I felt like I'd already lost him.

SIX

"Who's the hot guy waiting for you in reception?" Layla, the new receptionist, asked as she loitered behind me at my workstation.

"Eh?" I pressed send on the email I'd been typing and swivelled my chair around to face her.

"There's a guy in reception." She gestured in the general direction of the front desk which was obscured by the partitions of the office. "He said he's come to take you out to lunch."

Alex's flight must have been delayed. I'd been waiting all morning for him to give me a call before he boarded his plane to New York, but I hadn't heard anything. I knew that it wasn't due to take off until 2pm but perhaps it had been put back a few hours. He must have listened to what I'd said about us making more of an effort for each other and came to my office to surprise me.

"Oh right, you've not met Alex before, have you?" I said, pulling my hair out of its tight ponytail and reaching into my bag for my lipstick and a mirror. Layla had only been with the firm for a few weeks and while we got on really well during working hours, our friendship was yet to develop outside of the office environment.

"Alex?" Layla perched her brightly-clad bottom on the edge of my desk, flicking her long, bejewelled braids over her shoulder as she did so.

"Yes. Alex. You know, my husband."

"Oh right. Sorry, I forgot that was his name. It's not him though because this guy said his name's Saul."

I snapped my mirror shut. Saul? Bloody hell. I tried unsuccessfully to hide the tingle of excitement which must have flickered across my face, as Layla raised a perfectly shaped eyebrow at me. This was a turn-up for the books. I couldn't remember telling him the address of where I worked, but how lovely of him to look me up. Long gone were the days when Alex would have done something like that, so I should have realised that it wasn't him who'd come to take me out for lunch.

I stood up, smoothing out the creases in my shirt from where I'd been seated at my desk all morning.

"You look fine," Layla appraised me, making me feel suddenly self-conscious.

With Layla hot on my tail, I rounded the corner to the reception area and found Saul seated on the edge of one of the two long navy sofas that flanked either side of the room like sentinels. He was flicking through a dog-eared magazine but stood as soon as he saw me, placing it back on the nearest coffee table with the rest of the well-fingered reading material. I couldn't help but notice how good he looked. Poor old Alex always seemed somewhat uncomfortable in a suit, but Saul's suit appeared as though it had been stitched on around him.

"Hey, Ellie." He pushed his hair back from his face in what was becoming a familiar gesture. "How're you doing?"

"Hi!" We both stepped towards each other, and he leaned in to kiss my cheek, leaving me no option but to reciprocate. I came away feeling almost heady. He smelt amazing. "This is a surprise."

He laughed. "Yeah. I hope you don't mind. I was just passing and saw the sign for *Pasternacki & Co.* I remembered it was where you worked, so thought I'd just pop in on the off chance. See if you were free for lunch?"

"Oh. Right. Yes, well, I'd love to." I looked at my watch. "Although I've got a meeting in half an hour." Damn it.

"No worries. It was just on the off chance anyway." Saul backed away a little. "I should've called, but I don't have your number. I…look, never mind." He seemed embarrassed and I immediately felt bad for him. It had been lovely to have him turn up with the offer of lunch, and I hated to have to turn him down.

"Look, I can grab a few minutes. Why don't we just go for a stroll in the park over the road? It was quite nice outside last time I looked out the window."

"Sure, why not."

It *was* a beautiful day, and, despite the sharp bite of the March wind, when the sun peeked around the clouds and graced my skin, it instantly warmed me up.

It seemed like we weren't the only people who'd had the idea of making the most of their lunch breaks in the park either as office workers were scattered around on benches eating sandwiches from paper bags, and a group of young children littered the grass with a noisy game of tag.

We wandered slowly, side by side, along the gravel pathway lined with daffodils which meandered its way through the small park. While the trees weren't yet fully dressed in greenery due to the cold winter months, it warmed my heart to see some blossoms starting to colour the sky.

"Lovely, isn't it?" Saul had followed my gaze.

"My favourite," I told him with a smile. "One day I'd like to go to Japan to see the cherry blossom during Hanami. It's on my bucket list."

"That'd be amazing." I felt Saul's eyes on me. "Why haven't you done it already?"

"Oh, you know…one thing or another." I didn't want to tell him that Alex and I had been supposed to go there for my thirty-fifth birthday. Two whole years ago now. Of course, it had been called off after Alex's bike accident, which was fair enough, but the prospect had not come up again since. We'd actually not gone anywhere together following the accident, even though Alex was away on work trips all the time without me. I supposed I felt a bit cheated if I was honest with myself. "What about you?" I turned the tables on Saul. "Ever been to Japan?"

"Nope. But I'd like to one day. It's the kind of place you go to with someone special, isn't it? Hey look, there's a bench over there. Shall we sit?" He gestured to a weathered-looking bench before nudging me playfully with his elbow. "Or shall we just hop on the next plane to Japan? I'm game if you are!"

I knew it was just a silly joke, but as I stole a look at his lopsided smile, and his hazel eyes which had crinkled at the outer edges with good humour, the temptation to throw caution to the wind and book a flight immediately was immense.

Instead, I laughed away his expansive offer, taking him up on his first, more reasonable suggestion. We sat down, and I closed my eyes, holding my face up to the sun and letting the rays wash over my skin, dulled by months of winter.

"So, is there no one special in your life, then?" I was brave with my eyes closed.

"Not anymore."

There was a hint of sadness in his tone, and I turned to see him hunched over, arms resting on his knees, his gaze firmly on the ground beneath his well-shined shoes.

"I'm sorry, I didn't mean to pry."

"Hey, it's fine." He looked up at me. "Onwards and upwards, eh? Like I said the other day, if something isn't right, you just have to move on, don't you." He grinned that lopsided smile of his.

"Don't you think some things are worth fighting for?" I asked.

"Maybe, maybe not. Maybe you shouldn't have to fight so hard if things are right in the first place."

My fingers went to my necklace. I knew Saul was talking about his own situation, but I couldn't help but see the reflections of my own. It all seemed like an effort with Alex at the moment. I turned my sycamore seed pendant around and around, along with Saul's words. He had a point. Surely relationships shouldn't be such hard work. It's not like I wanted much from Alex, was it? Just to feel…I didn't know what. Wanted…loved…special.

The day we were supposed to fly off to Japan, I'd gone with Alex to one of his physio appointments. He still wasn't able to drive, so I'd take him and sit and watch the sessions from the sidelines instead of just waiting outside in the car. I knew he hated me being there, hated me seeing him so weak. I hated it too. He was supposed to be the strong one in our relationship, and it broke my heart to see him unable to do the simplest movements that his therapist asked him to do.

That particular day, we were both fed up. Alex was struggling to deal with his fragility, and I was struggling to deal with Alex. All I could think of while he swore and sulked his way through his physio session was how unfair this new shitty life was. In a parallel universe, we were on the trip of a lifetime to Maruyama Park in Kyoto where we'd planned to celebrate my birthday underneath the cherry blossom trees. Instead, we were both stuck in our local hospital, in an ugly room full of complicated equipment, and steeped in the frustration of my husband. It was a poor substitute.

I knew that in the greater scheme of things, we had to go through this, and getting Alex better was more important than anything else, but I still couldn't help feeling like life had struck us a crappy blow. I'd felt cheated and forgotten and I'd made the mistake of telling him how I felt. As the words had come out of my mouth, they'd sounded selfish even though I hadn't meant them to. I really hadn't. But I guessed they sounded that way to Alex as he'd told me not to bother coming to his sessions anymore. In fact, he'd told me to piss off altogether.

I felt tears springing up in my eyes at the memory and I tried to blink them away, not wanting Saul to see.

"Shit, are you OK? Oh my God, you're crying."

"It's fine. I'm fine. It's just the wind making my eyes water." I swiped at my eyes with the back of my hand.

Saul's expression told me he didn't believe me. "Hang on, here, take my handkerchief. It's clean, I promise." He held out a white cotton handkerchief and the sweet gallantry of the gesture made me want to cry even more. "I'm so sorry. I didn't mean to make you cry. I should keep my opinions to myself."

"It's not you, honestly." I dabbed at my eyes with the soft material, grateful that Saul had such an old-fashioned yet charming habit of carrying an actual handkerchief. "It's just that what you said made me think."

"Ah. Thinking's overrated sometimes." He smiled and patted my hand with his, letting it rest there a heartbeat longer than necessary. "Your hand's cold." He picked it up and rubbed it between his warm palms, and just like his gesture with the handkerchief it made me feel…cherished. It had been such a long time since I'd felt like that, and I was thankful for his thoughtfulness. I gave him a watery grin. "That's better." He smiled back. "Now come on, you. I had hoped to inject some fun into your day instead of sadness. Next time maybe I'll sing to you, and that'll really make you want to cry!" He cleared his throat and started the opening verse of what sounded like a Celine Dion song.

"No! Make it stop!" I laughed, swatting at him with the handkerchief, as he ducked out of the way.

"Hey, who am I to give advice anyway." Saul chuckled. "All I know is that I'm sitting on a bench in the Spring sunshine with a very beautiful woman, who deserves to be treated like a princess!"

"Yep, I'm like a regular Cinderella." I felt heat pinching my cheeks. "Speaking of which, I'd better get back before the Ugly Sisters send out a search party for me."

Saul jumped to his feet and held out his hands to me. I took them gladly and allowed him to pull me to my feet, our faces coming only centimetres apart. I stepped back, somewhat regretfully.

We re-traced our steps through the park towards my office, and I noticed that the children who had been playing had either become bored or worn themselves out, their excitable cries replaced with calm birdsong.

At the entrance to my building, we paused, and I felt suddenly awkward as to how we should part ways. Saul took charge and leaned in once more to brush his lips against my cheek before reaching into the pocket of his coat and holding out a small oblong card.

"Here's my number. I don't want to overstep the mark, but if you ever want to talk, just call me. I'm a pretty good listener."

I brushed my fingertips over the richly embossed gold writing on the dark grey card. Saul Faulkner. “Thanks,” I told him. “I might just do that.”

“Do.” He smiled that asymmetrical grin at me again. “Take care, Ellie.”

I watched him walk down the road towards the town centre, waiting until he turned the corner before entering the building. A glance at my watch told me I was cutting it fine before the meeting with my boss so I raced up the stairs to the office, not wanting to wait for the notoriously slow lift to arrive.

“How was lunch?” Layla was ready for me with an unctuous wink as I raced through reception.

Without pausing, I stripped off my coat and rolled my eyes at her. “He’s just a friend.”

“Uh-huh.”

SEVEN

The house felt empty when I got home now that Alex had gone away again and I walked from room to room, picking up stray items that he had left lying around, claiming the house as my own once more.

I'd hoped he might have left me a little note somewhere. He used to do that all the time. I'd open a kitchen cupboard and there'd be a post-it note stuck to a mug telling me he loved me, or sometimes I'd go to pull on a sock and find a rolled-up note inside. There was nothing like that these days, not even any flight details stuck to the fridge.

"At least *you* still love me, eh?" I stroked Mr Jones who on hearing the klaxon call of a packet of cat food being opened had come clattering through the cat flap, glueing himself to my ankles. He meowed his confirmation, then abruptly turned his back on me as I placed his bowl on the floor. "Typical man. The way to your hearts is always through your stomachs."

I opened the fridge and took out a covered dish which contained the leftovers of the lasagna I'd made the night before. It'd do as I couldn't be bothered to cook anything different just for myself. I pierced the clingfilm on top with a fork and popped it in the microwave for a couple of minutes, watching it go round and round as I contemplated the evening stretching ahead.

I always felt a little lost when Alex went away on a work trip. The feeling passed eventually when I got into my stride, but for the first couple of nights, I would find myself casting about for something to fill the void that he'd left. It was the same even when we weren't getting along.

I knew I should probably take up a hobby. Learn to paint or play the guitar or something, but I just couldn't focus enough. It was easier generally to just open a bottle of wine and lose myself in its calming effect, alongside whatever mind-numbing rubbish awaited my attention on the TV.

The microwave beeped as I unscrewed the lid of a bottle of Pinot Grigio that I'd bought on the way home, and the noise startled Mr Jones, who glared at me for interrupting his meal.

"Get over it," I told him, pouring myself a large glass of wine before adding a couple of ice cubes. I couldn't wait for it to chill in the fridge.

Using a tea towel, I transferred my dinner to a tray and peeled the clingfilm away from the edges of the dish, scalding my fingers as the steam plumed out from the over-heated food. Swearing under my breath, I grabbed a fork and then carried my sad little meal for one into the lounge.

I ate, accompanied by the cast of Coronation Street on the TV screen. I supposed this was one good thing about Alex being away, as he always moaned about the unrealities of life on the cobbled streets of my favourite soap opera. I didn't care whether it was realistic or not. They were my make-believe friends, and unlike him, *they* were always there.

Even they weren't doing it for me tonight though. There was some storyline about a historic affair and a secret child who'd made their way back to live on the street and was about to marry his sister. It'd all been done before. Maybe

Alex's constant nitpicking of the programme had finally worn off on me.

After the credits rolled, I made myself get up and brought my tray back to the kitchen. I scraped the burnt leftovers of my lasagna in the bin before stacking the plate in the dishwasher and topping up my glass with another hefty dose of wine. It had chilled enough now so that I didn't have to bother with ice cubes, which was a good job, as I'd run out. I noticed that Mr Jones had once again left the building and feeling thoroughly fed up with my lonely status, I plodded back to the sofa, pulling my legs up underneath myself. My feet were cold, and I knew that I should really go and get some warm socks to put on, but I just couldn't be bothered. Instead, I just pulled over a cushion from the other end of the sofa to cover my feet. It would do until I could find the energy to get up again.

"Well, this is shit," I announced to the empty room, the beginnings of self-pity starting to creep in. I may as well not be married at all if this was what it was going to be like. It wasn't even as though Alex was away for work in the army, or on call as a doctor or something equally important that would take him away from me. It was just a poxy management job. A job that had seemingly become more important than everything else. For him, of course, it was a vague link to his past world, getting to launch new cycling products overseas, but it was hardly worth ruining our marriage for, surely?

Not for the first time, I wondered if it was even the best thing for him to be doing. It must rub his face in it, not being able to ride like he used to. I'd tried to broach the subject with him before, but he'd just brushed me off, so I'd left him to it. Now, though, I was wishing I'd been more insistent.

Maybe I should've just married someone who didn't like risking his own life doing stupid stunts for other people in the first place. Someone who wouldn't have run the risk of breaking his stupid back doing tricks that should be left to teenagers. A grown-up. A man who would look after me and treat me right. Someone who would be here when he said he would. Someone who'd actually *want* to be here with me.

I couldn't remember the last time that Alex had done something to make me smile. When he was at home, he was always complaining about being too tired to do anything. Claiming that he was worn out from work or had too much to do to prepare for his next trip away.

The thought of him even making the effort to meet me for lunch was laughable, let alone saying I should be treated like a princess. I couldn't lie, today had been lovely with Saul, and while I would have liked it to have been Alex who'd met me for lunch, a little part of me was glad that he hadn't.

The thought of Saul gave me a feeling of exhilaration. One that I hadn't felt for a long time. It wasn't just that he was attractive, but he showed an interest in me and I hadn't realised quite how much I'd missed that feeling.

I reached into my bag to find his business card, and, as I rummaged around the cavernous space, my hand touched a soft fabric. Saul's handkerchief. Oh my God, of course. I hadn't given it back, had I? I pulled it out, opening it up on my lap, and caught a subtle fragrance from it, which drew me straight back to when he'd kissed my cheek. I held it closer and inhaled. God, it smelled good.

I saved Saul's number into my phone and, emboldened by the wine, I wondered if I should text him and thank him for coming to see me today. It wouldn't be inappropriate, would it? In fact, it would be the polite thing to do after he'd been so lovely. I tapped out a quick message.

Hi, it's Ellie. Just wanted to say thanks for today x

Nice and simple. Nothing suggestive about that. Yes, I'd put a kiss on the end of it, but I did that to everyone. I pressed send and the text flew off with a whoosh. Busying myself, I watched the opening titles to *MasterChef* and folded Saul's handkerchief back up, placing his card inside it. He probably wouldn't even reply.

Ping. My phone let out its familiar tone to say I'd received a message and my heart started to beat a little faster. It was Saul.

Hi, Ellie. Great to hear from you, and it was my pleasure. Maybe we can do it again another day when you have more time? x

He'd put a kiss on his reply. Did blokes do that? I read and re-read the message a couple of times, resisting the urge to respond too quickly, not wanting him to think I was sitting there waiting. I watched the contestants on the television putting on their aprons and readying themselves to make their first concoction, while I concocted my response in my head.

That'd be lovely x

God, I was out of practice.

Fully expecting that to be the end of it, I sighed and pushed myself up to go and get a refill of wine in the kitchen. What an idiot I was, opening communication with this guy. I shouldn't even have texted him in the first place. I was with Alex, and I'd hate it if he was texting someone else that he found attractive. Not that anything was going on. Saul was a friend, and nothing more. As I poured my drink, I heard my phone ping from the other room. I rushed back in.

So, what are you up to this evening?

My heart pounded in my chest. Now? He's asking if I'm free *now*? The little dots on the screen moved up and down to show me he was still typing.

Oh crap, that came out wrong. Sorry. I didn't mean we should meet up now.

He'd added a laughing emoji face to the end of his text, and I let out my breath.

Phew. I typed back. *Thats a relief as I'm not exactly dressed for company. I'm sat watching MasterChef on my own with a big glass of wine if you must know.*

I neglected to tell him that I was wearing my oldest, saggiest jogging pants with a face devoid of make-up.

That sounds great. Other than you being on your own. Hang on a minute...

Well, I wasn't exactly going anywhere. I took a sip of wine and watched Ronnie, aged forty-seven, from Wolverhampton explaining to John and Greg about the dish he was about to prepare for them.

Ping. Saul was back.

Thats better. I've got a glass of wine too now, and what channel is MasterChef on? We can watch it together if you like?

Oh my God, that was such a great idea, and a smile spread across my face. *Sure,* I typed back with a thumbs up. *It's on BBC1.*

OK, now, who's the guy with the handlebar moustache? and who the hell is he trying to poison with that plate of food?

By the time the programme had finished, there was only around an inch of wine left in the bottle and I'd managed to spill my guts to Saul about how miserable I was being on my own all the time while Alex worked away from home.

It was so cathartic being able to talk to someone who didn't know Alex. Helen was great to talk to but she'd known Alex ever since we'd first got together, and while she was a good listener, I knew that she loved him to bits. Sometimes, it felt like she was judging me when I complained, just the tiniest bit.

Well, you can always talk to me, Saul had replied after I had told him my feelings. *I won't judge you because I've been there myself.*

So, what is your story? I asked him. I was dying to know as each time I'd raised the question so far, he'd skirted around the issue. It shouldn't really bother me, but a mixture of good old-fashioned curiosity and a low-grade crush seemed to have formed inside me. Not a proper crush, obviously, but the kind you cultivate over untouchables like Bradley Cooper or Tom Hardy.

God, it was taking him ages to respond. I hoped that I hadn't annoyed him by being too nosey. But then he knew all about me, so it only seemed fair. I switched screens over to Facebook to see what was going on and noticed an update from Helen. A photo of her with Chrissie out for drinks in some bar, looking all loved up. I knew it was wrong of me, but I felt a stab of jealousy at how happy my friend was while I was stuck at home alone, again, with nothing but the TV and a nearly empty bottle of wine for company. Sighing, I pressed the heart emoji underneath the photo, more because it was the expected thing to do rather than because I wanted to.

Ping.

Ooh, a response.

Stepping back from Helen's on-line happiness I wasted no time in opening the incoming message.

It's no big story really, he'd replied. *I was married, but now we're separated. It turned out that we just weren't right for each other, so we decided to—*

Ping. Another message dropped down from the top of the screen. Alex. Oh, finally he deigned to get in touch after leaving me waiting all day. Filled with indignation, I brushed his message away, choosing instead to continue reading Saul's. Alex could bloody well wait for *me* for a change.

EIGHT

The weekends were always the worst. While I could fill the weekdays with work, and the evenings with wine, weekends stretched out like a road to nowhere across the Australian outback. The mirage of Monday shimmered way, way ahead in the distance.

It was already late morning when I woke up, and I rolled over, used to making the most of the cool, unslept-in covers on Alex's empty side of the bed. Despite the time, not much light was managing to force its way around the edges of the curtains, which told me that the day was going to be a typical grey English March day. Maybe I should just stay where I was.

Tempting as that was, I forced myself out of bed, threw on my fluffy robe and shuffled my feet into my waiting slippers before making my way downstairs. There was no sign of Mr Jones anywhere, so I grabbed a packet of kibble and opened the back door from the kitchen. The cold air immediately seeped its way inside and around my body, making me pull my robe around me a little tighter. The few daffodils that had braved the inhospitable chill in our back garden looked as though they were fighting a losing battle with the weather and, like me, were probably wishing that they'd stayed in their warm beds a little longer.

"Jonesy!" I called, giving the packet of kibble a good shake. "Come on in. Come and get your breakfast." Normally he'd come leaping over the back fence at the sound of his food, but there was no sign of him this morning. Assuming he'd ingratiated himself with a neighbour, and too cold to hang around waiting for him, I pulled the door closed, making sure his cat flap was unlocked for whenever he deigned to join me once again.

I'd left my phone charging in the kitchen overnight and turned it over to see if there was anything further from Alex. I'd called him back last night after I'd finally read his text which had said nothing much other than he'd arrived safely in the States. He'd spoken quietly as though he didn't want anyone to overhear him, and immediately claimed he couldn't talk for long as he had so much work to catch up on. I tried to let it go, and not to feel as though I was second place in his life, but it did make me wonder why I'd bothered to ring him back at all. His text had obviously been no more than a duty. A box ticked so that I knew he was OK. He hadn't actually wanted to talk to me at all.

I'd refused to give in immediately, though, the wine making me a little more forceful than normal as I pushed him for details about his flight and what the hotel was like. It had been like getting blood from a stone. The journey had been 'fine', and the hotel was 'nice'. It was all just a bit generic. Kind of like us these days, I supposed. It was only when I'd found myself reiterating back to him what TV programmes I'd been watching to fill my time that I realised I was just as bad as he was. Maybe there just wasn't anything to talk about anymore. Perhaps we'd reached the stage where we knew everything there was to know about each other, or at least all we wanted to know about each other.

As I'd suspected, there was nothing more from him this morning. Just the usual myriad of social media updates decorating my screen and a voicemail from Helen, which I opened straight away, her familiar Scottish tones demanding that I return her call a welcoming distraction to my pity party.

"Ellie!" she'd shouted at me down the phone. "I've been ringing you all morning! Where are you? I have news! Call me!"

She was speaking in exclamations, and I wasn't sure my low-grade hangover could deal with the full force of Helen just yet. I put the kettle on to make myself a coffee and flicked idly through Instagram while I waited for it to boil.

Spring definitely seemed as if it was in the air everywhere other than in my immediate vicinity this morning. My feed was full of images of blue skies, sunny primroses, and shiny happy couples. All flaunting their colourful lives while I was existing in black and white. I was obviously following the wrong people's profiles.

As the kettle came to a boil, my phone trilled to life and Helen's smiling face popped up on the screen.

"Hi Hels," I greeted her resignedly. "I was just about to call you back."

"Where have you *been*?" she wailed. "I've been trying to get hold of you for *ages*."

"I know, sorry. My phone was on silent."

"Never mind. I have news!"

"Go on." I poured milk into my steaming mug of coffee. "I'm all ears."

"You should sit down. Are you sitting down? Sit down, Ellie."

"What are you on about? OK, I'm sitting down." I lied, putting the milk back in the fridge.

"I'm getting married!" She ended with a squeal, and I had to hold the phone away from my ear as her excitement nearly pierced my eardrum.

"Oh…my God." I sat down at the breakfast bar, the stool spinning as I did so, a little like my head. "I…wow!"

"I know, right? Can you believe it? Me? Getting married!"

"Hels, that's fantastic news, and of course, I believe it. I'm so happy for you. For both of you." I rubbed at my wine-sore temples which were not helped by Helen's enthusiasm.

"I wanted you to be the first to know, after Ma and Ba, of course." Even though Helen had lived in the United Kingdom for pretty much her whole life, she still referred to her parents using the terminology she'd been brought up with by her Chinese parents. I loved it.

"Oh, Hels, it's fantastic news. How did it happen? Was it romantic?" I knew Chrissie must have popped the question. If Helen had done it, I would have heard about it way before now.

"It was so romantic. I can't wait to show you my ring. We're going shopping today to get one for Chrissie, too."

"That's brilliant." I sipped at my too-hot coffee, the liquid burning my tongue. "When do I get to see you? So we can celebrate properly?"

"I'm popping down the week after next to see Ma and Ba, so we could do something then? Are you around?"

I laughed ironically. I was always around. "Yep, I'll be here," I told her.

"Great. I've got to go, Ellie. I need to hit some jewellery shops. Give my love to Alex."

"OK, you go and say congratulations to Chrissie, too."

"I will, I will. Gotta go. Love ya. Bye, bye, bye." Never content with just the one goodbye, she tailed off the conversation with multiples to re-join her glittery bubble of joy at the other end of the phone.

The kitchen felt suddenly very quiet with no sound but that of the ticking wall clock. It wasn't nearly enough to fill the void.

In the old days, if Alex was here, I would have told him about Helen's phone call and we would have jumped around the room together, thrilled at her news. Maybe I should call him and let him know. I knew it was difficult for him to talk if he was working, but it would still be the early hours of the morning in New York so he shouldn't have started work yet. He was bound to be up already thanks to jet lag, and surely this would be something he'd want to know about. Besides, it would be good just to hear his voice.

I scrolled through my phone and called his mobile, rehearsing in my head what I was going to say. I didn't have long to think about it as, instead of ringing, the number went straight to voicemail. His phone must be switched off. Deciding not to leave a message, I ended the call, tucking away my disappointment. It'd be better to tell him in person, anyway.

Behind me, the cat flap clattered open and Mr Jones sauntered blithely over to his food bowl like the lord of the manor gracing his lowly serving staff with his presence. And like the most obedient servant, I got up and filled the small ceramic dish with stomach-churning globules of meaty cat food. He meowed his approval as I placed it in front of him, his tiny nose nudging my hand out of the way.

"Helen's getting married," I told him as he worked his way methodically through his breakfast. "Really?" I replied to myself. "Yes. Exciting, isn't it?"

Mr Jones licked his lips, and then made his way back towards the door, glancing at me en route as if to say, 'You still here, then?'

"You treat this house like a hotel!" I called out to him as he left.

Now what?

NINE

I hadn't meant to ask Saul out on a date, but now that I was sitting waiting for him at a secluded table for two at The Royal Oak I certainly felt as though I was about to embark on one.

Don't be so stupid, I told myself sternly, taking out my compact from my bag to check my makeup. It's not even a date. He's just a friend.

It wasn't like I'd texted him to ask him out for lunch, anyway. I'd just wanted to share Helen's exciting news with someone…anyone. I'd tried Alex about five times before giving up, and I couldn't exactly ring Helen to share her own news with her. Other than that, there was only my dad and my brother, both of whom now lived in Spain, and I'd not been close to since Mum died. No one else would be bothered by my secondhand news. I'd hit a brick wall.

That was when I'd thought of Saul, and while he didn't know Helen, I could tell he was genuinely happy that I'd called to share the news with him; and technically *he'd* been the one who'd said we should celebrate. Who was I to argue with that? It wasn't like I had anything else to do.

So, here I was, in my smart jeans, the ones without the frayed bottoms, and a top that drew a fine line between casual and alluring, waiting with what felt like pre-date butterflies in my stomach. A feeling that I'd almost forgotten existed. It was nice.

The Royal Oak had been Saul's suggestion. I hadn't been there before even though I'd driven past it often enough. It was lovely inside, a real traditional English pub with low ceilings, dark wooden beams, and plenty of ornamental brass decorating every available inch of wall space.

It was busy inside, and we'd been lucky to get a table, thanks to a last-minute cancellation according to my waiter whose eyes flitted around the room as he took my drink order, alert to the possibility of any raised hands requesting his presence. He'd brought me my wine, and a menu on a large sheet of thick cream-coloured card which I'd now scanned nervously about five times, looking up each time I heard the door creaking open.

Taking a sip of my chilled Pinot Grigio, I looked around the room at the other lunchtime patrons and wondered what their stories were. A raucous family of seven were over to my right, two middle-aged men on my left, and, behind them, a table of what looked like two couples who'd been out walking, if their muddy boots were anything to go by.

Where was Saul? Oh God, please don't let him stand me up. I'd be mortified to be left sitting here on my own. It was bad enough having to do that at home, let alone in a crowded room. Should I ring him? I looked at my watch and noticed it was ten minutes past one. God, was that all? It felt like I'd been sitting there much longer, and the lowered level in my glass suggested the same. I pushed it away, not wanting to be too tipsy by the time he got here, even though a bit of hair of the dog was helping with this morning's stuffy head.

At a quarter past one, the door opened emitting another chattering group into the dark confines of the pub, the bright sunlight behind them etching their silhouettes out in the doorway. I blinked, watching them move forward as one being, before seeing one of their number break away, an arm waving above their heads. Waving at me. Saul.

I breathed a sigh of relief and a smile spread across my face as he reached me. I rose to greet him and was enveloped in a hug which felt like it came more from the large coat he was wearing than from the man inside. Outside's cold air clung to the fabric, transferring to my skin and raising goosebumps.

"I'm so sorry I'm late." He shrugged off his coat, laying it over the back of the wooden chair opposite mine. "Traffic was a bloody nightmare. You look great by the way."

A burst of laughter from the family's table meant that I didn't have to formulate a reply. Instead, I smiled my thanks at his compliment before sitting back down and raising the over-sized menu in front of my face to obscure the blush which threatened my cheeks.

"What can I get you?" Our waiter had materialised at Saul's side.

"I'll join my friend here in a glass of…actually no, why don't you just bring us a bottle, please?" I started to protest, and Saul turned back to me. "Is that OK?" he asked. "Did you have anything special to do this afternoon? Sorry, I should've asked first." Both he and the waiter focussed on my response.

"I literally can't think of one reason why not," I told them both, and the waiter nodded his assent before practically clicking his heels together and heading off to fetch our wine.

"So, great news about your friend."

"Isn't it? I miss her so much now she's moved away, and with Alex gone all the time with work, well, it's a bit…" My words trailed off.

"Hey." Saul reached across the table and covered my hand with his own. "I get it. We all feel alone sometimes, even when we're surrounded by other people, eh?" He waved his other hand around the room at the other tables which were overflowing with good cheer. He'd managed to hit the nail on the head as to how I was feeling, and it was lovely to be understood. I was like a tiny island in the middle of all these people, and it felt good to have a companion next to me for a change. When he finally moved his hand away, a part of me wanted to grab it back and hold onto it.

The waiter arrived at our table with the wine and poured out two hefty glassfuls before taking our food order and heading back into the throng of merriment which swallowed him up wholeheartedly into its midst.

"Here's to your friend." Saul raised his glass. "Let's celebrate."

"To Helen and Chrissie." I lifted my glass, and we clinked them together before taking a sip.

"Helen and Chrissie," repeated Saul, without losing eye contact. "May they find the meaning of true love."

"Soppy bugger." I laughed, not feeling entirely comfortable with how my insides were responding to the heady mix of his words and the way he was looking at me. Surely, I was reading more into it than was meant to be. We were just friends, after all.

"Yeah, I suppose so." He gave me that compelling grin of his.

"So, what do you think everyone else is celebrating in here today? The family over there. What do you reckon? A birthday?"

Saul turned in his seat just as another burst of laughter came from the group. "Yeah, definitely. I'd put money on all the waiting staff coming over with a cake later and singing "Happy Birthday"."

"God, really? Even our waiter?" It seemed unlikely that Pete, as his name badge had declared, would be the type to enjoy bursting into song.

"Yeah, I reckon Pete secretly goes to karaoke every Tuesday and serenades his long-suffering partner with his repertoire of Cher classics."

I threw my head back and laughed at the image. "OK, then, how about the two couples over there?"

He swivelled the other way to look at them. "Hmm, tricky one. I think the women are rich sisters, the men are their husbands, and judging by the mud on their boots, they have been in the woods burying the bodies of their parents who they have just murdered so that they can claim a hefty inheritance."

"Bloody hell, Saul! I'm learning a bit about the way your mind works. I just had them down as enjoying a walk in the countryside." I took a big swig of my wine, enjoying the game. He laughed and followed suit.

"What about those two?" he asked, nodding towards the two men seated together. "Your turn."

"Oh God, I don't know." They didn't look as cheery as some of the other tables' occupants. "Looks a bit like one friend commiserating with the other one because his wife's left him for a life of travelling around the world in a combi van, getting stoned and enjoying the surf with her hippy lover, while he's left behind to pay off all her debts." I looked over at Saul, anticipating his laughter. "What do you think?" His face had dropped.

"Saul? What have I said?"

"It's nothing." He flicked his hair out of his eyes and took a gulp of wine. "It's probably a bit close to home, that's all."

"Oh God, no! I'm so sorry. I didn't mean to—"

“It’s fine, honestly. You weren’t to know.” His lips formed a smile that came nowhere close to reaching his downcast eyes.

What an idiot I was to make up such a stupid story. He’d mentioned before today about his broken relationship which had clearly affected him, and I’d gone and done that. Guilt twisted its way through my thoughts. “Do you want to talk about it?” I asked. “After all, you’ve listened to all my tales of woe. I’m pretty sure I owe you.”

“I’m not great at talking about it.” His eyes remained firmly on the table.

“I understand.” I felt my hand reaching out this time, and my fingertips brushed his just as he pulled them away to lift his glass again. “But if you ever wanted to...”

“Thanks.” He lifted his eyes to mine with what looked like a great effort, and I could clearly see the pain behind them. “It’d probably do me the world of good and you’ve been so honest with me.” I smiled encouragingly and he took a deep breath. “I guess it started when—”

“One wood-fired Napoli Forte pizza, and one salmon, avocado, and new potato salad,” announced Pete who had appeared, stealth like, at our side once again, cutting off Saul mid-flow. “Can I get you any sauces? Chilli oil?”

“We’re fine, thanks,” I told him, and he took his leave as subtly as he’d arrived. I turned back to Saul. “Go on,” I urged.

He ignored the cutlery laid out in front of him and instead tore a slice of pizza, trailing mozzarella from the rest of the dish, which hung over the edge of his plate. “Some other time, eh?” He offered a grin. “We’re here to celebrate, remember, and this pizza looks too good to let it go cold.” He curled the edges of the slice up and put enough in his mouth to put a halt to any more words for a while.

———

As the waiting staff rounded off the last tone-deaf notes of "Happy Birthday", Meghan blew out the candles on her cake and the rest of her family cheered rapturously.

"Told you so." Saul smirked with a triumphant glint in his eye, and we both joined in along with the other tables in the pub, clapping furiously at her good fortune in turning sixteen while she cringed at the attention and took endless pouting selfies.

Clearly traumatised after his enforced musical performance, Pete placed our bill on the table accompanied by a couple of after-dinner mints and, as I reached for the slip of paper, Saul whipped it out of my grasp.

"You've got to let me at least go halves with you," I insisted, conscious that we'd managed to work our way through two bottles of wine during lunch.

"No way," he replied, reaching inside his coat pocket for his wallet. "It's my shout. If you like, you can get it next time." He winked at me and I had to remind myself sternly again that this was not a date. It wasn't.

Nevertheless, I was still glad that he wanted to see me again. It had been fun. Lots of fun. And that was something that had been sorely missing in my life for a long time. While he hadn't opened up to me in the end about his own situation, which was clearly too painful for him, we had instead put the world to rights, celebrated Helen's engagement again and again, and laughed solidly for the last three and a half hours. My stomach almost ached from all the laughter, and even the two men at the table next to ours had joined in with the convivial atmosphere in the room. It turned out that Nigel was celebrating his big promotion at work with the help of his brother, Richard. I was relieved my stupid prediction hadn't been correct, and we'd raised a glass to him as well.

"Your taxi's on its way," Pete informed us after we'd asked him to call for one, and I couldn't believe the time had passed so quickly - for us, at least. I imagined our waiter was probably dying for everyone to leave so he could finish his shift and put his feet up.

We wound our way through the room, waving goodbye to our newfound acquaintances, best of friends for the duration of a drunken afternoon and unlikely ever to be seen again.

Stepping outside, I was struck by the chill in the air and I shivered despite the warmth offered by my winter coat.

"Cold?" Saul asked, and I nodded, the motion making me realise that I was drunker than I thought I was.

"Come here, let me warm you up a bit."

He pulled me into his arms and rubbed his hands briskly up and down my back. I could feel the heat of his body warming me through his open coat, and I rested my slightly woozy head on his shoulder for a moment, inhaling the scent of his aftershave which was starting to become familiar.

"Thanks for celebrating with me today." I pulled back slightly to look at him.

"My pleasure. I wasn't going to leave you on your own, was I?" he replied. "You deserve better than that."

I did deserve better. He was absolutely right. I rested my head back down on his shoulder, and could have quite happily stayed there, had a car not pulled up, beside us, its arrival noisy on the gravel of the car park.

"That'll be the taxi," Saul said.

"Hmm," I murmured, looking back up and regretfully stepping back from his embrace. "How're you getting home? We can share the taxi if you like?" I offered, looking to prolong the company before going home to an empty house once more.

"Ah, no, it's fine. I'm not far from here, so I can walk and have a smoke on the way." He pulled out his vape from his coat pocket. "It's been such a great day, though. We'll definitely have to do it again…if you'd like to?"

His words warmed me just as much as his embrace. "That'd be great."

Feeling suddenly awkward now we had to part ways, I leaned in to kiss him goodbye on his cheek, just as he did the same, and our lips brushed like the lightest touch of a butterfly wing. I felt a jolt of pure electricity go through my being, and as I pulled back, I struggled to meet his eyes.

"I should..." I half turned towards the car.

"Yes." I thought I heard the essence of a missed opportunity in his voice. "Take care and text me to let me know you got home safe."

I waved at him through the window of the taxi as it pulled away from the pub, and watched him disappear into a plume of vapour, like a magician.

"Good afternoon was it, love?" the driver asked.

"Yes, it was, thanks," I told him, saved from a sentence of small talk by my phone ringing shrilly from inside my bag. I fished it out, and the display flashed with Alex's face. He was finally getting back to me after making me wait for nearly the whole day to return all my calls. Saul was right…I couldn't quite remember what we'd been talking about at the time, but I did deserve better than this. I pressed the red button on the screen and let Alex go through to my voicemail. Two could play at that game.

TEN

I must have dozed off shortly after I got home as I woke up on the sofa in the dark, the muted television screen flickering silently on the far wall. At least I'd had the foresight to pull a blanket over myself, although I couldn't remember getting it out of the cupboard in my drunken stupor.

I really hadn't meant to drink so much over lunch. In fact, I hadn't planned on more than a couple of glasses, let alone a couple of bottles. No wonder my head was pounding, and my throat felt like the bottom of Mr Jones' litter tray.

I remembered getting in and curling up on the sofa with a cup of tea, hoping for a cheesy afternoon movie on the TV. I'd only closed my eyes for a minute to stop the room from revolving quite so quickly, but now it was just after eight, my tea was stone cold, and I had the early signs of what was going to be a grim hangover starting to kick in.

I fought my way out from under the confines of the blanket and made my way to the kitchen where I swallowed down some paracetamol with a glass of water, hoping that it wasn't too late to flush the alcohol from my system. I still felt woozy, but I knew it wasn't just the wine that was making my head spin as I remembered the touch of Saul's lips. I brushed my fingertips against my own and closed my eyes, recognising the feeling of longing that fluttered through my body.

This wasn't supposed to happen, I told myself, knowing full well that it was a pointless one-sided argument, and that deep down, given half the chance, it was always going to happen. There'd been a spark between us the very first time we'd met, and I'd become wrapped up in it, like some kind of infatuated teenager. Even now, I couldn't stop myself from reaching for my phone to look up Saul's Facebook profile. As I took the phone in my hands, the screen came to life showing me a message from him and my heart sped up despite the rest of my body feeling so crap.

How's your head?

I tried to resist the urge to message back straight away but caved in after about thirty seconds and hated myself for being so needy.

It's been better. How's yours?

He seemed to reply before I'd even finished adding the question mark to my message.

LOL. Not too bad. I had a great time today x

I paused before replying, soaking up his message and the kiss on the end of it which caused me to touch my lips yet again.

Me too x

The phone went silent. Oh God, I should have asked a question to keep the conversation going. I tucked the phone into the back pocket of my jeans and turned towards the sink to get myself some more water, almost tripping over Mr Jones who had decided to lie prone across the floor. He looked up at me with disbelief that I'd dared to disturb him.

Pouring myself another glass of water, I took it back to the lounge and collapsed onto the sofa, pulling the blanket back over myself to keep warm. Alex always had the thermostat turned down low when he was at home, and I hadn't got around to turning it up like I usually did when he went away. I checked my phone again. Nothing. Aargh, maybe I was reading too much into things. I was obviously just a sad, lonely idiot and Saul was just a nice guy taking pity on me.

My phone pinged.

Can I be honest with you Ellie?

Before I had time to formulate a response, the phone pinged again.

Actually, I'm just going to be honest anyway.

Oh. I felt nervous as I waited for him to continue.

The thing is, I like you. I really like you, and if I'm honest I wish I'd kissed you properly earlier. I know that you're married, but you've also told me that you aren't happy, and I think you deserve to be happy.

I sat frozen, trying to swallow the lump which had formed in my throat. He continued.

Anyway, look, I probably shouldn't have even said all that so I'm sorry. And if you want to just ignore it and carry on as friends then that's fine. But if not, well, I just wanted to be honest.

Aware that my whole body had stiffened, I forced my shoulders to drop and took a deep breath before typing.

I don't know what to say. That's beautiful. It's all a bit unexpected x

I added the kiss and removed it, before putting it back again. Was it unexpected? I wasn't sure. I was fully aware that we'd not known each other for long, but during that time, we'd talked so openly, maybe too openly. There was an undeniable connection, but as he'd said, I was married, even though it didn't always feel like it anymore.

My fingers went to my necklace where they started to twist it round and round in their familiar pattern as I re-read my as-yet unsent words.

My phone pinged.

Ellie? Are you OK? I'm sorry. I honestly don't want to put you in an awkward position. I guess I just thought that maybe life is too short to not take the chance of happiness...for either of us. Hey, if you don't feel the same, we can just put it down to the wine talking. LOL. Think I'm probably still a bit pissed to be honest.

Suddenly realising I'd been holding my breath, I let it out slowly. He was giving me an escape route if I wanted it, but I just wasn't sure. How could I have such conflicting feelings? How could I still love Alex while I was being drawn so incomprehensibly towards someone else? I deleted my previous message and started to type once again.

OK, I'm going to be honest with you too.

I pressed send and could imagine Saul holding his phone watching the cursor flash, just like I'd been doing.

I like you too. Very much. Probably more than I should, and today when we said goodbye, I wanted you to kiss me too. Actually, I haven't stopped thinking about it. I pressed send before continuing, knowing he'd be able to see I wasn't done. *But...* I added, pressing send again.

He replied quickly before I could write more.

No. No buts. Let's just leave it there. I like you and you like me. Let's run off together and live happily ever after.

A smile crossed my lips, and I touched them again, closing my eyes at the thought of kissing him. It would be so easy, so easy to just dip one toe into the water. Just one.

I opened my eyes and they fell to rest on the mantlepiece that hosted a whole array of my and Alex's happy moments caught forever on camera. No one captures the miserable ones for prosperity, do they? Just the rose-tinted memories.

And this was why, I realised, as they served as a reminder as to why I was wearing that ring on my finger when my husband wasn't here to let me know.

I can't, I typed. *I want to, but I just can't.*

I waited a moment before pressing send, savouring Saul's words for just a bit longer before having to close the door on them. Then, with more than a little regret, I pressed the button. It was done and my phone remained depressingly silent in my hand. Now I was carrying two loads of guilt. Firstly, for even contemplating doing anything behind Alex's back, and secondly now for having let Saul down. I felt a rush of unexplained anger towards Alex. He was making *me* unhappy and now Saul, too.

Trudging up the stairs, and feeling extremely sorry for myself, I got changed for bed, leaving my clothes lying on the floor where they fell. I didn't have the energy to tidy them up. Alex's bad habits were obviously rubbing off on me, but who cared when there was no one else there to worry about? Taking my phone with me, I climbed under the duvet and rolled onto my stomach, propping myself up on my elbows to read through the messages once again. Why hadn't Saul replied? I'd undoubtedly hurt his feelings when he'd been brave enough to put himself on the line. Perhaps I should send another? Tell him I was sorry? Maybe I should just let sleeping dogs lie.

As if reading my mind, my phone pinged back into life.

It's OK. I get it. I honestly do. And while I think we could have something really special, I respect your decision and I'll take a step back. I hope we can still be friends x

Relief flooded through me. Friends was good. It was better than nothing.

ELEVEN

It had been five days since I'd seen him, not that I was counting, but I really missed him.

In fact, it felt like the old days when Alex had first started travelling abroad for work and I would literally count down the days and then the hours until I was going to see him again. Only now, of course, it wasn't Alex that was encompassing my waking thoughts. It was Saul.

He'd stuck to his word and not contacted me, respectfully giving me the space that I'd asked for. The only issue now was that I was left with a hell of a lot of empty space to fill which gave way too much time to think about my situation.

There'd been barely any contact with Alex, as usual. It was always the same when he was at a convention. Obviously, the time difference between here and New York didn't help, but he always claimed it was difficult to talk anyway, no matter where he was. The most we had managed after the weekend were a few texts, and jealousy plucked at my skin at the thought of all the after-hours schmoozing he'd be doing at different restaurants and bars. He'd always told me that all the dinners and drinks do's that he went to were a boring necessity, just another part of his job, but it irked me nonetheless when I was left to eat meals for one in front of the TV.

We had managed to talk briefly on the Sunday after Saul and I had called time out on our blossoming friendship and I'd finally been able to tell him about Helen and Chrissie's engagement. While his tone had still been restrained, it had been so nice to hear his genuine excitement and happiness for our friend creeping into his voice. It was like speaking to the old Alex, the one that used to lift me up and spin me around when either of us had good news to share. Bolstered by his rare positivity and filled with a new resolve to heal our flagging relationship, I'd suggested that maybe the two of us should go away together once he'd finished his latest convention tour. Take some time to reconnect.

"I'm not sure," he'd told me, immediately crushing my idea before it was even fully formed. "I'm just going to be so knackered when I get back so all I want to do is to spend some time at home."

"But we could go away somewhere relaxing where we can just lie on a beach in the sun and do nothing together." I heard a wheedling tone creeping into my voice. "You wouldn't have to do anything. I could plan it all."

"Let's talk about it another time, eh? My head's so full of work that there isn't any room for planning anything else right now. Besides, all I've done is be away from home and I'm not sure I've got it in me to just pack up and go somewhere else as soon as I'm back. I'm sorry, Ellie."

I could've screamed in frustration, despite his apology. Why couldn't he see that it was what we needed as a couple? Time away together, to relax and reconnect, and who knows, maybe even try to start a family of our own at last. At least then I wouldn't be on my own the next time he went away. But no, all he could think of was the fact that *he* was tired, that *his* job took precedence, and that *he* needed to be at home. I'd gazed outside at the gloomy weather, wallowing in self-pity. What about me? What about what I wanted? It felt like he'd stopped loving me, so was it really any wonder that I'd allowed someone else to offer me solace?

All week I'd managed to keep the demons at bay. Staying occupied at work wasn't a problem and at home, I'd had my regular dose of my *Coronation Street* friends to keep me company along with some new ones on *EastEnders*. I knew Alex would moan about my extra soap opera viewing when he came home, but it was tough. I needed something to block out the solitude.

Up until now, I had coped with thoughts of Saul just filtering into my head while I was awake, but I'd woken up this morning with his name on my lips and an ache throughout my body. I knew before I even opened my eyes that I was going to contact him.

As the opening credits to *MasterChef* rolled onto the TV screen that evening, I finished off my first glass of wine and sent him a message.

So, what are you up to?

I placed my phone on the arm of the sofa where it remained resolutely silent while the contestants on TV did battle to impress John and Greg with their dishes. I'd already decided who I thought should win, but he was getting some stiff competition from a couple of others.

I picked up my phone after ten minutes just to make sure that I hadn't left it on silent. I hadn't. It was just being quiet of its own accord. Something else that had decided to ignore me, just like my husband and Mr Jones. I honestly wondered sometimes why I bothered having a cat at all, for all the company he gave me. Alex had always been his favourite, which I had accepted, but one of the main reasons we'd got him was to keep me company when Alex went away. Instead, the stupid creature just took it as his cue to do the rounds of the neighbourhood instead.

I wasn't overly worried about him as his food bowl was emptied on a regular basis, so I knew that nothing had happened to him, but still, it'd be nice to have him around a bit more. Perhaps we should have got a dog.

I checked my phone just to make sure that my message to Saul had sent properly. It was green and time-stamped underneath, fifteen minutes ago now. I sighed. Perhaps he'd moved on already. I mean, he was a good-looking guy, and it wasn't like he was going to struggle to meet anyone else. Someone who didn't come with all the problems that I did. It just went to show that he obviously didn't care that much anyway, even though he'd claimed to.

I poured a second glass of wine for myself to accompany the rest of the programme. I knew I shouldn't be drinking too much on a weeknight, but hey, they were making a fish course next, so it only seemed like the polite thing to do. I pondered whether I should make myself a nice bit of fish tomorrow night, knowing in the back of my mind that when it came down to it, I'd just do something easy instead.

Still no reply from Saul. The logical part of my mind told me that he was probably just busy, out with some mates or…someone. A sigh escaped my lips which I dampened down with a sip of wine, but it just fuelled the illogical part of my mind which put forward the suggestion that I'd pushed him away.

I'd obviously upset him. After all, *I'd* be bothered if I had told someone that I liked them and then got turned down. If only circumstances were different. Perhaps I should have explained things to him properly, face to face. After all, the tone of text messages could come across wrong sometimes, couldn't they? He could have taken offence when I had no intention of hurting him.

I scrolled back through our messages from the weekend, but nothing seemed hurtful from my words, other than the ultimate rejection, of course. The time of my last message still showed up at the bottom. It had been well over an hour now. Damn it.

Perhaps I should stop obsessing about whether I'd hurt Saul's feelings and ring Alex instead. After all, he was my husband, whether it felt like it or not. A quick Google search showed that it wasn't quite 5pm in New York, so I needed to wait for a bit longer before trying him.

Wine glass empty and looking for a distraction, I pushed myself up from the sofa and made my way to the kitchen to pour myself another drink. I knew I should just stick to the two glasses, but who cared? One more wasn't going to hurt, was it? I grabbed a box of kibble to shake in the doorway, to try and entice Mr Jones to come inside and spend some time with me and was surprised to find the back door unlocked when I tried it. I was always going on at Alex for leaving it unlocked so it irked me that I had stupidly done the same. Not that I would tell him.

"Jonesy?" I called, my breath pluming out into the chill of the air. "Come on in, boy. Mmm, yummy kibble." I gave the box another shake.

From the right side of the house, I heard a clatter, and before long Mr Jones came skidding over like a cartoon character to arrive on the door mat.

"Where have you been, mate?" I bent down to scratch behind his ears, and he brushed past me, heading straight for his bowl, where he stood looking back at me, waiting for his slave to fill it up. If he could have tapped his paw impatiently, he would have. I obliged, obviously.

Mr Jones now in residence, and the back door locked up, I took my wine to the lounge and dialled Alex's number. It started ringing, which was a pleasant surprise as I'd become used to it just diverting to voicemail straight away.

I drummed my nails on the arm of the sofa while I waited, imagining his phone vibrating in his jacket pocket, no doubt flung on the back of a chair while he stood elsewhere talking passionately about gear boxes or something equally as dull.

"Come on." I urged him to answer, taking a large sip of wine.

"Hi, you've reached Alex Thompson—"

I cut off the voicemail message that I knew so well, and immediately re-dialled. Surely, if I rang him enough times, I'd force him into answering the bloody phone.

"Hi, you've reached—"

Damn it. Redial. Sip of wine.

"Hi, you've—"

"Oh, for God's sake, Alex!" I slammed my fist down on the sofa. "Answer your sodding phone!"

I didn't like leaving messages. I used to leave them, and they were full of how much I missed him and worried about him while he was away. These days it just wound me up that I could never reach him, and then I'd end up leaving some snotty voicemail with an edge to my voice, which obviously never inspired him to call me back. Maybe I'd try one more time and then give up. I steeled myself and redialled.

"Hi, you—"

I closed my eyes and forced myself to breathe deeply. I just had to write off tonight and start afresh tomorrow. I couldn't take it personally. I *shouldn't* take it personally. But then why the hell did it all feel so bloody personal? I felt unwelcome tears moistening the corners of my eyes, and I tried, unsuccessfully, to blink them away.

Not for the first time, I wondered if Alex was where he claimed to be, and an uninvited vision of him with another woman lying on a vast hotel bed, expensive bedsheets tangled around their entwined naked limbs gatecrashed into my mind's eye. It was so at odds with everything that I thought I knew about him, and the image sat uncomfortably, making me feel like a voyeur within my own head. I shook it away, mentally and physically, and I stood up, walking over to the collection of photos on the mantlepiece.

My favourite image had been tucked behind an ombre grey vase, which I must have moved the last time I'd dusted the mantlepiece. Tutting, I pulled it out and carried the silver frame back to the sofa, where I studied our faces. Caught unawares, we'd been sharing some private joke on our wedding day, and the photographer had been there to immortalize the moment. My head was thrown back in laughter and Alex was looking at me as though I were the most wonderful thing he'd ever seen. I sighed, holding the frame face down against my heart, trying to remember the silly joke he'd told me to make me laugh so much. Something about the day being so emotional that even the wedding cake was in tiers. It was daft, but that had been Alex all over. It was one of the reasons why I loved him so much. His irrepressible ability to find joy and to spark it within my own heart. It seemed a million years ago now, and I wondered where the couple in the photograph had gone.

Maybe I'd try to call him one more time.

"Hi, you've reached Alex Thompson—" I let the voicemail play out, leaving nothing but silence in its wake.

I turned the photograph face down on the cushion next to me, and let my head drop against the back of the sofa, giving in to the tears which formed tiny rivulets down the remnants of today's makeup which still lay heavy on my face. I sat in the same position for a while, half listening to the evening news, before eventually finding the energy to reach for the remote control to silence the voices. At least I could control the ones outside of my head.

As the TV screen went dark, my mobile phone emitted a muffled ping from where it had become sandwiched between the sofa cushions. I retrieved it, fully expecting the usual dismissive text from Alex excusing his inability to take my calls and saying he'd get back to me when he could.

Hey, sorry I missed you earlier. Still awake? My whole being flooded with hope.

It was Saul.

TWELVE

I stared unseeingly at my computer screen at work, the words in front of me a complete blur as my mind wandered down a lane which was decorated with freshly made memories.

After Saul had replied to my text last Thursday, we had messaged each other long into the night, and my initial suspicions about him meeting someone else were quashed as he told me he'd just wanted to stick to his word and give me some space, which I couldn't help but admire.

I would've replied to your message quicker, but I was in the cinema, he'd explained.

I hadn't asked who he'd been with, but I was stupidly relieved when he told me later that he'd been with a friend. I might have told him so, but I couldn't remember properly as the wine I'd drunk had muffled the edges of some of what I'd said, although I knew I'd said a hell of a lot.

I'd told him all about the rot that had insidiously crept into my marriage, about how much I wanted to have a family of my own and how Alex wouldn't even entertain the idea. I felt a semblance of guilt for sharing secrets that I'd only previously shared with my husband, but I'd had to let it all out to someone, and Saul had been easy to talk to.

Encouraging. It was rare that someone let you share your own thoughts without bringing the narrative back to themselves. Maybe I'd said too much. I'd have to go back and check the messages, but there were so many to go through now.

What I did know was that by the time I had eventually gone to bed, the texts had slowly and insidiously become sexts, and reading those back to myself afterwards without having my confidence boosted by wine, made me blush.

I'd hoped that he would suggest us meeting up at the weekend and when he didn't, I'd taken the bull by the horns and put the idea forward myself. I was emboldened by Pinot Grigio and so high on Saul's attention, that I'd thrown my usual caution to the wind. Besides, Alex was off doing who knew what with whoever he did things with. I was done with sitting around waiting for him.

I'd love nothing more, he'd told me, *but I have to go to a family thing.* A tearful emoji had followed. *I know where I'd rather be though.*

Never mind, I'd typed back, minding immensely but not wanting to give too much away, although I'd suspected it was possibly too late to play the cool cucumber card.

I'd resigned myself to yet another boring weekend for myself, but it hadn't been too bad in the end. I'd kept myself busy tidying the house and going shopping. I'd even gone out on a limb and treated myself to a bit of salmon from the fish counter in Tesco's, inspired by all those *MasterChef* recipes.

As he'd promised, Saul had sent me messages whenever he could, and each one kick-started my heart, reminding me what it was like to feel wanted again.

I wish you were here, he'd told me.

I wish I was too, I'd sent back.

Maybe next time, you could come with me.

His messages had told me that he wasn't just thinking of the here and now. This was something that could go somewhere. Somewhere that I'd quite like to be. Included in someone's life, instead of just left alone, slowly wilting like a plant starved of light and water.

The skies had cleared briefly on Sunday, and I'd taken myself out for a walk, wishing that Mr Jones was a dog, so that I could have a bit of company. Saul kept me company instead, though, ringing me from the car on his way back home. We'd talked for about an hour as I'd wandered through woodlands, and I told him more of my hopes and dreams for the future while he had listened, truly listened, unlike Alex, who always had one eye on the television.

I couldn't believe how much we had in common, almost as though he had been put on the planet specifically for me. If this were a cartoon, I'd have birds and small woodland creatures accompanying me as I walked, relishing the warm Disney-like happiness that emanated from me. It would probably have been sickeningly sweet to anyone else, but not to me. It made me joyful.

I smiled at the memory, and rustled through some paperwork on my desk, trying to look busy, as I caught my boss approaching from the corner of my eye.

"Morning" he boomed at me. "How was networking this morning?"

"Morning, Mr Dickinson. It was good, thanks."

My boss had never invited me to call him by his first name, which was fine by me. He was a dick by name and a dick by nature and most of us in the office called him 'Dickhead' behind his back.

He nodded curtly and continued his path to the glass-fronted office to the right of my desk where he would languish for the rest of the day, requesting coffee every hour until it was time for me to leave.

Angling my in tray a little further round to block his view of me, I resumed my reminiscing. Technically it was work-related as my thoughts centred on that morning's networking meeting. Tuesdays had become my new favourite day of the week, and for someone who had always loathed getting up before the sun to attend these events, there had been an abrupt shift in opinion as I'd known I was going to see Saul.

We'd sat together at the back of the room, thighs touching, and hands brushing at any given opportunity. Such small nods to intimacy, but each of them feeling like a bolt of electricity. I had been surprised that the other attendees couldn't hear the crackles of electricity emanating from us. As far as we had been concerned, there could have been no one else in the room. It was like a switch had been flicked, transforming what was usually a drab conference centre room, which smelled of stale carpets and cheap aftershave, into a romantic backdrop fit for a movie screen.

Saul had taken hold of my hand as we sat in the hotel lobby at the end of the meeting, ostensibly talking shop to anyone who passed us by. My eyes had flicked around the room to see if anyone might notice, but the only other person nearby had been a suited man with a small case who stood at the reception desk waiting for one of the disinterested reception team to look up from their mobile phones so that he could check out. I'd left my hand where it was. His hand had felt nice, smaller than Alex's, but the unfamiliarity in itself was new, enticing.

"Meet me for dinner on Thursday night?" he'd asked, and my heart had crested high with excitement before plunging back down on the tracks of its emotional rollercoaster.

"I can't," I'd told him. "I'm meeting my friend, Helen." Something that I'd read to be disappointment had flickered across Saul's face as his gaze had dropped down to our interlinked hands.

"Can't you blow her off?" He'd looked back up at me, his thumb stroking the top of my hand, a lopsided smile sending my stomach flip-flopping.

"I wish I could, but I haven't seen her in months. I've already promised her we're going to celebrate her engagement, and it's the only night she can do while she's down here."

Saul's lower lip had stuck out in a parody of a small child realising he wasn't going to get his own way.

"Don't give me that hurt bunny face," I'd told him, making him laugh, his eyes crinkling up at the sides, making me want to just lean over and kiss him. "Are you free another night?"

"I can do Friday."

It had been my turn for my face to drop. "I can't."

"Ah." Realisation had dawned on Saul's face as he'd sat back in his chair, pulling his hand away from mine. "He's back then, isn't he?"

I'd nodded. He never spoke Alex's name, and the mere fact of him not doing so meant that I said it less often, too. It somehow made him less present. Now, suddenly, he may as well have pulled up a chair to sit with us, as reality flooded back in.

Saul had crossed his arms, looking past me to the sliding doors which had whooshed open to allow entry to a young couple who'd breezed their way over to the elevators, too wrapped up in each other to even register our presence. I could tell he was feeling fed up, and who could blame him? He hadn't asked to be in this situation, in fact, he'd tried his best to give us both a way out. I was the fool who had taken us all a big step deeper.

"Hey, perhaps I could meet you for a drink after I finish with Helen on Thursday?" I'd put to him, needing to see a smile back on his face. "She's staying at her parents' place, so she'll have to head off fairly early anyway."

He'd looked back at me and gave me a sad smile. "Maybe. Let's see how we go." He'd put his hands on the arms of the chair and pushed himself up to standing, before holding out a hand to me. "Come on. You need to get back to work before you're late. I'll text you later."

And here I was, sitting at my desk, replaying the scenario over in my head and wondering why I hadn't heard from him yet bearing in mind it was now nearly lunchtime and we would normally have messaged each other at least twenty times by now.

I was just about to get up and make Dickhead a cup of coffee before he asked for one when my desk phone rang shrilly. I could see it was an external call, and I let it ring four times before answering, knowing that it would annoy my boss that I hadn't picked up on the third ring. Like I said, dickhead by name, dickhead by nature.

"Good morning, Mr Dickinson's office. How can I help?"

"Ellie! It's me! Why aren't you answering your mobile?"

"Helen?" She never rang me on my work phone, so I was surprised to hear her voice when I'd been expecting a client call to come through.

"Duh. Of course, it's me. How's it going? Can you talk?"

"Not really," I whispered, covering the mouthpiece. "Dickhead's in his office. How come you didn't ring my mobile?"

"I did, about a million times!"

I grabbed my bag and started rummaging through it. I must have left it on silent this morning, which would explain why I hadn't heard anything from Saul, either.

"So, what did you want?" I asked, tucking the phone under my chin and pulling items out of my bag one by one and placing them on my desk. Purse, umbrella, shopping bag.

"Nothing major. Just checking that you're still OK to get together on Thursday. Wondered if you fancied meeting me straight after work and coming wedding dress shopping with me?"

I pulled out a diary, notebook, five pens, paracetamol. "Are you kidding me!? I'd love that!" I was conscious of my boss watching my every move from his glass-fronted office, and I lowered my voice again. "Look, I can't talk right now, but I'll meet you at 5pm on Thursday. I can't wait to see you."

I hung the phone back up and emptied my bag, letting what little contents were left drop onto my over-crowded desk. No phone. Damn it, I must have left it at home this morning in my haste to get out of the house so early.

"Everything OK, Eleanore?"

"Fine, thanks Mr Dickh…inson. Sorry about the mess. I'll get it tidied up. Would you like a coffee?"

"Later. Come into my office, would you?"

THIRTEEN

"So, what did Dickhead want?" Helen's voice filtered out through the luxurious floor to ceiling dressing room curtains, her words at odds with our surroundings.

"Helen! Mind your language!" her mother shouted back. She was perched next to me on the edge of a rose-pink velvet chaise lounge inside 'Wedding Belles' bridal boutique while Helen tried on what felt like every single dress in the shop.

"Oh, Ma," she called back. "He really is a dickhead! Tell me what happened Ellie."

Mrs Leong tutted before relishing a sip of her second glass of free Prosecco and looking towards me.

"Well, obviously I thought I was going to be in trouble, because well…anyway, it turns out that he wants me to take on some extra responsibility with one of our clients, and if it goes well then I'll be getting a bit of a pay rise."

"Oh my God, Ellie. That's so cool." Helen's head popped out from between the curtains, her glasses skewed, and her hair all messed up from pulling layers of tulle over her head.

"It is," agreed Mrs Leong. "We should celebrate your good fortune. Cheers!" She raised her glass and drained what was left in it, before rolling up the sleeves on her home-knitted, highly-decorated cardigan and whipping out a fan from her black M&S handbag. "Is it hot in here or is it just me?"

"Bloody hell, Ma, if you do much more celebrating, you aren't going to make it through dinner." Helen rolled her eyes before whipping her head back through the curtains.

"It's great news, Ellie." Mrs Leong ignored her daughter and patted my knee. "What extra work will you have to do?"

For as long as I'd known Helen, her diminutive powerhouse of a mother had been like a surrogate parent to me and, while it brought home the fact that I missed having an actual mother of my own around anymore, I relished the fact that she cared so much about me. I turned towards her, keen to share my news but not wanting to blow her mind with the boring technicalities.

"He's basically trusting me to see a property purchase through from beginning to end."

"That's a big responsibility. Good for you."

"She can totally do it!" called Helen, making me smile at her confidence in me. Like mother, like daughter. "Can I get some help in here please?"

A smartly dressed shop assistant hurried over to the dressing room and disappeared behind the curtains, closely followed by much rustling, puffing, and panting.

I turned back to Mrs Leong. "It's not that big of a deal. The contracts are already all drawn up and the searches are done now too, so it's really just the final stages I have to see through this time. I already do a lot of the work myself, but it's normally supervised."

"You shouldn't do yourself down, Ellie." Mrs Leong ceased fanning herself and smoothed her almost white hair back into regimented order. "They obviously have confidence in you, so you should have more confidence in yourself."

I pulled at a loose thread on the sleeve of my suit jacket, twisting it around my forefinger before pulling at it sharply, only to unravel more of the stitching. I tucked it inside the hem deciding I'd deal with it later. She was right, of course, and it wasn't that I doubted my ability as such. I supposed my lack of excitement was more due to the fact that other big things were jostling for position in my mind. I made a mental note to buck my ideas up and try to be more present instead of mooning around about my increasingly complicated life. Just as I was giving myself a strict talking-to, a squeal came from the dressing room.

"Oh my God! This is it! This is the one!" Helen was speaking in exclamation marks again. Beside me, her mum sat up straight, and it felt as if the wall-lined rows of frothy fabric around us were all holding their breath to see which one of them had been chosen. "Are you ready for the big reveal?"

I put my glass of Prosecco down on a little glass topped side table and started a muffled drum roll against the cushion of the chaise lounge. "Of course, we're ready. Show us!"

Helen flung the heavy-looking curtain aside, and stepped out, lit up from all angles by perfectly placed spotlights. Mrs Leong gasped and grabbed hold of my hand as we both stared in awe at Helen. She looked gorgeous as she twirled around in a sea of white chiffon. It fitted her perfectly, with what looked like hundreds of tiny buttons up the back of the bodice, and cascaded like a waterfall from her hips. For someone who never classified herself as a 'girly' girl, she looked like a princess. I felt a lump in my throat as I looked at the glittering delight in my best friend's eyes.

"Well? What do you think?"

"Oh, Hels," I managed to get out before her mum burst into tears. I pulled a tissue from a discrete box placed on the ornate table next to me and handed it to her, before grinning back at Helen. "I think we've got a winner."

Back in her regular uniform of jeans, plaid shirt, and Converse pumps, Helen and I had escorted her mum a few doors down to a cute little pizzeria. Mrs Leong had dried her eyes and insisted on a third celebratory Prosecco in the bridal shop before we left, and the shop assistant, happy in her sales commission had had no issues whatsoever with topping up our glasses.

Now, despite eating most of a very large Pepperoni pizza, Helen's mum had also managed to share a bottle of wine with me and was starting to slur her words. For a small woman, she could certainly put it away.

Helen shook her head despairingly as Mrs Leong wound her way to the ladies' room, holding onto the backs of several chairs as she went, and pausing to tell other diners that her daughter was getting married.

"Sorry, I'm going to have to cut our evening short," Helen said as she arranged for a taxi to come and pick them both up. "I think it's all been a bit overwhelming for her. She probably never imagined me getting married at all, let alone in a dress." She laughed. "God, can you imagine what she'll be like on the day?"

I laughed with her. "Don't worry, she's having the time of her life, and we can catch up again another day."

"Are you sure?"

"Of course. I said I might meet up with a friend later anyway." A frisson of excitement ran through me at the thought of now being able to see Saul, and I reached for my phone to fire off a quick text to him.

"What? You have other friends!?" Helen adopted an expression of mock disgust. "Should I be worried?"

"Never. You'll always be my number one."

"So, what's going on with you anyway?" Helen asked, sipping her drink. "I know Ma's talking enough for everyone, but you don't seem your normal self."

"I'm fine," I confirmed, surprised that she'd noticed anything amiss, and not wanting to burnish the good time we'd had that afternoon with talk of failing marriages.

She looked at me sternly, eyebrows inching down below the frame of her glasses in a frown. She knew me too well. "Seriously, Ellie, I can tell something's up. You *can* tell me you know."

"It can wait."

"Ellie…" There was a warning tone in her voice.

I took a deep breath and exhaled noisily. "I…well, I guess I've met someone." I couldn't look at her as I spoke the words. Instead, my gaze flitted around the room before coming to rest on the mangled remains of my pizza in front of me.

"What? But you're…do you mean like another man?"

I nodded and took a sip of my chilled white wine, holding tightly to the stem of the glass as though it were a lifeboat.

"Are you fucking serious?" Helen's voice demanded my attention return to her, and I risked a look, seeing that her eyes were wide. She put her vodka and coke down on the table and stared at me open-mouthed. That alone would have told me she was shocked. Helen puts a vodka and coke down for no man. "Jesus Christ, Ellie, why didn't you tell me before? How long's it been going on? I thought you and Alex were happy."

"We are. I mean, we were. We haven't been *really* happy for a while." I was struggling to look my best friend in the eye. She loved Alex just like everyone did, other than me, apparently. "We just don't talk anymore." As I said the words they felt like a cliché. "Actually, we barely see each other as he travels with work all the bloody time".

"But he can't help that, can he?" Good old devil's advocate. Thanks, Helen. "After all it's not like he'd choose to do it, would he?" She looked almost upset, and I wasn't sure if it was because I'd been seeing someone other than my husband, or because I was only telling her about it now.

"Yeah, I know, but it's pretty much constant now. When he's at home, we just skirt around each other like strangers and when he's away, well, who bloody knows? I just get the odd rushed phone call or text before he has to go off to another meeting or another dinner or I don't know what." I felt my eyes welling up, and I knocked back a big slug of wine. "I can't help thinking he's been seeing someone else."

"Not Alex, surely?" She looked distraught at the suggestion.

All I had were my suspicions, but as I relayed them to my friend, they cemented themselves even more firmly in my mind.

"Shit. I had no idea." Helen traced her finger through the condensation on her glass before picking it back up and taking a sip too. "Why didn't you tell me sooner? Before it got to this?"

"I wanted to tell you. I just…I don't know. I haven't seen you since you moved away, and it didn't seem real until now. It wasn't supposed to happen. I wasn't looking for anyone else, I promise." My friend knew me well enough to know I was speaking the truth. "It's just fortunate that he came into my life when he did, and he's been such a shoulder to lean on. He's made me realise that I don't have to put up with things the way they are. Honestly, I don't know what I would've done without him lately."

Helen's eyes narrowed at my words, and I wondered whether she had taken them as a criticism of Alex or of herself.

The text alert on my phone went off saving me from her immediate response and I reached for it, the message it displayed making me smile.

"Is it him?" I couldn't read Helen's expression for once as it seemed caught somewhere between disapproval and curiosity.

"Yes." I turned the phone so she could see the message.

Hi gorgeous. Are you OK? I can't wait to see you x

I quickly fired off a reply before putting my phone back in my bag, where it pinged once again almost immediately. This time I left it.

"Well, he certainly seems keen. I assume he knows about Alex?"

"Yes."

Helen exhaled dramatically. "Have you slept with him?"

"No. I've not even kissed him. It's just…I don't even know *what* it is. A bit of texting. It makes me feel good. And we talk, you know? We talk a lot. He's actually interested in what I have to say. Alex stopped listening to me a long time ago, and then I just ran out of things to say to him."

"Oh God, Ellie. Please be careful."

"I am," I assured her. "Nothing's going to happen."

FOURTEEN

By the time I got to the bar where I'd arranged to meet Saul, the place was packed, but he had somehow managed to secure a spot for us against a wall-mounted shelf which served as a table, along with two bar stools. It was perfect, tucked away discretely at the back of the room where we wouldn't be noticed. Music pumped from a speaker fixed to the wood-panelled wall behind me, and I told myself that was the reason why I moved my stool closer to Saul's, in order to hear him. Positioning my knees between his, I didn't complain when his hand moved to my leg and stayed there, his thumb brushing my thigh. It made me feel as if I'd been lit up inside.

I'd missed this feeling so much. That kind of electric spark you get when you first start seeing someone new and realise that it could be something special. I supposed I must have felt it when Alex and I were first together, but it was so long ago that I couldn't be sure. Maybe I hadn't felt it at all, not like this.

"I'm so glad you came," Saul told me, the intensity of his gaze even more intoxicating than the wine I was drinking.

"Me too." I gazed back at him, all the alcohol I'd drunk already that day making me brazen and easier to shove thoughts of Alex out of my head. It was like a line from a cheesy romance novel, but I really felt lost in his eyes. It was as though he was truly seeing me, and me him, in bright technicolour. It was dazzling after the monochromatic lens I'd been living behind for so long and throughout the next couple of hours, I couldn't help but keep glancing at my watch, willing time to slow down so that the evening wouldn't end. At that moment, I could quite happily have turned my back on my normal life so that I could stay here forever, in this dark corner, sustained only by the electricity zinging between us.

"You know I'm falling for you, don't you?" he told me, his eyes not wavering from mine, and I felt like all the oxygen had been sucked from my body. I nodded, unable to form words. "You don't have to say anything," he continued. "I know it's not an easy situation, but I just wanted you to know how I feel."

Feelings. The last time Alex had shown any kind of emotion was when we found out that the possibility of us having a family might have been stolen away from him after the accident. He'd wept that day. Wept freely like a small child while I held him. After that, it was as though he'd packaged those emotions up neatly, put them in a box, and locked them away in a steel cabinet, never to be opened again. It changed him. It changed me. It changed us.

The rational part of my brain knew that it was ridiculously quick for such strong feelings to be involved in my fledgling relationship with Saul, but it had been so intense already. Secretive, illicit, and emotionally heightened. I'd shared so much with him in just the course of a few weeks, meaning that it didn't feel quick at all. The feelings were very much there for me, too, but they were all tangled up like a big ball of yarn. Messy, confused, and hindered by too many glasses of wine.

"So, he's back tomorrow?"

I knew Saul was referring to Alex, and his change of topic broke my temporary hypnotism. The muscle memory in my fingers sent them immediately to the chain around my neck, twisting the pendant round and round. "Yes. In the afternoon."

Saul's face fell and his gaze dropped down to our interlinked knees. "I guess I won't see you for a while, then?"

I shook my head and sent my pendant spinning around, before twisting the chain back up again. Saul's eyes followed its progress, and I saw emotion flicker behind them before he blinked it away.

"I hate the thought of you sharing a bed with him."

"I know. But you know we don't have that kind of relationship anymore. We're just like friends skirting around each other. Not even particularly *good* friends these days." I felt another layer of guilt come to rest on my shoulders. Now I was hurting Saul as well as Alex. At least Alex was unaware of the situation, whereas Saul's pain was sitting right here in front of me, making me feel like I had to make it all better. "He'll be gone again next week. This is just a pit stop for him to do his washing and catch up on sleep before he leaves again for the second part of the convention." I took Saul's hand in mine, and he lifted his gaze back up to my face once again. "Let's make the most of tonight," I offered, wanting to make amends. "I'll get us another drink, shall I?"

Saul took his hand from mine and pushed his hair back from his face, looking as though he was trying to shake off the negativity that had crept in on us, and re-setting his expression back to what it had been previously before any mention of Alex. "I'll get them. You sit tight."

I sighed as he headed off to the bar, taking my phone from my bag as a distraction while he was gone. There was nothing from Alex, which was unsurprising, but there *was* a text from Helen that I opened straight away.

Please d*on't do anything stupid tonight*, it read.

I won't, I assured her, my fingers stumbling across the small letters on my phone, my inebriated brain cells unable to concentrate on typing a longer sentence.

I looked across the dwindling crowd to the bar where Saul was paying for our drinks and sharing a joke with the woman serving him. She smiled at whatever it was he'd said to her, and a spike of jealousy pricked at me. Not that I was in any position to feel jealous. I had to remember that. My phone beeped at me, and I was glad of its interruption. Helen again.

Just make sure you sort things out with Alex first. If Saul is decent, he'll wait.

I knew she was right. Of course, she was right, but as a timely break in the music collided with the tinkly, flirtatious laugh from the barmaid, I knew I couldn't keep Saul waiting for too long if I wanted him in my life. As I dashed off a suitably pacifying response to Helen Saul re-joined me, placing our drinks on the shelf to our side. A large white wine for me and a coke for him as he was driving.

"Was that him?" He nodded at my phone, still in my hands.

"No, just Helen looking out for me."

"What do you mean, looking out for you?"

"Oh, you know, telling me not to do anything daft, like jump into bed with you." I giggled as I spoke, the idea having already crossed my mind on more than one occasion.

"And why would that be daft?" Saul obviously didn't find what I'd said that funny.

"Well, not daft exactly." I swallowed down my smile, realising too late that what I'd said may have been hurtful. "She's just looking out for me." Oh God, I'd done it again. Put my massive great foot in it by being insensitive. "She just thinks I should sort things out with Alex…with *him*, first."

Saul perched back on his stool, pushing it further back from me as he did so. "It sounds like maybe she cares more about his feelings than yours."

"Oh God, no. No. Of course not." The fact that I'd had the same thought myself recently flickered brightly, before dimming back down again. Helen loved Alex to bits, but she was my best friend in the world, and she just wanted the best for me. For both of us.

"You know what? Maybe she's right. Maybe you should sort things out with him first." Saul lifted his glass to his lips, then put it down again without taking a sip. "Maybe we should just nip this in the bud now before things get too out of hand."

I felt my heart crash down to the pit of my stomach as though it were strapped into a high-rise lift and its wires had been cut. I couldn't rationalise it, but Saul had become incredibly important to me, and I panicked at the thought of losing him. Tonight wasn't supposed to be like this, not in my head anyway. Not that I had any idea of how it should have played out either.

"But I…" I couldn't finish, as I didn't know what to say. Saul looked at me expectantly and I felt like weeping at the thought of being all alone again. "But I don't want to nip things in the bud."

"It's obviously putting pressure on you, Ellie. Pressure that you don't need. Maybe your friend is right, and I should just do the right thing and back away. You'll be fine. You'll probably sort everything out with him and live happily ever after."

It felt like he was slipping away from me, talking himself out of the situation that we'd found ourselves in. Talking me out of it, too. I couldn't help a tear from trickling down my cheek at the thought of being all on my own again. I wiped it away angrily, but it was no good, as more followed.

"Oh, Ellie, please don't cry. I can't bear it." Saul jumped to his feet and drew me into his chest, his arms wrapped securely around my back. "I didn't mean to make you cry."

I rested my cheek against the warmth of his body, breathing in the scent of him, and relaxed inside the circle of his arms. Safe in his embrace, I let my tears fall, and I felt him kiss the top of my head before he took my face gently in the palms of his hands and kissed away my tears. "Don't cry, baby," he whispered, his kisses on my cheeks. "Please don't cry." He drew back and looked at me as if seeking some sort of approval. I closed my eyes and let him kiss me.

FIFTEEN

The car pulled up to the curb outside my house and we sat facing forward for a moment, the engine idling quietly. It was late, and all the neighbours' houses were wrapped up in darkness, the only light coming from the pin pricks of stars above and one streetlight at the very end of the road, which flickered intermittently.

"I meant it, you know." Saul twisted in his seat to face me. "What I said about falling for you."

"I know." My eyes dropped down to my lap.

Saul reached across the centre console of the car, and gently turned my head to face him, his hand warm and soft on my skin. "Hey, don't be sad." His thumb stroked my cheek and I leant into the palm of his hand, relishing its warmth and the scent of him.

"It's just all so confusing," I opened up, looking him straight in the eye. "I feel like I'm falling for you too, but…"

"Don't say any more." Saul placed his fingertips against my lips, his crooked smile inching across his face. "Let's just leave that sentence there. Let's run away together, make beautiful babies, and be happy."

I smiled at the thought. The chance to start again, have a family of my own. The possibility floated around us like a bubble that I didn't want to pop by using words.

Saul leaned in towards me and brushed his lips across mine. The gentlest butterfly wing of a kiss, before pulling back, his eyes questioning if it was OK, and the unspoken acknowledgement between us that there would be another. "Let me make you happy, Ellie. You deserve to be happy."

Any reservations that I may have felt were soothed by his words. I did deserve to be happy. I did deserve this. Our lips met again, and it was as though I had never kissed anyone else before, nor wanted to kiss anyone else again. My heart soared and my body responded to his touch in a way that it hadn't done in so long. I felt like I could stay sitting in this car, kissing this man, forever, and it was only when a light went on in a nearby house that I pulled back, suddenly aware of the reality of the situation. Conscious that any of my neighbours could see me sitting in a car outside my house, kissing this man that wasn't Alex.

"I should go," I told him.

"Please don't."

"I have to."

Saul sat back in his seat, the expensive leather upholstery creaking as he moved away. "Why?" he asked. "It's not like there's anyone at home, is there?"

Stung, I looked away from him, out of the windscreen towards a light which had now come on in my next-door neighbour's house. I could see shadows moving, muted behind the blind that covered the pane, and I felt a brief jealousy for what must be their easy lives within.

"Ellie, I'm sorry. I didn't mean it like that. You know I didn't." I felt Saul's hand take mine. "I guess I'm just feeling confused, too. Look, why don't I come in with you, just for a bit? We could talk." I turned back to him and met his beseeching eyes. "Please, baby?"

He must have seen a softening in my expression, as he pulled me towards him again, the solid curve of the car's centre console digging into my side. My thoughts, still blurry from alcohol and high on dopamine kisses longed to just give in and say yes, but Helen's words came unbidden into my mind, brusquely pushing aside what the rest of my body craved. I couldn't do it to Alex. No matter how crap our relationship now was, I still had too much respect for him to let this go any further.

"I really have to go," I whispered, pulling away for a second time, and watching a frown etch onto Saul's brow. "I have to sort things out with Alex before anything else can happen between us."

With a sigh, Saul pushed his hair from his eyes and gave a small nod. "I get it. Honestly, I do." Silence filled the short space between us briefly, making me wonder if he did understand. "Come on, I'll walk you to the house." With that, he turned away and opened his door, causing light to flood the interior and making me blink, feeling like an unprepared actor on a floodlit centre stage. If only I'd been given some lines to memorise. Saul got out of the car and walked around the back of it before opening my door for me.

I staggered a little as I pulled myself to my feet, and I felt embarrassment flooding my cheeks at the realisation that I was far drunker than I'd considered myself to be. Saul chuckled kindly and offered his arm for me to hold on to as we walked the short distance up the driveway to the house, which sat dark and empty as usual. I wished I'd left a light on when I'd headed out that morning.

Rummaging around in my bag, I tried to feel for my keys in the darkness, and eventually grasped the small silver keyring that they hung from. Drawing the cat-shaped piece of metal out, I fumbled with the keys, dropping them at my feet on the doorstep. Saul leant down and retrieved them with a grin on his face.

"Allow me." His words were indulgent for the inebriated woman who stood in front of him and I laughed awkwardly, letting him manoeuvre me to one side and open the door. "Are you going to be OK on your own?"

God, how I wanted him to stay. I wanted him to carry me upstairs, throw me on the bed and make love to me. And even worse, he *knew* that it was what I wanted, too. I could see it in his eyes as they twinkled, daring me to give in. I couldn't.

"I'll be OK," I told him, stepping inside and putting my bag down on the floor before straightening back up and seeing him standing there, just inside the threshold, leaning against the doorframe. Still blanketed in darkness, I traced the outline of his face with my fingers, unable to help myself while he was still in such close proximity. "I'm sorry you can't stay." I pre-empted his question before it arose.

"Are you sure?"

"I'm sure."

As the last vestiges of the words left my mouth, his lips fell once again onto mine, and I welcomed them. Welcomed them like a starving woman who wasn't sure when she'd be able to eat again. He pushed me against the wall, our kiss deepening, and the darkness in the hallway thickened as he shut the door behind him with his foot.

SIXTEEN

"Stop!" I pushed him away from me. "I can't do this. It isn't right." My coat was puddled at my feet, jacket unbuttoned, and shirt untucked around my waist, where only a moment ago Saul's hands had been hot against my skin. My breath came quickly as I tried to gain some control over the situation and the thoughts which galloped through my head.

We were still standing in the darkness of the hallway, although my eyes had now adjusted enough to the gloom to be able to see the flicker of annoyance in Saul's eyes as he staggered backwards. The look was gone before it was able to make itself at home though, and he shrugged with seeming good nature. "Hey, you can't blame a guy for trying."

"I'm sorry." I tucked my shirt back into my waistband as I spoke, avoiding his eyes. "I want to, I just…"

"I know. It's difficult. But I want you so much, Ellie. I want to be with you. We can do this, make it happen."

I risked a look at him, stood with his arms in supplication, speaking words that I wanted to hear so much, but it was confusing to hear them uttered from Saul's lips.

"Be with me. I know it's hard, but once it's done, we can be happy, really happy. You know it makes sense."

It did make sense. All I had wanted from my life was to be happy. I didn't want a big career or to earn a fortune, I just wanted to be confident in my choices. To live a happy life with my own family and to be loved and needed by the husband that I had chosen. My husband. "Saul, I—"

He didn't let me finish. "Be with me, Ellie. Let's make this happen while we're both still young enough to have a family of our own. I want to give you that. I want to give you everything you need."

His words were almost physical as they swirled around me. I wanted what he offered so much. This beautiful man depicting in words exactly the life that I'd envisioned for myself. How could I possibly say no?

As if sensing indecision, Saul leant towards me, his hands firm on my shoulders, holding me in place. I did want it. I wanted everything that he was serving up to me. A man that loved me, needed me, and children of my own that would secure my place in the world and give me a reason, a purpose. I wanted it all, desperately. But I wanted it with Alex.

The realisation shook me, knocking the thick cloud of befuddled inebriation from my mind, and I took a step back from Saul's hands, stumbling among the tangle of my coat. I steadied myself with a hand against the hallway table, sending God knows what tumbling to the floor around us.

"Shit," I muttered to myself, holding steadfastly to the relative solidity of the cheap IKEA furniture as Saul bent down to pick up some of the mess. Before I could chicken out, I forced myself to speak the words that had to be said. "I'm sorry. You need to leave. I can't do this anymore."

He straightened back up immediately. "Ellie, please don't do this. You're not thinking straight."

"That's true, I haven't been thinking straight at all. Helen's right. I need to sort things out with him…with Alex before I do anything else. It's the only way."

Saul visibly flinched. For weeks now it had been easier for us both to pretend my husband wasn't real, but he *was*. He had a name and he deserved for it to be spoken out loud. Somewhere along the way, I'd forgotten that. "I need to do the right thing."

"The right thing for *him*," Saul countered. "What about what's right for *me*?"

Guilt seeped through my veins. "This is for all of us. It's been so quick, we need to slow it down. Take a step back."

"So, basically, you've led me on." Saul's sudden change of tack hurtled at me like a slap, and now I could clearly see the anger in his eyes.

"No, I—"

"You've led me on with all your sob stories, making me think that we stood a chance. Christ, what a fucking joke." He pushed his hair back. "My husband doesn't love me anymore. He doesn't give me what I need." The expression on his face was ugly and the mimicry of my words was cruel and cutting. "All you've done is get my hopes up when really you were always going to go running back to him. You don't give a shit, do you?"

"It's not like that. Please, Saul, don't do this." I hated the wheedling tone of my voice but I couldn't stop it. "I do care. I'm just so mixed up. Please can't you just give me some time?"

He moved away from me, opening the front door, and casting himself in silhouette once again. "Take all the time you fucking need. Just don't expect me to be waiting for you when you finally make up your mind."

With that, he turned away and left, slamming the door behind him so that it rattled in the frame.

Leaning back against the wall, I slid down it to land amongst the creased ruins of my coat. Too shell-shocked to cry, I just stared straight ahead of me, trying to compute what had just happened.

Suddenly, more than anything in the world, I wanted to hear a friendly voice. I pulled my bag over to where I sat and found my phone among the contents. Dialling the familiar number, I listened to it ringing for what felt like an age before it was finally answered.

SEVENTEEN

When my alarm went off at seven o'clock, I felt like I wanted to die. I'd drunk way too much the night before, which I wouldn't normally do on a weekend, let alone when I had to get up for work the next day. I pressed the snooze button and lay in bed, staring at the shadowy shapes made by the bedroom furniture, and contemplated calling in sick. Not that it was an option, now I had my new workload to deal with.

On the bedside table, my phone flashed brightly into life, showing a lot more enthusiasm than I felt, and I rolled over to pick it up, a wave of nausea coursing through me at the movement. It was a message from Helen.

U ok?

She'd been shocked when I rang her late last night, her initial grumpiness at being woken so late, soon replaced by worry.

"Jesus, Ellie. The guy sounds like a dick. You're better off without him."

I'd wept, then, gulping for air between sobs. The realisation that I'd come so close to ruining my life irreparably had finally started to dawn on me, and the pent-up shock had released itself in a cascade of tears and snot which had run unbidden down my face as I'd rambled, still half inebriated, down the phone to my friend in the middle of the night.

"Go and get some sleep," she'd told me once I'd eventually calmed down. "It's nearly one in the morning, and you've got work in a few hours." She was right. I'd had no idea of the time. "Will you be OK?"

"I'll be fine. Thanks for listening."

"Alright, well, if you're sure? I'd better go and get some beauty sleep too before Chrissie gets here."

To my shame, I'd forgotten that Helen's fiancée and her parents were due to arrive. It would be a big deal – the first time the in-laws would actually meet. I'd been so wrapped up in my own ridiculous situation that I hadn't even considered what was going on in her life.

"Oh God, I'm sorry. I shouldn't have rung so late. Go on, you go."

"Don't be daft. You're my best friend. You can always call me."

All I could do was blub out a thank you at her sentiment.

"You'll feel better in the morning. Well, maybe by the afternoon, at least."

A small smile had forced itself onto my lips, and I'd gone to bed feeling slightly less desolate than before.

And here she was again, checking in on me to make sure that all was well. She was a good friend.

I fired off a quick reply.

I'm fine, other than a banging head and wanting to throw my guts up. Sorry for waking you last night.

I manoeuvred my legs off the side of the bed, pushing myself into an upright position, and my head swam, meeting the tidal wave of nausea head-on somewhere at the back of my throat. The minute my toes made contact with the carpet I knew that I was going to throw up. Staggering as quickly as I could to the bathroom, colliding against things en route, I only just managed to wrench the toilet seat up in time before my stomach emptied itself of its contents.

Pulling the seat back down after I'd finished retching, I reached up and flushed the toilet, before sitting back on the cool tiled floor and resting my head against the wall. At least my stomach had calmed a little now, even though my head was still throbbing painfully. From the bedroom, I heard my phone ping, and then again, quickly afterwards. I stayed where I was. Helen would have to hang on for a bit, while I got my equilibrium back. She'd understand.

After a while, I gingerly pushed myself up using the toilet for support and I brushed my teeth to remove the acidic taste of vomit and stale alcohol from my mouth. Never again, I told myself, knowing full well that I was kidding myself even as the words filled my head.

Tying my hair back to stop it from getting wet, I forced myself under the shower. I let the water run cooler than usual and stood, drained, in its flow, just letting the droplets pour over me. The pattering on my skin was soothing, and I fought the urge to sit down and stay there until the water ran cold.

As I towelled myself off afterwards, I could hear my phone pinging again from the other room. Undoubtedly Helen as she would always send five or six short texts instead of writing one long one without a break.

I grabbed some paracetamol from the cupboard and quickly washed them down with water from the tap before heading back to the bedroom to get dressed. The time on my alarm clock announced that it was already nearly eight-thirty, so there was no way I was going to make it to work on time. Helen would have to wait a bit longer before I replied, I thought, as I grabbed my phone and thew it into my bag before rushing downstairs. It beeped at me angrily from its confines.

I hadn't got around to tidying up the mess in the hallway last night, and, conscious that Alex was due home later, I quickly scooped up the contents of the large ornamental bowl that I had up-ended the night before, then dived into the kitchen and topped up Mr Jones' bowl with some kibble. For once I was relieved by his absence, as it meant I wouldn't have to listen to his judgemental meows as I closed the front door on him to rush off to work.

Once inside my car, I turned up the heating to full blast, thankful that at least there hadn't been a frost the night before. The windows had still fogged up, though, so I angled the air vents to the windscreen where they slowly started to clear the glass as I drummed my fingers impatiently on the steering wheel, wishing I'd worn gloves.

My phone pinged again, and I wondered if maybe it wasn't Helen, after all. I knew from sad experience that it was unlikely to be Alex, but perhaps his return flight had been delayed, and he was trying to let me know. I reached into my bag on the passenger seat, my movements cumbersome in my thick Puffa jacket. My smart work coat still hung on its peg in the hallway in an effort to get rid of all the creases made the night before.

As I turned my phone over in my hand, the screen jumped to life and showed me the messages stacked up on the screen. Seven of them, and all from Saul.

EIGHTEEN

"Jesus Christ!" I stared at the number of messages that sat there, stacked up like a row of index cards, ready to be opened. I cast my eyes quickly over the first one, feeling them widen further as I took in his words.

How could you do this to me Ellie? it read. *I really thought we were going somewhere. Instead, you seem to have back-tracked on everything that you said.*

Why couldn't you have been honest with me from the beginning? You said you were unhappy, and all I wanted to do was to make life better for you. For us.

You said you were falling for me, and yet you won't be with me. Surely if you meant what you said you'd want to leave him and be with me. Maybe you never had any intention to leave him at all?

It was a litany.

Ellie? Please answer my messages, he went on, before changing tack, maybe realising that he'd been too accusatory.

Please message me back. I'm sorry if I sound angry but you must understand how hurt I'm feeling.

I've not felt like this about anyone for a long time. I'm sorry if you think I over-reacted but its only because I care so much about you.

I don't want to lose you.

My heart pounded heavily in my chest, giving my head some competition, but I couldn't tell whether it was beating so hard out of shock from all the discomforting messages or the fact that I still couldn't help having feelings for him, even though I knew it was stupid. I sat motionless for a moment, not knowing what to do other than watch the last vestiges of condensation melt away from my windscreen while I concentrated on slowing my breathing. I let it hypnotise me into a semblance of calm, before putting the phone back in my bag where it immediately pinged again indignantly. Ignoring its tenacious noises, I turned down the heater to stop its roaring, released the handbrake and manoeuvred the car into the road. I was going to be late, and I just hoped that Dickhead wasn't already in the office, making note of every minute I wasn't there.

I knew that I shouldn't have been driving after the skinful I'd had last night as my brain felt muddled and my reactions were not as quick as they should be. I was undoubtedly still over the limit, so I overcompensated by driving at a snail's pace and by lowering the driver's side window to let in some of the biting air from outside, hoping it would act like an adrenaline shot.

I arrived at the office car park twenty minutes late and the only space left was the tricky spot in the corner by the wall. As I didn't have the time or the mental agility to try and reverse into it, I parked as close to the wall as possible before having to clamber over into the passenger seat and out through the passenger door. Grabbing my bag, I squeezed through the narrow space between my car and the one next to it catching its wing mirror with the strap of my bag as I went. Thankful that I hadn't caused its alarm to go off, I angled the mirror back in place and then ran into the building.

Before heading to the office, I went to the ladies' toilets to catch my breath. I was already late, so a few minutes more wouldn't matter now. I flung my bag onto the low shelf which housed the sinks and rested my hands on the lip of the pale pink porcelain, letting it take my weight. I gazed at my reflection in the strip of mirror which lined the wall behind the row of sinks and was unsurprised to see that it showed me what I had expected. Dishevelled clothes, hurriedly scraped back hair which needed a wash, and a pale unmade-up face. I looked a state. I ran my hands under the cold tap letting the water run over the pressure points on my wrists for a moment and then patted my wet fingers to my clammy forehead. Small rivulets of water ran down my face, and my phone pinged again. Wrestling it from its confines, Saul's name glowed from its screen.

I'm sorry if I went in too heavy. Please can we talk?

We can go at your pace, I promise.

Please talk to me.

God, I was confused. He'd obviously had time to calm down and was regretting his earlier words, but I couldn't speak to him now.

We'll talk later, I typed out, before putting my phone on silent and throwing it back in my bag. It was time to go and face the music in the office.

Layla looked up as I opened the glass doors, and her expression changed from one of polite welcome to curious concern. "I was just about to send out a search party for you. Everything OK?"

"Yeah, fine." I grimaced. "Is he in?" I nodded in the direction of my boss's office.

"You're lucky. He's in a meeting. If you sneak around the far side of the office, he won't see you. You can make out you got in earlier."

"You're a life saver. Thanks."

"Are you sure you're OK?"

I nodded, slapped an apologetic expression on my face, and made my way to my desk which was piled high with files that needed my attention.

Somehow, I made it through the day with limited interaction with anyone, including my horrible boss. I'd taken paracetamol at four hourly intervals to try to keep my hangover at bay, and during my lunch break, I'd booked out one of the meeting rooms and rested my head in my hands on the shiny wooden conference table for as long as I could.

Despite looking at me warily when I'd brought him his coffee, Dickinson hadn't mentioned anything about me being so late that morning and didn't question me as I left at my usual time of half past five. Layla's cover plan seemed to have worked.

I was desperate to get home and see Alex. I knew that his flight had been due in at lunchtime, so he was bound to be home before I got there. For once, I couldn't care less if he'd left a mess everywhere or if he was asleep and snoring on the sofa. After all that had happened over the last twenty-four hours, all I wanted to do was to throw myself into his arms and for everything to be better again. I wanted 'us' back.

I burst through the front door, almost falling over his work shoes, which he'd blatantly just stepped out of and left where they lay. I didn't care. I turned the hall light on and moved the shoes against the wall before closing the door behind me.

"Alex?"

The house was strangely quiet. None of the lights were on, and the TV in the lounge wasn't emitting its usual background noise of sport. It was very odd. He'd obviously been back as his footwear had tried to trip me up and his coat was hanging on its usual peg. Perhaps he'd gone out to get some dinner for us. I hadn't been able to contemplate food at all earlier, but now the thought of a takeaway made my stomach rumble.

I made my way to the kitchen, turning on lights as I went, and plonked my bag on the worktop next to an envelope with my name printed on it and a notepad covered with Alex's handwriting. I picked up the pad, anticipating his words, my face dropping as I read them.

Sorry, but I've gone to bed early in the spare room. Got a splitting headache. This card was hand delivered for you.

NINETEEN

I knew the card was from Saul before I even opened it, and the knowledge coiled like a snake at the pit of my stomach waiting to strike as I slit the envelope open with my finger. I pulled out a cream-coloured card, it's texture expensive, the front adorned with an image of a single cherry blossom flower.

I opened it up and its folds bloomed into a tiny 3D structure of a cherry blossom tree, so intricate and beautifully crafted that it made my breath catch.

Let's make this a reality, were the words written across the card. Underneath was an 'S' and a kiss, that was all. That was enough. I slammed the card closed, as though just by having it open, I had invited Saul inside the house.

He'd been here. Been here at the same time as Alex. My heart pounded. Had he simply posted it through the letterbox and left, or had he knocked? Had Alex seen him? Answered the door? Spoken to him? The thought of it was too awful to contemplate. I scrabbled in my bag, suddenly remembering how I had silenced him that morning, unable to deal with his tirade of messages. Now I worried that instead of being able to buy some time to deal with things when I felt better, I'd only exacerbated things.

There was nothing.

For some reason, the fact that there wasn't another glut of messages on my phone from Saul made me feel warier than if there had been. Used to hearing only niceties from his lips, his angry words this morning and last night had shocked me. It had shown me a side to him that hadn't raised its ugly head before. It made me realise that we really hadn't known each other for that long, and while I had poured my heart out to him, I didn't actually know that much about his life. I'd excused it before, thinking that certain things were too painful or awkward for him to talk about, but it now made me feel on edge that he held all the cards.

As I stood in the quiet of the early evening contemplating what to do next, the cat flap rattled into motion behind me, making me jump and sending my heart into overdrive. Mr Jones wound himself around my ankles, and I was at least relieved to have some company in the still of the house, even though his entrance could have been a little less dramatic.

"Are you trying to give me a heart attack?" I asked, lifting him and nuzzling his soft head. Pulling away from my affections, he looked plaintively over towards his bowl. "Yes, yes, it's coming," I assured him before lowering him back to the floor and retrieving his food from the cupboard. "What do you think I should do?" I asked him, filling the bowl. He ignored me, finding his dinner much more interesting.

Part of me wanted to just come clean to Alex, but I wasn't sure if we were anywhere near the right place for that to happen. Maybe it would make more sense to wait until the second part of his convention was done and dusted, and then we could sit down together and get all our feelings out in the open. Try and find a way forward from this mess.

I leaned back against the worktop that ran underneath the kitchen window with my arms crossed, watching Mr Jones eat. "You couldn't give a toss, could you, Jonesy?" I asked him. "As long as you're fed and watered."

He continued to munch away at his food, the crunching of the biscuit the only noise in the quiet room, and my eyes fell again to the card which lay on the breakfast bar like a poisoned chalice. I didn't find it endearing. In fact, it felt the opposite. Intrusive. He'd been to the house. Uninvited.

I shivered. No doubt Alex had already re-adjusted the thermostat to drop the temperature in the house, but it was more than the cold. Little pin-pricks of unease trickled up my arms to the skin on the back of my neck and I suddenly felt exposed in front of the windows. Lit up and on display to an unwelcome audience in the darkness outside.

TWENTY

Saturday morning dawned sunny and bright, which made a welcome change from the dreary weather of the week before. I loved mornings like this when Spring was starting to make an effort and the sunlight glinted off everything it touched, making me squint my eyes as I went around the house opening all the curtains. I could almost lull myself into believing that everything was OK.

I hadn't wanted to risk throwing Saul's card into the bin, just in case Alex happened to come across it, so I'd hidden it away in the bottom of my underwear drawer last night. I was safe in the knowledge that it wasn't somewhere that Alex would be visiting anytime soon. Thankfully, Saul hadn't tried to contact me any further that evening, which gave me plenty of time to sit and kick myself for having been such a bloody idiot for getting involved with him.

I had to try and make the most of this weekend with Alex before he left again on Monday morning. I couldn't help but wonder why he bothered to come home at all in between the New York leg and the London leg of his convention, but I was grateful for the opportunity for us to spend some time together so we could start to make things better.

As I waited for the kettle to boil, I wondered if perhaps I should suggest a bike ride to him. We hadn't been on one in such a long time so, surely, he'd leap at the chance to get out of the house and do something that he used to love. The fresh air would be a tonic for us both. As the tea brewed, I wondered where my bike helmet was. No doubt covered in dust in the garden shed. I'd have a look after we'd had our tea.

I stirred in sugar and milk and grabbed a packet of Digestives to bring up to Alex who hadn't yet surfaced from bed. I could've sworn I'd got a packet of his favourite Jammie Dodgers biscuits last time I went shopping but I must have imagined it. If I'd been in a better state on Friday, I could have got some stuff in to make us a fry up. Never mind, though. The Digestives would have to do for now, and then maybe I'd treat us to a nice lunch instead.

At the top of the stairs, I popped the biscuits under my arm and tapped on the door of the spare room where he'd slept the night before. There was no answer.

"Alex?" I called softly. "Are you awake?"

Still nothing.

I didn't know whether to go in or not. It was just after half past eight, which wasn't that early, but if he was still on New York time it was some un-Godly hour of the morning. I stood outside the door, shifting from foot to foot unsure about waking him up, but then took the bull by the horns and opened the door. He had to adjust back to UK time anyway, I told myself as I tip-toed in and put the mugs down on the bedside table. There was just enough light in the room filtering around the curtains for me to be able to see his sleeping form in the bed. I perched on the edge and touched his shoulder gently.

"Alex? I brought you tea."

He still didn't move.

"Come on, lazy bones, wake up." I gave him a little shake. "It's a beautiful day outside and you're missing it." I got up and moved around to the window, cracking the curtains open just enough to allow a shaft of morning light into the room, dust motes dancing down its length.

There came a groan from the bed. "God, Ellie, what are you doing? Close the bloody curtains." The shape rolled over to face away from the sunlight.

"Come on, you. You've got to get up and fight the jet lag, remember? You'll be no good in London if you're like this on Monday."

Alex groaned again. "Just let me sleep. Please? I'm so tired."

I walked back around the bed and sat on the edge. "You can't go back to sleep. I've made you tea, and I thought once you were ready, we could go on a bike ride together. What do you think?"

He rolled onto his back, covering his face with his forearm, and groaned again.

Unperturbed, I kept going. "We could ride up to the Mount, what do you think? Check out the views over the whole town. I bet you can see for miles on a day like today." He moved his arm and squinted one eye at me. It looked like I had his interest. "Then we could freewheel down and go for lunch at the pub, maybe?" Despite his obvious tiredness, a ghost of a smile touched his lips. "I just need to find our bike helmets. Here, sit up and have some tea."

Alex pushed himself up, looking at me warily, and I handed him the mug, before picking up my own.

"Do you think they're in the shed? The helmets? I can't think where else they'd be. Maybe I'll go and have a look after we've had our tea." I reached for a biscuit just as Alex started coughing.

"Are you OK?" I asked, putting the biscuit back down again.

His coughing came to a rattling halt, tears in his eyes. "I'm fine. My tea just went down the wrong hole, that's all." He put his mug back down on the side table and cleared his throat. "Look, I'm not sure I'm really up for a bike ride today. I'm sorry, but I'm just so knackered."

My heart dropped at his words, but I scooped it back up again quickly, ready with a backup plan. "Well, if you don't fancy the bikes, how about we just go out for lunch? What do you think?" I could see the doubt in his eyes. "It doesn't have to be anywhere fancy."

"Ellie—"

I headed him off. "Just the pub? A sandwich or something?"

"I'd really rather not. All I've done is eat out over the last few weeks, and I want to just be at home before I have to head off again."

"But Alex—"

"Please, just let it go. I'm so knackered." He shifted his weight, so he was lying back down, his hand reaching out to hold mine. A small gesture of consolation, but it felt so good.

"Tell you what…" I was determined not to give in just yet. "I'll let you rest a bit longer and we can see how you feel at lunch-time."

"Sure." He didn't meet my eyes, instead pulling his hand away and tucking it under the duvet.

I collected up the mugs and the packet of biscuits and turned to leave the room.

"Ellie?"

I turned to look at him. Maybe he was going to tell me he loved me or ask me to curl up with him so we could spoon under the covers together. Nothing more, just that feeling of closeness.

"Can you shut the curtains before you go?"

Alex had really pissed me off with his parting words, but instead of telling him so, I decided to punish him by making as much noise as I possibly could to hinder his blissful fall back into sleep. I slammed the kitchen cupboards, clanged the bin lid, and put the radio on, turning up the volume and singing along to Girls Aloud. I even contemplated getting the hoover out, but decided against it, sitting down in the lounge with a sigh at the realisation of how petty I was being.

It was late enough for people to be up and dealing with the day now, so I grabbed my phone to call Helen. I knew I could rely on her to talk sense to me. She could calm me down and help me get my head around the fact that maybe Alex wasn't just thinking about himself, no matter how much it felt like it. Besides, I hadn't spoken to her since the early hours of Friday morning when everything had gone so disastrously wrong. I could update her on what had happened since.

As I turned it over in my hands, the screen lit up with its usual backlog of notifications. WhatsApp's from a group I belonged too, suggestions of who I should be following on Twitter, and Oh God, another bundle of messages from Saul.

Thoughts of talking to my friend were shoved rudely out of my mind, as I opened the messages, watching them cascade downwards like a fold-out story book.

06.55 *I hope you liked the card.*
07.13 *I think we need to talk. Don't you?*
07.28 *I really want us to work things out.*
08.01 *Ellie, why aren't you answering me?*
08.16 *It's because he's there isn't it?*

08.32 Please don't tell me you've gone running back to him Ellie. I thought you were unhappy. You told me you cared about me.

08.40 ELLIE, PLEASE ANSWER

09.10 Please respond to me or I'm coming round.

It was the last message in the bundle and as my mind took the words in, I heard a car pulling up outside. I looked at the time on my phone and felt sick. Nine forty-five.

TWENTY-ONE

I ran over to the lounge window and looked out to the street. My breath was caught in my throat, and I scanned the road for Saul's car. I couldn't immediately pick it out among the parked vehicles, and I craned my neck to try and see the full length of the road.

Hearing a car door slam to my left, I whipped my head around, expecting to see him emerge through a plume of vape smoke like some evil villain. Instead, I spotted my elderly next-door neighbour retrieving his shopping from the boot of his car. One arm laden with bags, he lifted the other in greeting as he spotted me at the window.

I waved back, forcing a rictus smile on my face, and tried to keep my wobbly legs from giving way beneath me. The imminent threat now past, I grabbed my phone and called Saul. There was no time for texting back and forth. I didn't have a clue where he lived, and he could be seconds away from my door. I had to stop him before it was too late.

"Ellie." He answered with a smile in his voice on the third ring. "This is a nice surprise." I could hear he was driving and wondered how far away he was.

"What are you playing at?" I hissed down the phone at him. "You can't come here."

"Why? Scared I'm going to rock the boat?" he asked.

I turned away from the window, leaning against the sill. "You know why. This isn't right."

"Well, that's not what you said when you were kissing me, was it? I seem to remember you saying you had feelings for me."

"I know I did, but…" There was a thud from upstairs, and I held my breath momentarily before continuing in a whisper. "I told you I needed to sort things out at home. This can't happen."

"But we need to talk, don't you think?"

I heard an indicator flick on at the other end of the phone. Jesus, where was he? He could be turning into my road right now.

"Please, Saul? Please don't come here. Fine, we should talk, but not now. I'll meet you after work on Monday, OK?"

"Monday's no good."

"Tuesday, then? Let's meet for coffee instead of going to the breakfast meeting?" Only silence answered me. Silence and the ticking indicator. "Saul?"

"Fine. I'll meet you at that cafe we went to before at eight." The indicator quietened.

"I have to go," I whispered. I wasn't sure, but I thought I'd heard Alex's tread on the stairs. "I'll see you on Tuesday." Before he could reply, I ended the call and slid the phone into the back pocket of my jeans just as the door to the lounge was pushed open. My husband filled the frame.

"You're up!" I announced brightly, overcompensating for my guilt.

"Yeah, I couldn't get back to sleep, and then I thought I heard voices down here."

"Sorry, I was just trying to ring Helen."

Alex looked at me strangely and then shuffled over to the sofa where he fell back, stretching along its length and aimed the remote control at the TV. It sprung into life, and he wasted no time finding some rugby to watch.

I didn't have the energy to complain and instead, I collected my coat and bag from the hallway and left him to it with the offer of going to the shops to get something nice for lunch. I was determined for us to get through the weekend without an argument.

To be fair, we both did really well with our uneasy truce, and while Alex still felt somewhat distant from me, there had been moments where it felt as if we properly connected again, albeit fleetingly. He seemed to take some delight in my hand-me-down chatter about Helen's upcoming wedding, and despite him not wanting to do much of anything, we took advantage of the weather closing in on Sunday, deciding to put on a cheesy afternoon movie.

Alex stretched out his long legs on the sofa, and Mr Jones immediately took it as his cue to jump onboard, sprawling along the length of Alex's thighs so he was in prime position for a belly rub. Accepting defeat, I curled up in the armchair underneath a blanket and pressed play on the remote control.

We were just in time to see a familiar scene on the screen in front of us. A starry night hosted the silhouette of trees, amongst which rested a spaceship. Before long, men with flashlights flooded the area, chasing a small alien creature, separated from his group. Unable to return to the ship in time, he is left behind, alone in, what is to him, an alien world. The film was *E.T. – The Extra-Terrestrial.*

I couldn't believe that this film was on, of all the millions of movies that could've been shown that afternoon. It was our thing…our film. Something that we'd always watched with fondness.

Ever since I'd changed my surname to Thompson when we got married, Alex had nicknamed me *E.T.* as they were my new initials. I'd always protested that I hated it, but both of us knew that I secretly loved it. He'd often leave messages for me on my mobile when he wanted me to call him, using the silly little voice that the alien had in the film, asking me to "phone home." It was cute and *E.T.* was cute if you could get past the odd features. The fact that this film was on right now was like a sign. It was meant to be.

I turned to Alex with a soppy grin on my face. "It's *E.T.*"

He smiled back, a real smile, and held out one finger towards me, the trademark of the little alien character, and it made my heart swell so big that I really thought it could burst. It made me feel as though everything may not be lost after all, and I watched the rest of the film with my mind mulling over plans for our future once again.

It wasn't until the evening that things took a turn for the worse. I only really had myself to blame, trying to push things just that little bit too far, but after our moment of closeness, it felt right. Well, maybe not right, but not completely wrong, either.

I'd cooked a roast dinner for us, and we sat at the dining table to eat it, awkward in our formality when normally we'd sit with trays on our laps in front of the TV. This time, I wanted us to be together without distraction, but it was only once we were seated opposite each other that I wished I'd at least put the radio on to soften the silence.

"Maybe once the second half of the convention is over, we can spend some more time together again?" I put forward tentatively as I poured gravy over my food.

Alex nodded, his eyes focussed on his knife which was carving into the slightly over-done chicken breast on his plate.

I took that as a positive and carried on blithely. “We could start cycling again. Properly. I know how much you must miss it. I mean, I know I used to moan about it, but it was nice when the weather was good, and the ground was flat.” I laughed. “Although we do live in England so both of those are pretty rare.”

Alex nibbled on a small piece of meat and started moving a potato around on his plate.

“Perhaps we could move to the Netherlands,” I carried on, trying to make up for his silence. “Apparently, it’s pretty flat over there. Alex?”

He looked up, eyes grazing my face before dropping back to his plate. “Perhaps.”

“Actually, how cool would that be? We could have a fresh start in a new country. We could learn Dutch, visit the tulip fields.” I was warming to my theme and if I wasn’t mistaken there was a glimmer of a smile on Alex’s face. I breathed in and took advantage of his slightly upturned lips. “We could even talk about starting a family again. You know, maybe get in touch with the cryobank.”

As soon as the words were out of my mouth, I knew I’d made a mistake. A shadow had passed over Alex’s face like a cloud covering the weak rays of the winter sun.

“I mean, not now,” I backtracked. “Not straight away.” It was like trying in vain to catch something slippery that was fast falling out of reach of my fingers. “We don’t have to…not yet.”

Alex put his knife and fork down and pushed his plate away from him. “I think I’m done.”

“But you’ve barely touched your food.” I pointed out the obvious.

“I’m not very hungry.”

"But—" I stopped myself just in time from telling him how long I'd slaved over the oven. "Alex, I'm trying to make an effort for you…for us."

"The time isn't right, Ellie. I can't deal with this at the moment."

"But the time is never right, is it? Can't we at least consider things? It doesn't mean we have to jump straight in. I just meant once the convention's done and you aren't travelling so much for work, we can get back on track and make some plans for our future."

"What makes you think I won't still have to travel?"

"What are you saying?" I heard an unplanned brittle edge creep into my tone, and my husband stayed silent. "Alex?"

"Just that I'm not always going to be here." He either couldn't or wouldn't look me in the eye.

I pushed my own plate away, my knife clattering from the plate onto the table, leaving a trail of gravy behind it. I was sick to death of his attitude.

"Oh my God, Alex, what's going on? You're never here as it is, and even when you are it's like you're somewhere else in your head. We can't carry on like this."

"I know."

"So, what are you saying?" My eyes bored into the top of his blonde head while he continued to look downwards, the wood grain of the table apparently fascinating. "Do you want a break? To split up?" I fired at him. I watched his head shake from side to side, but I wasn't sure if it was in disagreement or exasperation. "Is it me?"

"Not everything's about you."

"What the hell is that supposed to mean?" I was shocked at his comeback and suddenly confronted with self-doubt.

Alex shook his head again. "Nothing."

"Well, if it's not me then is it someone else? Are you seeing someone else?" There, it was out there. I'd heard about these men who lied that they were going away for work and instead went to stay with their girlfriends. I would never, ever have put Alex in such a category, but then he'd never seemed so detached before. It was like he'd become a completely different person over the last few months.

At least my question caught his attention and he looked at me fully for the first time that evening. And while I totally understood the two-facedness of my question, I waited for him to confirm that there was no one else and never would be.

"Well?"

My husband's face registered utter disbelief and instead of quashing my suspicions with reassurance, he started laughing. Not like what I'd said was funny, but as though he found me ridiculous. His derision hurt me, only serving to provoke my irritation even more.

"Don't laugh at me," I shouted, knowing as I did so, that it wasn't going to help the situation, but unable to stop myself, nonetheless. "You're away all the time, you never call me, and when I ring you, you never answer your phone. What am I supposed to think?"

"I can't always call you *or* answer the phone because I'm working." He continued to speak calmly without raising his voice, which wound me up even further.

"But you don't work all night, do you? You could call me back when you finish. I rang you over and over again last Thursday night and you never even got back to me."

"My battery had died."

There was something about the way his eyes shifted away from me as the words came out of his mouth, and I could feel myself verging on hysteria. Getting more and more ramped up in response to his measured replies. This was probably what we both needed. To have a damn good argument. To scream and shout and clear the air, instead of tiptoeing around each other all the time.

"Look, I'm sorry," Alex continued before I could carry on my litany, "but it's just the way things are at the moment." He stood, calmly tucking his chair under the table, blatantly trying to bring an end to the conversation.

"I don't want an apology, Alex," I bit back, determined not to give in to his wishes. I wasn't done yet. "I just don't want it to happen. You've changed so much lately, and it feels like you don't care about me anymore. Maybe you don't. Maybe all you care about is your stupid job." Even as I spoke the words, I knew they weren't true, but I wanted him to come back at me, to escalate the argument so we could both confess our transgressions and then fall into each other's arms, cleansed from sin. If anything, though, it seemed as if my words just made him retreat even further from me.

"You know that's not true," he whispered as he picked up his plate and took it out to the kitchen.

Leaving mine on the table, I followed, not wanting to give up, but trying a different tack to keep him with me. Keep him talking. "Please don't go to the hotel tonight."

"I have to. I need to be there in the morning."

"Please!" I begged him, grabbing hold of his hands. "We need to talk."

"There's nothing to talk about." His expression was passive, and I knew there was no point in pushing things any further. I let go of his hands and turned away from him.

Running up the stairs to the bedroom, I tripped and fell, hurting my knee in the process. It wasn't the pain that caused the tears to start falling, though. Not the pain in my knee, anyway. The pain in my heart was worse.

I must have cried myself to sleep as I woke up in the muted light of my bedside lamp to feel Alex pulling the duvet over me. I allowed myself to bathe in the simple gesture of love, and I reached up and flung my arms around his neck, drawing him down towards me and breathing in the familiar comfort of him.

"Tell me everything's going to be OK." I whispered into his neck.

He pulled back, the lamp behind him making his expression unreadable. "Go back to sleep, Ellie. Everything will be fine, I promise." He stroked my hair before leaning over and kissing my forehead.

TWENTY-TWO

I hated every second of work on Monday and for once it wasn't just because my job was crap. In fact, now that I'd been given my extra responsibilities, it had the potential to make my working life a bit more interesting at last. For once, though, I could do without having to concentrate on what I was doing so that I could mull over what was going on in my personal life. I couldn't get the disagreement with Alex out of my head, and I found myself going over and over the argument that we'd had the day before.

By the time I left the office at the end of the day, I'd barely touched my in tray, finding it much easier to stick to my old mundane tasks instead, which included making copious amounts of coffee for Dickhead. It also had the added advantage of keeping him off my back while allowing me to autopsy the words that Alex had spoken, searching for clues as to why he was acting the way he was.

I ignored Layla's inquisitive gaze as I rushed through the reception area, choosing my departure to coincide with her being tied up on the phone. I wasn't in the mood for conversation, and, instead, I just gave her a wave, mouthing 'see you tomorrow' while she rolled her eyes at whoever it was that was taking up her time on the phone.

The roads were busy on the way home, dark and slick with an incessant drizzle which seemed to necessitate a lot of stopping and starting and the pressing of car horns. By the time I neared my house, it felt as though I'd been driving for hours. As I pulled into my road, the dashboard clock read six twenty-two and I wondered if I could hold off pouring a glass of wine until seven o'clock. Who was I kidding? I knew that as soon as Mr Jones was fed and my dinner was heating up in the microwave, I'd undoubtedly be filling a glass. It'd be six forty at best.

As I parked on our single driveway, the car headlights lit up the front of the house and I was surprised to see what looked like a flower delivery on the doorstep making my breath catch in my throat. Once prolific, it had been the longest time since Alex had sent me flowers, and after the initial delight had calmed itself, it was followed closely by the suspicion that surely, the flowers weren't for me and that they must have been delivered to the wrong house.

Locking the car behind me, I ran to the shelter of the small awning over the front door and picked up the pastel bouquet. Tucked amongst the soft petals there was a small envelope with my name on it which I wasted no time in plucking out and opening to reveal a card.

Written inside were two words, *I'm sorry*, followed by a kiss. I closed my eyes and breathed in the combined scents of the flowers. Typical of Alex to put such a short message, as he had always been a man of few words. Still, this was an acknowledgement that he knew things needed to be better, and that knowledge along with the sweet fragrance of the blooms soothed my tired mind. Maybe things were going to be OK after all.

Inside the house, I headed straight to the kitchen and selected my favourite vase from the cupboard under the sink, filling it with water. I carefully undid the florists' wrapping and introduced the flowers to their new home, their subtle colours immediately bringing cheer. I carried them through to the lounge with me and positioned them on the low table in the centre of the room where they'd be sure to catch my eye constantly, reminding me that things were going to get better.

Filled with hope, I perched on the arm of the sofa and dialled Alex's number, wanting to thank him for his gift. I hoped that he'd answer this time as obviously, the flowers meant that there was a brighter future ahead for us, but when my call was greeted by his usual voicemail message, it dimmed my newly found optimism a little. Undeterred, I left a message anyway.

"The flowers are beautiful. Thank you. Call me when you can." My finger hovered over the end call button before returning the phone to my lips once more. "Love you."

Despite the colourful bouquet in the middle of the room, I couldn't help but feel a little deflated that I hadn't been able to speak to him, and my hand reached for my necklace to twirl the sycamore seed to comfort myself. There was nothing there. In a panic, my fingers scrabbled around my neckline, confirming the absence of the delicate chain.

I pulled off my jumper, checking the folds of the fabric, and then my top just in case it had come loose and fallen to land in my bra but there was still nothing. Maybe I'd not even put it on this morning. I didn't like to sleep in it just in case the chain got caught and broke, and I supposed it could be entirely possible that I'd overlooked that part of my morning routine. A routine that I carried out so regularly that it was like driving a car on a familiar route, and then reaching your destination and not remembering how you actually got there.

That was it. I'd just forgotten to put it on. It was undoubtedly still sitting, curled up in the little china pot that I kept on my dressing table. Taking the stairs two at a time, and nearly falling over Mr Jones who was stretched out along the landing, I arrived in the bedroom with my heart beating a little faster than it was used to. I lifted the lid of the pot which had my star sign painted on it in gold, and poked around the small collection of chains, earrings, and rings that nestled inside.

Eventually, I tipped the contents onto the duvet, separating everything, but there was no sign of my necklace. Damn it. I knelt at the side of the bed and racked my brains trying to think of the last time that I'd worn it. I didn't always put it on at weekends, but every weekday, like clockwork I would put it on before I went to work. It was part of my morning ritual, and I wore it like a talisman. Something to touch and ground myself with when I needed it.

I knew I hadn't worn it on Saturday or Sunday, and Friday was a bit of a blur. God, I had been so hungover that I was barely able to remember my name, let alone anything else. There was the distinct possibility that I'd not worn it on that day, either. So, Thursday must have been the last time I'd worn it. Yes. I could remember I'd twirled the little pendant around and around when I was in the bridal shop with Helen and Mrs Leong as I'd been reminded of when I'd tried my own wedding dress on.

I retraced my steps from that point. The pizza restaurant, and then the bar…with Saul. The sudden memory sent goose bumps up my arms like a Mexican wave. The first wave was of illicit delight, but it was closely followed by the tsunami of shame and horror at how the events of that evening had panned out.

I'd been so drunk and so unbelievably stupid, and the humiliation of the scene in my hallway was now doubled by the realisation that it was probably the point when I last had my necklace. The delicate chain could easily have snapped during the events of that night. Saul could have pocketed it out of cruelty, or it could have fallen to the floor amongst all the contents from the bowl that I'd knocked over in the hallway as I'd careened about like an inebriated fool.

Pushing myself up from my knees, I ran back down the stairs, this time circumnavigating Mr Jones, who was still stretched out on the landing, blissfully unaware of the drama around him.

It could be in the bowl. Perhaps I'd scooped it up along with all the rest of the junk that normally resided in there. It could have been tangled up with the rest of it.

Back on my knees, but now in the hallway, I emptied the contents of the bowl onto the floor, separating keys, pens, shopping lists. All the rubbish that never found a more permanent residence in the house. I did find my sunglasses, which had been abandoned after the last sunny days of Autumn, and a lipstick that I'd not worn in ages, but there was no sign of my necklace.

For the second time in a matter of days, I sat on the floor, back against the wall, surrounded by junk, and cried. I couldn't believe it. I couldn't believe that I had lost the one item that meant so much to me.

I sat there until the remnants of daylight melded themselves into darkness. It wasn't that long, but time enough for pins and needles to attack my left leg as I eventually brought myself to scoop everything back into the bowl once again and hoist myself up. I positioned it back on the table, and, as I flicked on the hall lamp, I heard my phone beep in the lounge where I'd left it. I hoped it was Alex as I hobbled back into the room, turning on the overhead light as I went, hoping to chase away the shadows.

I was overjoyed to see his name glowing on the screen, and I wasted no time in opening his text. I needed his words, his calmness…him. And there was his message. Short and to the point as usual.

What flowers?

TWENTY-THREE

Oh my God. The flowers weren't from Alex. I tried to put off admitting the knowledge of exactly who must have sent them by throwing out possible alternatives but none of them would have sent me flowers with those words in the attached card. There was only one other candidate. Saul.

Jesus, why would he do that, though? Why send an apology after being so angry and so…threatening. The dramatic change of direction completely threw me off my tracks. He'd accused me of leading him on and then all but threatened to turn up and tell Alex what had been going on. Now the guy was sending flowers and apologising. I didn't get it.

Also, had the flowers been delivered? Or had he just turned up with them and left them on the doorstep? The thought of him coming to mine and Alex's house yet again sent a shiver through me and, feeling suddenly vulnerable in the lighted room, I strode across the carpet to the window, pulling the curtains sharply closed.

Turning back to face the room, the flowers, once a source of joy, now seemed to sit smugly on the table. I knew I should probably just throw them out, but it would be a futile defeat. Instead, I picked up the vase and marched it into the small dining room where only yesterday Alex and I had argued over our roast chicken. They could stay in there with the ghost of our disagreement, where I didn't have to look at them. Then, in the morning, I'd wrap them back up in their cellophane jacket and return them to Saul at our pre-arranged meeting. To hell with him.

I closed the door to the dining room behind me and, with my body awash with shame, I fired off a text to Alex, trying for some belated damage control.

Oops, turns out they were from Helen as a thank you for going wedding dress shopping with her. Helen. Christ. I should really text her, too. *There was no card on them, so I just thought they were from you.* I hated the fact that the lie had come so easily, but what else could I tell him?

All my earlier hopes and dreams upon receiving the beautiful flowers had been trampled on and I now felt completely bereft. Going into auto pilot, I filled up Mr Jones' food bowl and, not really feeling the urge to eat anything myself, I emptied the remains of a bottle of wine into a glass instead, almost filling it to the brim. The bottle hadn't looked like there was that much left in it, but never mind.

Taking the near-over-flowing glass back into the lounge, I sat in my usual spot on the right-hand side of the sofa and sipped at my drink while I scrolled through some old photos on my phone. Most had been taken before Alex's accident, and our happy faces shone from the confines of the past, showing off how in love we'd been. It broke my heart how much had changed after the accident. I scrolled forward to some more recent pictures. I'd taken them on one of the rare occasions when I'd managed to get Alex out for a walk on a beautiful summer's day. He hadn't wanted to go, but I'd forced him into it, pushing the point that gentle exercise was good for his rehabilitation.

We'd paused on a bench during our walk which overlooked a beautiful lake, ostensibly to take in the view, but really for him to rest. While we'd sat there, quietly gazing out at the sunlight dappling the water, I'd whipped out my phone and taken a selfie of us both before Alex could argue. We looked tired and somewhat dulled by recent experiences, despite the bright sunshine, and my gold sycamore seed rested on its chain against my skin. I felt the sadness of its loss all over again and, even though I was aware it was just a piece of jewellery that could easily be replicated, I knew that a new one wouldn't be the same. It wouldn't contain all our dreams for the future and our love for each other. It felt as though I'd lost my connection to our happy past. My talisman.

A tear trickled down my cheek and I left it on its course, moving onto the next picture. This one was just of Alex on the same day. Same walk. Same bench. It was his side profile and the way that the light fell caused shadows around the small scar by the side of his left eye. Just another reminder of what he'd been through. I traced it with my finger, causing the image to move around on the screen. I removed my finger and let the image drop back into place, and as I did so, my phone burst into life, Helen's name flashing up on the screen.

Normally, I'd never avoid her calls, but I just couldn't face her effervescence tonight. She'd undoubtedly want to talk about the wedding, and I just didn't have it in me to find the enthusiasm for it. I guiltily let my friend go through to voicemail and finished off my glass of wine, continuing to scroll through photos.

By nine o'clock, I'd had enough of sitting on my own in the lounge. I hadn't even bothered to put the television on for company for a change and judging by the empty bowl in the kitchen, it looked as though Mr Jones had eaten and left me to wallow in self-pity. I didn't blame him.

Deciding that I may as well go to bed, I dragged myself up the stairs and into the bedroom, not bothering to switch on the ceiling light as I walked through the door. I padded over to the window in darkness to close the curtains before putting the bedside lamp on. As I pulled one curtain across, I could see the people in the house opposite sitting in their lounge, watching their TV. The screen flickered, animating their still faces. I never could understand the way some people left their lights on and their curtains open for all to see. They either couldn't be bothered to move, or they wanted people to see their framed slice of domestic bliss. Whatever. I didn't need to see it.

I reached for the other curtain to shut out their diorama and as I did so, a sudden movement caught my eye over by the trees to the left of the neighbours' house. I squinted into the darkness, struggling to see with the light from the hallway falling into the room behind me, hampering my view a little. I wrapped the curtain behind me so I could see better, and as I did so, my heart leapt into my throat. There was a figure, a man, tucked cleverly into the shadows, looking towards my house…my window…me.

Whipping the curtain back around and in front of me, I stumbled back, my right heel scraping against the end of the bed painfully.

"Ouch," I cried out, falling back onto the bed and rubbing my foot until the pain dissipated. "Stupid sodding bed." I wanted to kick it, and emboldened by anger at an inanimate object, I got back up and pulled the bedroom door closed, blocking out the light spilling in from the hallway, before stomping back to the window ready to confront whoever was out there. Without thinking twice, I wrenched the curtain back, gazing down towards the trees. There was no one there.

TWENTY-FOUR

Saul was already at the café when I arrived in the morning for our pre-arranged meeting, and as I entered the bustling room, he rose from his seat with that lop-sided smile of his on his face as though nothing bad had happened. I really wanted to slap it off, but I restrained myself, allowing him to lean in towards me and graze my cheek with his lips. I let it happen, too stupidly polite to pull away, and I once again noted that heady scent that he wore. I hated myself for still liking it and letting it evoke the memory of what it was like to kiss him.

I sat down opposite him, shrugging off my coat onto the back of the seat, just as a waitress arrived with a tray.

"Who's for the cappuccino?" She held out the oversized cup and saucer, and Saul directed her to me, before accepting his espresso. The waitress also placed two muffins on the table, which I'd assumed was for someone else's order. They seemed too frivolous for us.

"I got you blueberry," Saul pointed out, pushing his hair out of his eyes. "I know you enjoyed it last time."

I pushed the muffin away from me, annoyed that he'd been so presumptuous. "I'm not hungry, thanks." Stirring my coffee, I forced myself to look at him. “So, what did you want to talk about?”

“Did you like the flowers?”

Damn it. The bloody flowers! I realised that I’d left them at home in the dining room. Out of sight, out of mind in my usual morning rush to get out of the house. I should’ve put them in a place where I would’ve seen them, and I was annoyed that I wouldn’t now get to shove them back at him.

“You shouldn’t have sent them,” I told him. “I’ve thrown them away.”

As I spoke, I saw that glimmer of otherness behind his eyes again. So fleeting that it was easy to miss, easy to mistake for a change in the light. I knew better though, didn’t I? I’d met the anger that hid just beneath the surface.

“That’s a shame.” He took a sip of his coffee, the tiny mug all but swallowed up in his hands. “They were meant to be an apology, nothing more.” He placed his mug back down, his coffee already drunk. “I know I might have over-reacted on Thursday, and I just wanted to see you to explain that.” Saul’s eyes stayed downcast as though trying to read his fortune from stray coffee grounds in his mug.

“And the texts?” I asked. “The phone call? You scared me.”

Saul looked back up, his eyes pinning me to my seat. “I didn’t mean to scare you. You have to believe me. It’s just…just that…well, I’ve fallen for you, Ellie. Don’t you get it? When you ditched me just like that, *you* scared *me*. That’s why I reacted the way I did.”

I fidgeted in my seat, uncomfortable under his gaze. Was he being serious? Was it possible that I had caused him to flip out like he had done? I *had* been pretty drunk, after all, and my memories of that evening weren’t crystal clear.

"You made me feel like I wasn't good enough for you, Ellie. One minute you were kissing me and the next, you didn't want me anywhere near you. It freaked me out. I lost the plot, I know that. But baby, it's only because I care about you so much. I'm sorry. Please forgive me." Saul's eyes were beseeching, and he reached one hand across the table towards me. "Give us another chance, please? We can take it slow, go at your pace. I'll wait until you're ready to leave him and be with me."

I didn't take his hand, feeling it would almost be like shaking on a deal, giving into what he wanted. But his words had touched me more than they should have. They'd made me question the reality of the situation I was in once again. Had he over-reacted *that* much really? Perhaps I'd blown things out of proportion in my drunken state. "I don't know, Saul, I—"

"Don't make any decisions yet," he interrupted. "Please just think about it. Think about how happy we were before all this silliness happened. Our lives could be brilliant together. You told me that you weren't happy with him, remember? You said those words."

"I know, but I just—"

"I'll give you all the time you need. Like I said, we can take it slow. I want to give you what you want, baby. We could be so happy, start our own family. I know how much you'd love that, right? Just think of it. I want to give you all that. I want to give you everything that he won't give you."

I *did* want a family. He knew that, and he was offering me everything that Alex wasn't. But something was still holding me back. The memory of his anger, battling with the words now coming from his mouth.

"I've not felt like this about someone since...well...since my ex left me. I don't ever want to go through that pain again. Please don't give up on us over some silly argument, Ellie."

I couldn't think straight. He was saying all the words that I wanted to hear. Painting a vision of myself as seen through his eyes, and a future that was intoxicating. But I just wasn't sure I wanted it with him.

Saving me from an immediate response, my phone rang shrilly from my bag, and I reached for it.

"Can't you leave it?"

"I can't. It could be work. I'm supposed to be at the stupid networking group, remember?"

Retrieving my phone, I saw Helen's name and I swiped the call open, not wanting to talk but glad of the interruption.

"Hey," she started. "Where've you been? I tried calling you last night. Didn't you get my message?"

"I can't talk right now," I told her. "Can I call you in a bit?" I watched Saul's eyes assessing my side of the conversation and I heard disappointment creep into Helen's voice at my tone.

"Um, yeah. Sure. Are you OK?"

"I'm fine. I won't be long." I ended the call and put my phone away before turning back to Saul whose eyes had narrowed.

"Was that him?" he asked.

"What?"

"That was him, wasn't it?" His face was pinched, lips in a hard line. Suspicion and fury permeated his words.

I thanked God that I hadn't let him fully sway me with his beautifully decorated pitch for my affection. This man was not sincere. He was not decent, and I had now seen his mask slip yet again as he realised that he was not going to get what he wanted. The realisation that Saul was quite possibly sociopathic made me take a deep breath and swallow before I spoke. I took time to formulate my words carefully and I looked him straight in the eye, trying to convey more confidence than I felt. "I've thought about what you said. My answer is still no. Please just leave me alone."

As if I'd just renounced the devil, he stood, chair scraping back across the linoleum. He stared at me without expression, a fighter sizing up his ring opponent with no kiss of the gloves to follow. "You're going to regret this." Each word landed like a slap before he turned away and walked straight out of the café.

I sat still, breathing heavily to stop the panic inside me from completely taking over, and was startled when I felt a tap on my shoulder.

"Are you OK love?" Our waitress was at my side, surprising me that there was still good to be found in people after my interlude with Saul. "Have an argument, did you?" Perhaps it was just nosiness then after all.

I slapped a mask of my own in place with a smile. "I'm fine, thanks."

"Well, that's good. Here's your bill, love." She headed back to the counter, leaving me to pay for my untouched breakfast and horrible experience. I wouldn't be leaving any reviews on Trip Advisor for this visit, that was for sure.

By the time I got to the office, I was running late again. At least I narrowly avoided having to park in the horrible corner spot in the car park though, thanks to someone else who worked in the building leaving in their Mini just as I pulled in. My tardiness was starting to become a regular habit and I hoped to God that I could break it before it was noticed. Still, now that the situation with Saul was over, maybe I could get back to a bit more normality.

I threw my bag on my desk and switched on my computer, ready to get started with the mountain of paperwork that seemed to have multiplied overnight. There was so much to get through, but I felt sure it wouldn't be a problem. My head was already clearer, and I made a mental note to cut back on the wine in the evenings, too. I was ready to focus.

I shuffled my work into some sort of order with the bulky Kelsey-Williams file on top. Their house purchase was due to exchange and complete soon, so I'd make them top priority today.

"How was the networking meeting this morning?" Mr Dickinson had materialised behind me, and I swivelled my chair around to face him. I felt at a disadvantage being seated while he stood.

"It was fine. The same as usual, really. Would you like a coffee?"

"Good speaker, was it?"

"Um, yeah." I grasped for some inspiration and worried at a small catch in my tights which would undoubtedly run by the end of the day. "It was an estate agent talking about the fluctuating market." I was impressed with the speed of my improvisation.

"Right, I see." My boss shook his head and straightened his already straight tie. "Well, I must have been at a very different networking meeting, because the one I pay you to attend had a talk about data entry this morning. I enjoyed it. It's a shame you weren't there."

TWENTY-FIVE

This was not good. My boss had just caught me in an outright lie, and now my phone was ringing merrily in my bag, making me look even more unprofessional. I mentally kicked myself for forgetting to put it on silent before coming into the office.

"Do you need to get that?" Dickinson asked, nodding towards my ringing bag.

"Um, no. Sorry. I'll turn it off." My face felt like it was on fire, and I was glad to turn away from him. I found my phone, noting that it was Helen ringing again. I had no choice but to send her off to voicemail once more.

"Perhaps you'd better come into my office." It wasn't a suggestion but more of an order.

I trailed behind my boss into his office, and he shut the door behind me gesturing me towards a chair.

"Take a seat, Eleanore."

I did as requested, noting the smell of stale body odour. I hated having to spend any length of time in here that meant I couldn't hold my breath.

"I can't help but notice that you've been a bit 'under par' lately. Is there anything you want to tell me?" Dickinson had positioned himself in his worn, high-backed leather seat, elbows resting on the desk and fingers steepled in front of him. His expression seemed like it was trying its best to convey concern but seemed to have given up halfway there and opted for the easier option of exasperation instead.

"I'm sorry," I told him, forcing myself to look up at him. "I've had quite a lot going on at home. I promise it won't get in the way of my work anymore."

Dickhead Dickinson looked at me over the top of his glasses and gave a smile laced with condescension. "I do hope not, as I've entrusted you with a lot of responsibility." I half expected him to end the sentence with 'young lady'. Thankfully, for both of us, he didn't.

"I know, Mr Dickinson. I won't let the firm down, I promise."

He pressed his lips together and continued to regard me for a moment as though assessing my words, before averting his gaze to his desktop. "Jolly good." He picked up some papers in front of him and jostled them together before moving them to another spot on the desk, which gave me the impression that his pep talk was over, and I'd been dismissed.

I stood to leave his office, one hand on the doorknob, ready to go back to my desk when my boss called out behind me.

"Don't forget that coffee, Eleanore."

Arsehole.

I made a concerted effort to get my head down for the rest of the day, even giving up my treasured lunchbreak just to show some willing. I had figured it wouldn't go down too well if I'd waltzed off for an hour when I'd arrived so late. Luckily Layla bought me a sandwich from the local supermarket when she went out, so at least I'd had something to eat when my stomach started rumbling.

Dickhead had taken huge advantage of my new focus on work and brought out two more files for me to deal with, each more important than the last, so he said. I got on with them both without complaint and was surprised when I eventually looked up from the second one to find that the office was empty other than one of the senior partners and the cleaner, who I could tell wanted me out of the way so she could hoover around my desk.

By the time I finally got home, I was worn out. The high emotion of the day had got to me and all I wanted to do was to curl up in a ball on the sofa with Mr Jones and a glass of wine. Although, maybe I should give the wine a miss, bearing in mind my recent promise to my boss.

The house was in darkness when I got home, which was odd, as I could've sworn that I'd left the hall light on that morning. Having said that, I'd forgotten to pick up the flowers in my rush to get out of the door, so why would I remember to leave a light on? Flicking the switch and illuminating the hallway, I took off my coat, immediately feeling the chill in the air through the thin material of my shirt. Damn it. Another thing I'd obviously forgotten to do was to crank the thermostat back up. Unusual for me to forget, as it was normally the first thing I did whenever Alex left. I adjusted the temperature gauge on the little unit to 25C and heard the welcome click that meant the heating would soon start to kick in.

Rubbing my hands up and down my upper arms to warm myself up, I ventured into the lounge, keen to shut the curtains before turning the lights on after my experience last night. I shivered at the memory of the figure standing, watching me from the shadows over the road, and I ran my fingers over the radiator, which had started to tick as it warmed up. Next, I went into the dining room. I never normally used that room when I was home alone, but something in me felt the need to do a sweep of the house before I could settle properly.

Those curtains were already closed, as they had been all day, but I poked my head round the door cautiously nonetheless before turning on the light. I gasped at the mess before me.

The flowers were scattered across the table and the floor, my vase was shattered, and water had pooled on the table, forming a small stream which had wound its way to the edge of the wood and dripped onto the cream carpet, staining it beige.

"Oh no!" I cried and ran to the kitchen to get a tea towel to mop up some of the mess. "Mr Jones, you bad, bad cat!"

I couldn't care less about the flowers now I knew where they'd come from, but I hoped the water hadn't stained the table, and the broken vase had been my favourite. Once I'd cleaned up as best I could, I collected the shards of china that used to be my vase. They were fairly large chunks, so perhaps I'd be able to glue them together again. I was pretty sure that Alex kept some super-glue out in the shed. Not that I'd consider going out there now in the dark, but perhaps at the weekend I could find it and have a go at fixing my vase. With a sigh, I put all the broken pieces in a bowl in the kitchen.

I picked up all the stems that had been scattered around the room. It was a shame to throw away something so beautiful, but I didn't want them inside my home. Saul had made them ugly. Unlocking the back door, I lifted the lid of the garden waste bin and threw them inside. I heard them hit the bottom unceremoniously. Good riddance, I told myself.

As I turned to go back into the safety of the house, a clatter from the far side of the garden shocked me into stillness and raised goose bumps over my flesh. Body poised for flight, I held my breath, listening, but nothing followed. Was the side gate locked? I never used it unless I was putting the bins out, and I was sure I'd put the catch back on after the last time. Positive. Wasn't I?

I edged along to the corner of the house, hands on the rough brick to ground myself against something solid, and peered down the side passage. All was in darkness. I could see that the tall wooden gate was closed, but I couldn't tell whether it was secured or not, and there was no way I was going to venture any further into the shadows without a torch. If only we had put up one of those motion sensor lights that we'd talked about a hundred times before. Hindsight was a wonderful thing.

As I stood just outside the pool of light that spilt from the open kitchen door into the garden, I felt the hairs on my neck stand up, and a feeling of being observed crept over me. An unwanted caress from someone's eyes, crawling over my skin, leaving another wave of goose bumps in its wake. It froze me to the spot, not wanting to move a muscle in case something leapt out of the darkness at me.

Forcing myself to move, I turned slowly, first my head, and then the rest of my body to look behind me at the garden. It was a still night, and nothing seemed to move among its nooks and crannies. I slowly exhaled and started edging back towards the safety of the back door.

And then the noise came again, from the deep shadows of the garden. Startling in the stillness of the night. I suddenly realised how very alone and vulnerable I was.

TWENTY-SIX

The noise kickstarted my limbs into gear, and I practically threw myself through the kitchen door, turning the key in the lock and leaning against it, breathing heavily.

Every reasonable bone in my body suggested that the noise was just Mr Jones or another neighbourhood cat, but there was a small voice that piped up to argue for the prosecution, convincing me, the jury, that it was something much more sinister.

And then it hit me. What if it was Saul? What if he was a total nutter and I'd tipped him over the edge this morning by telling him to leave me alone? He'd told me I was going to regret my decision, so what if he was some kind of crazy stalker who had snuck into our back garden and was watching me through the windows? After all, he knew where I lived, didn't he? And he'd threatened before that he would tell Alex everything.

Spurred into action, I pulled down the blinds on the kitchen window and moved away from the glass pane in the door so that I was out of sight of anyone who may be looking in. Even though I'd planned not to drink that evening, I poured myself a glass of wine with shaking hands, telling myself it was purely medicinal, while my mind continued to whirl around without a safety belt on.

It could have been Saul standing across the road the night before, as well. I didn't know why he'd do that other than to freak me out, but then what rationality did psychopaths have? Their reasoning wasn't the same as everyone else's, was it? I gulped at my drink and continued to rail at myself. God, what an idiot I'd been. How could I have been so bloody stupid to get involved with him in the first place? I had been the world's biggest fool.

I pulled out a seat at the kitchen island and sat down, eyeing the window in the back door, and wondering whether I should tape a kitchen towel over it so no one could see in. But that would make me crazy too, wouldn't it?

Crazy. That word summed it all up perfectly. Obviously, I had been crazy to get involved with Saul. But then, was that really my fault? If Alex hadn't started distancing himself from me, both physically and mentally, then I wouldn't have felt so lonely, would I? I let my fear turn into anger, which was comforting, although undoubtedly misplaced. But I didn't care. It wasn't just the fact that he was away constantly with work. If he still stayed in contact, then it wouldn't be so bad, and I wouldn't have felt the need to find company with someone else. He always used to make the effort to call me when he was on a work trip, but now there was nothing.

I toyed with the jagged pieces of broken vase in the bowl, letting my thoughts run away from me. The vase had been a Valentines present from Alex years ago and he had filled it with long-stemmed roses. If I closed my eyes, I could still visualise them, the velvety dark red petals, their scent filling my senses. But that was then, and this was now, and I just couldn't understand what had changed, couldn't pinpoint the decline of our relationship.

Yes, his accident had thrown our lives into turmoil, but we had started to claw our way back from it, at least I'd thought so. Then the new job had come along, and he'd thrown himself into it. That had been fine, too. In fact, I had been pleased that he'd had something to take his mind off things. The travel, in the beginning, was OK as well. He'd go away, but we still spoke to each other most days, still had that important line of attachment. Things hadn't been the same as they were when we were first together, but that was only natural. I knew that, but we'd still been OK. It was only in the last few months that things had gone really downhill. That he'd seemed to give up on us completely.

I couldn't get the thought out of my head that there was the possibility he may have met someone else, and it sparked a small fire of jealousy in my heart. I knew I was in no position to judge, but it wasn't *my* actions that I was dissecting. That was cause and effect. Alex had caused it and I had reacted. No, this was different.

I drained my glass and topped it straight back up so that it was half full, unlike my attitude. Alex could easily have met someone on one of his work trips. These things happened, didn't they? What goes on tour stays on tour. I'd never thought my husband was that kind of man, but who knew? I was all too aware after recent events that certain people fed on others' misery, turning it to their own advantage, and if you were in any way compromised it was easy to get sucked in.

I could imagine some glamorous American woman from Alex's New York office coming on to him. He was a good-looking guy, so why not? Who wouldn't want him in their life? Married or not. I could visualise her sitting next to him at one of their work dinners. Probably in her late-twenties, twirling her hair in her fingers and giving him undivided attention, unlike me, always scruffy and rushing around trying to keep the plates spinning. Too busy. Always too busy but never seeming to achieve anything.

The house was quiet, other than the clock ticking on the far wall, letting me know that it was already seven-forty. The wine had started to kick in, and while it had initially calmed my fear and fed my anger, it now started to make me maudlin. I had no urge to eat anything, and the thought of another evening spent alone depressed me even further. All I really felt like doing was pouring another glass of wine and taking it up to bed with me. I could read for a bit, maybe. Lose myself in the romcom that I was halfway through, and then get a good night's sleep for a change.

I finished my glass and poured a third decent measure. Yes, that was what I'd do. I stood and, with a glance towards the back door, I crossed the room and flicked off the light, bringing the world to life on the other side of the glass. Nothing moved.

I wasn't sure why I'd woken up so suddenly and I lay in the dark, still only semi-aware of my surroundings. The wine I'd drunk before bed had obviously dehydrated me, and thirsty, I reached over to my nightstand, taking a sip of water from the glass that sat there. The luminous digital screen on my bedside clock read 2.07am and I sighed at the realisation of the hour.

The bedroom was chilly, the central heating having clicked off at around midnight and I tucked my arm back under the duvet, hoping it wouldn't take long to get back to sleep. I closed my eyes, trying to recapture whatever dream I had stepped away from, and then I heard it. It wasn't loud, but it was…something.

Rolling onto my back, my eyes were now wide open and pinned to the doorway, my ears straining to hear. There was nothing other than the thudding of my heart, and I berated myself for imagining things. It was becoming a habit. Then, about to roll back over, the noise came again. I stayed still, not wanting to move a muscle, and listened. Again, the noise came. A rattle. Faint, but enough to worry me. It sounded as though it was coming from downstairs.

Fighting the urge to pull the duvet over my head and hide, I pushed myself up, the cover falling away and allowing the chill of the room to wrap itself around me. I looked across at the bedside table, expecting to see my phone sitting there, but it was missing from its usual spot. Damn it. I must have left it downstairs where it was of absolutely no use at all. I didn't want to, but I would have to go and get it. I couldn't just stay here in bed like a sitting duck. If there was someone in the house, I had to do something, even if it was just to hide somewhere else.

I reached around underneath the bed for a weapon to arm myself with just in case, finding nothing but dust bunnies and an old shoe which had obviously been kicked under there and forgotten about. I grabbed it anyway as the heel could probably do some damage, and, ignoring my slippers, I tiptoed out of the relative safety of the bedroom. The rattle came again, louder this time. It sounded like a door handle, and my heartbeat kicked up a notch as my mind struggled to remember if I had locked the kitchen door.

I thought about putting the lights on and vanquishing the shadows which jostled around me in the hallway, but, as in all good horror movies, I decided to leave them off. If there was an intruder, all that would do was alert them to my presence and I'd be stuck upstairs with no phone and no means of escape. If there *was* someone in my house, I needed to be in a better position to either defend myself or run.

I crept slowly down the stairs, bare feet silent against the carpet, and as I reached the hallway I paused, unsure which way to turn. Towards the front door and the safety of the street, or into the kitchen where I could grab a better weapon than the shoe I was still gripping.

Everything had gone eerily quiet, and I hoped to God that whoever or whatever had been making the noise had not now gained entry to the house. I decided that my best option would be to head out of the front door, and I looked around for my housekeys to unlock it. My handbag wasn't there, and the realisation hit me that it was sitting on the work-top in the kitchen, probably with my phone in it too.

I contemplated the bowl of random junk on the hallway table. There were spare keys somewhere in its depths but by the time I had rummaged through it, if there was an intruder, it would be too late. They would hear the commotion and be on top of me in a heartbeat. I had no choice but to either hide behind a sofa or risk entering the kitchen.

Shoe still in hand, I inched along the hallway with my back pressed up against the wall, holding my breath in case I made too much noise. As I reached the entrance to the kitchen, I let my breath out slowly, trying to ready myself for whatever was waiting inside. Just one more step and I'd be through the door. Should I creep in with the lights off and assess what was going on, or burst through the open doorway and flood the room with light? Either way, I had to be brave.

Reaching around the door frame, my fingers felt around for the light switch. Any minute, I expected someone to grab my wrist and pull me through, holding me against the wall with a knife to my throat. My fingers touched plastic, I found the switch, and just as I was about to apply pressure, there was an almighty clatter from the back door.

I yanked my hand back, flesh chilled into bumps with fear, an involuntary gasp breaking free from my mouth. Do it, I told myself. Just do it.

As if propelled by an invisible puppet master, my arm snaked back into the kitchen, fingers snapping on the light switch. I was bursting with adrenaline, breath sharp, muscles poised to either fight or flee, as I stepped through the doorway.

TWENTY-SEVEN

In front of me, in the middle of the kitchen, was the metal pedal bin, which was rocking back and forth on its rounded side, its contents strewn across the floor. My eyes shot around the four corners of the room, the sudden brightness making me squint.

The back door was closed and there was no one in the room unless they were crouched behind the island. I tiptoed around it cautiously, relieved to find Mr Jones hunched over on the door-mat.

"Jonesy?" I called out to him. "Come here, baby."

He ignored me, which was nothing unusual. I marched over towards him, expecting him to move so I could check the door was locked. He still didn't budge.

"Jonesy?"

Normally he'd at least grace me with a side eye if nothing else, but still no movement, which was strange.

"Jonesy? What's up, mate?" I bent down to his still body, my throat tight. "Jonesy?" A twitch. Was that a twitch? "Are you OK, baby?" I reached out to him, trying to mentally prepare myself for the worst, and failing.

I gently stroked his back. He was warm. Oh, thank God. I stroked him again. More firmly this time, hoping for him to roll over and let me tickle his tummy. I wasn't prepared for him to turn and hiss at me, sharp teeth bared, looking for all the world like he'd rip me apart if only he were three times bigger.

I pulled my hand back quickly, shocked at his reaction. And then I spotted it. Clenched in a death grip between his paws was a small rodent, still squirming around to get free. Jesus Christ! I'd never known Mr Jones to catch anything before, let alone bring it into the house, and my stomach turned at the thought of an autopsied mouse left as an offering for me.

At least it explained the carnage of the pedal bin and all the noises I'd heard when I was upstairs. Even though I was now faced with a new problem, the relief that there wasn't an intruder in my home washed over me like a wave, and I fell back to lean against the island.

Bloody cat! Mr Jones had turned away from me again to undoubtedly deal the fatal blow to his prey. I let him carry on, without the energy to do anything about it. It was mercifully quick, and with his toy now lifeless and no longer of any interest, Mr Jones got up on his haunches, gave himself a quick clean, and sauntered away with a glance in my direction that I interpreted as 'You sort it.'

Sighing, I pushed myself up and, donning a pair of washing-up gloves, I righted the bin and gathered up all the spilt rubbish from the floor, finishing up by wrapping the dearly departed in a blue and white checked tea towel. Placing him in the bin, I threw the washing-up gloves on top of the tiny mound, feeling guilty about giving the tiny creature such a disrespectful burial but there was no way in Hell that I was venturing back out into the garden at this time of night.

After a quick mop around the floor, I grabbed a throw from the back of the sofa in the lounge, wrapped it around myself and made a cup of tea. I couldn't face lifting the bin lid to throw the teabag away, so I took a leaf from Alex's book and just threw it in the sink. I'd deal with the bin tomorrow, although it was technically tomorrow already. I'd deal with it later. What a night.

I sat on one of the high stools at the island to drink my tea and calm myself down. Still too hot to drink, I blew on the liquid to cool it, and retrieved my phone from my bag, scrolling through my notifications. There'd been a missed call from Alex, which surprised me and warmed my heart, making me feel guilty for my thoughts earlier that evening. It was easy to place blame when he wasn't here to defend himself. Now that I knew he'd tried to call me, I just wanted him here with me more than ever. Wanted his arms around me, keeping me safe. God, how had we got ourselves into this situation where we were so far apart from each other? It made my heart ache with loss. We *had* to make things better between us again. Hell, *I* had to make things better.

There was a whole host of other messages piled up, and I blew on my tea again as I pressed the WhatsApp icon. The individual notifications paraded themselves in front of me. I read one, and then the next, and the third, and my heart sank.

"Oh shit."

TWENTY-EIGHT

It's always amazing how stupid you feel in the cold light of day, isn't it?

My phone had been filled with messages from Helen who had started by asking if I was OK as she hadn't heard from me, and then became increasingly frustrated at the thought that I was ignoring her.

You've not even asked how it went with the in-laws! she'd pointed out. *You know how important that was to me.*

My flaws as a friend had been put out there. It made me sound like I didn't have time for anyone but myself, but it wasn't true. I loved Helen. I just wasn't in a good place at the moment. It wasn't my fault that everything had spiralled out of control lately. Well, obviously I'd had a part in it, but I didn't know that things would lead to where I was now. It had made her upcoming nuptials pale into insignificance a bit.

Ellie, what's going on? Please call me. I'm worried, was her last message and, reassured that I still had her in my corner, I decided to ring her and fill her in on everything that had been going on as soon as I got a chance. That had been at around three-thirty in the morning and now it was lunchtime, and I still hadn't managed to get hold of her.

Things had been manic since I'd woken up to another cold and cloudy morning.

Yet again, I hadn't bothered with a lunch break as I had so much work to get through, and Layla had gone out with the offer of bringing me something to eat. It was so good of her to look out for me, and I made a mental note to suggest that we went for a drink or something after work one day. It'd be good to have some more friends, especially now Helen was so far away. Layla hadn't returned to the office yet, and my stomach was grumbling at the thought of what she'd bring back with her.

Struggling to stay awake after such a disrupted night, I could feel my vision blurring as I stared at my computer screen trying my hardest to focus on what I was supposed to be doing. I closed my eyes briefly, feeling the welcome relief it gave me, and it was an effort to crowbar them back open. It was no good, I'd have to get up and walk around a bit to wake myself up. Perhaps I could make a strong coffee to keep me going. I'd offer to make one for Dickhead, too, while I was up. I'd caught him glaring at me several times that morning, so maybe it'd put me in his good books.

I spun around in my chair and pushed myself out of it, noticing that my boss wasn't sitting, purveying his kingdom from his glass-fronted office like he usually was. I hadn't even noticed him go out. Good. It meant I could lean against the cupboard in the small kitchen with my eyes closed for five minutes.

Thankfully no one else was in there, as I wasn't in the mood to make small talk while the kettle boiled. I switched it on and took my mug over to the sink to give it a quick rinse. The sink was piled high with dirty cups and plates from everyone's lunches, and I wondered why it was so difficult for people to walk a couple of extra steps to the dishwasher.

Swirling hot water around in my mug, I gazed out into the carpark. I was in the crappy parking space next to the wall again today. I knew if I got in earlier, I'd have a better choice but until I got my act together, it seemed to be my penance. Better than nothing, I supposed.

As my gaze raked over the other cars, I noticed someone in a black hoody wandering through the parking bays. It seemed as if they were looking for a particular vehicle, as they kept pausing to look at number plates. I couldn't tell if they were male or female as they were faced away from me and the hood was pulled up, shrouding any features from sight. On the back of the hoody, I could see some kind of design which looked like the outline of angel wings with a word printed between them, but it was too small to be able to make out properly.

I turned the tap off and stood, watching as they approached the back row of spaces where my little Peugeot was squeezed tight against the wall. I saw them take out their phone as if checking something against it, and then they headed straight to my car, slipping down the passenger side. I watched open-mouthed as they walked the length of the vehicle, peering into the windows. This did not look good.

Dropping my mug into the sink to join its dirty friends, I hammered against the window and shouted, "Oi!"

Unperturbed, or perhaps unhearing, the person reached the back of my car and turned around. I struggled to see any facial features as a gloved hand pulled the hoody low, obscuring my view.

"Oi!" I shouted again, fingers struggling to open the catch on the window, but not having any luck. I spun around on my heels, and ran back through the office, grabbing my car keys from my coat. The startled faces of my colleagues tracked my progress as I ran to the fire escape which would get me to the car park much quicker than going through reception.

I hurled my body against the weighted door, slamming it open onto the brickwork of the dimly lit claustrophobic staircase which led directly to the car park. I leapt down the concrete steps several at a time, hanging on to the painted metal handrail, then crashed through the final heavy door into the cold air. Panting, I ran helter-skelter through the parked cars towards the back of the parking lot.

My car was still there, so at least it hadn't been stolen, and I slowed to a walk as I realised that the person in the hoody was no longer in sight, at least as far as I could see. Trying to catch my breath, I checked in-between parked cars as I went, just in case anyone jumped out at me. As I got nearer, I was relieved to see that the windows were still intact, and I breathed a sigh of relief.

And then I saw it. The huge, jagged scar that ran the length of the passenger side. The green paintwork split apart with the finesse of a low-rent graffiti artist holding a key in their hand. I gasped at the shock of it and felt all the adrenaline from my run drain through the soles of my feet.

I traced the disfigurement with my finger, feeling its rough edges against my skin, before opening the passenger door and climbing inside. I couldn't believe what was happening to me. It was one thing after another just piling up, and I felt like I was nearly at breaking point. Tears pricked at my tired, sore eyes, and I felt overwhelmed with the high emotion of everything that had been going on, along with the lack of sleep. As the tears started to fall, I buried my head in my hands and gave in, my shoulders shaking, my chest heaving. I didn't notice anyone approaching the car, and the knock at the window shocked me back into the here and now.

TWENTY-NINE

"Oh my God, are you OK?" Layla's concerned face peered through the window at me.

I looked towards her bleakly. There was no way I could try and cover up the fact that I'd been sitting, crying in my car so I didn't even bother trying. I shook my head, feeling embarrassed to make eye contact.

Layla cranked open the back door and manoeuvred herself onto the seat immediately behind me. She pulled the door closed behind her with a thunk, before sliding across to the far side so we could at least make eye contact if I chose to turn around. The smell of the hot pastrami bagels that she'd bought us both for lunch filled the car immediately, and my stomach growled as she placed the paper bags on the centre console, the hot grease from the cheese already starting to turn the edges translucent.

"Right, let's get some heat on in here to start with," she instructed, pointing towards the starter button for my car. "Then you can tell me why you're sitting out here sobbing, in the cold, without a coat on."

"It's nothing, I…I'm just having a bit of a hard time at the moment." I sniffed and turned on the engine as instructed, Harry Styles bellowing immediately from the speakers. I turned the volume down, turning to look at Layla apologetically. "Sorry, guilty pleasure."

"I'll say." She smiled indulgently and passed me one of the paper bags. "Here, have something to eat and it'll make you feel better, I promise. They don't call it comfort food for nothing y'know." She winked and patted her stomach with a grin.

"I should really get back. I've got so much work to catch up on."

Layla looked at me, her red-painted lips pursing in consternation. "It can wait a little while. You are entitled to a lunch break, right? And I don't want to sound rude, but it looks like you could do with a bit of nourishment."

She was making perfect sense, of course, so I complied, and the food alongside her company and the warmth of the car heater washed over me like a balm, edging aside some of the despair that had hit me moments ago. As I ate my lunch, twisted in my seat to face the back, I found myself filling Layla in on all the disasters that had beset my life recently. She let me talk, every now and again interjecting with a question.

"But he wouldn't do that, would he?" she asked when I told her my suspicions about Saul hanging around my house. "I mean, he seemed so nice. Normal."

I shrugged. "How well do we ever really know anyone?"

Layla dabbed at her mouth with a paper napkin before placing it inside her empty sandwich bag and scrunching it up. "True." She looked past me, through the windscreen, as if contemplating her own history, before turning back towards me. "So, you think he keyed your car, too?"

Now it was my turn to look away, out at the vista of vehicles parked in the depressing lot. It didn't seem like Saul's style, to be sure. More a thwarted act of teenage revenge than that of a man in his late thirties, but who knew? His threat from the day before was still fresh in my mind. I exhaled deeply. "God, I don't know. Someone's got it in for me, though, that's for sure."

"Hmm."

I flicked down the mirror in the sun shield to survey the damage wreaked on my face from my crying. It wasn't too bad, thankfully, and I licked my finger to swipe away a dried mascara rivulet that had run down my right cheek. I turned to Layla. "Will I pass?"

She looked back at me, smile lines making an appearance by the side of her eyes. "Course, you will. Are you feeling any better?"

I nodded. "Thanks for listening. It's been good having someone to talk to. Now I just need to get my bloody car sorted out."

"Well, I might be able to help with that, too, as it happens." My new fairy Godmother squeezed my shoulder and I looked at her in confusion, finding it hard to imagine the always glamourous Layla poured into a boiler suit doing part-time body work down at the local garage on a weekend.

"With those nails?" I ventured a small joke.

She laughed, lifting her hands to admire the long, painted talons. "Well, maybe not me exactly, but my brother can."

My eyes widened in question.

"Look, what're you doing tonight? If Taff can fit you in later, which he should be able to do as Lord knows he owes me enough favours, then we could drop your car over to him and go for a drink while he looks at it. Best case scenario, he'll be able to fix it up in a couple of hours. Worst case, he can't do it and you can bring it back to him at the weekend. What do you think?"

"I think you're a bloody star. Thanks so much."

Layla tucked in a braid which had escaped from the intricate knot she'd arranged to the side of her head that day. "Ah, no problem. What are friends for, eh?"

THIRTY

Layla's brother had agreed to sort my car out for me if we could drop it over to him straight after work and leave it overnight. He planned to work on it in the morning before his first customer was due. That was fine with me. I could get a taxi home tonight after drinks with Layla, and then catch the bus to work in the morning. It would take forever to chug its way across town, but it was a small price to pay, and if I made sure to only stay out for a couple of drinks, then it would be OK getting up early.

I managed to get through the rest of the afternoon without mishap, keeping Dickhead topped up with coffee offers on the hour. I'd often fantasised about swapping his three sugars for rat poison like the beleaguered secretaries had done in the film *9 to 5* and I couldn't resist humming the theme tune to myself as I delivered him his last cup of the day.

He eyed me suspiciously as I placed the mug in front of him, making sure to put it on a coaster. I'd learned like one of Pavlov's dogs never to place the mug directly on the shiny wooden surface of his desk.

Back at my workstation, I waited patiently for the digital clock on the lower right-hand side of my computer screen to make its way round to half past five. At five twenty-eight I pressed send on the email I'd just written, at five twenty-nine I closed all my applications down, and at five-thirty I hit the shutdown button on my keyboard and picked up my coat and bag.

Layla was waiting for me in reception, already wrapped up in her bright red coat and purple scarf. She was always so colourful, and I made a conscious decision to stop wearing so many dark shades. It was grey enough in England at this time of year, without me adding to it with my dull wardrobe.

The garage was only a couple of streets away from our office, and after I'd handed over the keys to Layla's brother and he'd reassured me that the car would be ready to collect after work the next day, Layla and I found our way to the nearest bar.

"I'm only staying for a couple," I pre-empted as Layla ushered me up the steps and into a trendy bar littered with comfy-looking armchairs and sofas.

"No worries," she threw back over her shoulder, and I followed in the wake of her perfume as she approached the bar. I could see the male bar tenders jostling for position like a pair of horny stags. I couldn't blame them, as she certainly managed to catch the eye with her long braids and thick lashes.

"What can I get you, ladies?"

While the question was ostensibly posed to both of us, it was really aimed solely at Layla, and I couldn't help but snigger to myself. It suited me just fine as I'd proved recently how badly I handled unwarranted attention.

Conscious that I wanted to take it easy, I was about to suggest a white wine spritzer when Layla announced to her wannabe lothario that we'd have cocktails.

"We'll start with Cosmos," she told him, and then catching the look on my face, "What? They're two for one until seven o'clock. We might as well take advantage."

I rolled my eyes. "Fine. Go on then."

Layla clapped her hands, a massive grin lighting up her face.

"I'll go and find us a seat." Unbuttoning my coat, I wound my way through the low-slung furniture, finding a well-worn leather sofa by the window. I laid my coat over the back of it and took out my phone which was blissfully free from notifications for a change. I fired off a quick message to Alex and then one to Helen, telling her I was out for a couple of drinks after work and promising to call once I got in.

"Can you believe that guy asked for my number?" Layla exclaimed a few minutes later as she bent to put the drinks down on the knee-height table in front of me, sloshing some of the liquid onto it.

"Er, yes," I told her. "I'd ask for your bloody number if I was that way inclined!" I laughed, wondering how Helen would react to my new friend, who had now removed her coat and positioned herself flawlessly on the sofa next to me, highlighting my general scruffiness even further. I could feel the bartenders' eyes flicking towards us and thought how useful it was that there were drip trays on the bar to catch their drool. I couldn't help laughing at the image in my head, and Layla looked at me, possibly wondering if I was alright.

The Cosmopolitan went down well, and surprisingly quickly, so it came as not much of a surprise when Layla suggested another. The bar had started to fill up with lots of other office workers, relieved to reach the end of another day. I'd known her suggestion for more drinks was coming, so I offered to get the next round in, confirming to myself as I put in my order for two Sidecars that this really would be the last drink and then I'd make my excuses and head off to the taxi rank.

By the time I'd wound my way back to our spot, managing not to spill too much from the over filled glasses, Layla was deep in conversation with a man perched on the arm of the sofa, his friend uncomfortably jiggling from foot to foot behind him. As I approached, Layla looked up with a big smile on her face, holding her hand out for her drink.

"Ellie, this is Nathan. We used to go to school together."

Nathan got to his feet and held out his hand for me to shake, meaning I had to wipe the spilt cocktail down the side of my trousers before taking his hand.

"Nice to meet you, Ellie. Layla says you guys work together."

I nodded and took a sip of my drink as Nathan stood to one side, introducing his friend.

"James," he announced as he lunged forward, taking my hand in a clammy grip that made me immediately want to have a shower.

"Ellie." I wiped my hand on my trousers a second time.

After listening to James talk unabashedly about his ball-bearing company for the next twenty minutes without so much as drawing breath, I put my now empty glass on the table and excused myself to go to the ladies' room. I didn't need to go, but I wanted to get away from his monotone company.

I stood in front of the mirror in the toilets and wiped a little blob of eyeliner away from my inner eye. I yawned at my reflection, noting how pale my face looked. While I had been enjoying Layla's company, she seemed pretty smitten with Nathan and I decided that I'd go back downstairs, make my excuses to Layla, and then head off. All I wanted was a good night's sleep for a change.

I headed back to the bar, tripping as I came through the door from the toilets, making me realise that the two cocktails I'd had, had already had an effect. As I approached the table, I was greeted by a cheer from Layla.

"Here she is!" Nathan exclaimed, with a shit-eating grin on his handsome face. "Layla said you were drinking sidecars, so I got you two each while Happy Hour's still on." He picked up one of the multitudes of glasses from the table and handed it to me. "Cheers!"

I clinked glasses with him, shooting Layla a look of consternation. She batted it away like a pro baseball player. I felt stuck. "That's really kind of you Nathan, but I can't stay."

His face dropped, obviously worried that I'd be taking Layla away with me. "Oh, I thought…"

Layla was frowning and mouthing something at me from behind him that I couldn't make out.

"Sorry. It's just I've got to get up early for work tomorrow, and I have to feed my cat."

"Oh, OK. Well, another time then maybe." Nathan had already moved on from the conversation, his eyes casting their way back towards Layla, who stared at me as though trying to hypnotise me with unspoken words.

"Could you come to the toilet with me, Ellie?" She took my arm, spinning me around. "Back in a sec," she told Nathan.

"But I've only just—"

"Yeah, I know, but I need you to come with me." Layla was already pulling me back towards the doors that led to the loos. As soon as they swung shut behind us, she stopped in the hallway.

"I thought you needed the—"

"Ellie," she wheedled. "Please don't go yet. Just one more drink, pleeease? I haven't seen Nate since school, and he is looking *fine*."

I couldn't help but laugh.

"Please say you'll stay and be my wing-man?" She'd obviously sensed a weakening in me. "You could do with having a laugh, too. A couple more drinks. Switching off from things. It'd do you the world of good."

"Oh, Layla…really?"

She adopted a big-eyed puppy dog face, tilting her head to one side. "Pleeease?"

I rolled my eyes. "Oh, for God's sake, fine. Just one more drink though and then I'm gone. You'd better move fast."

Layla whooped and hugged me tightly before dragging me back out to the bar where Nathan and James were waiting.

I reclaimed my drink from where I'd left it. I'd certainly need it to get through any more conversations with James.

THIRTY-ONE

"Last orders!" came the shout above the music which had been cranked up around an hour earlier.

I looked at my watch, finding it hard to focus on the tiny digital display. "Oh my God, Layla! Its nearly eleven o'clock! I've got to go. I've got to get home."

My friend unwrapped herself from Nathan, the pair of them jolted back into reality with my intrusion. I had no idea what had happened to James and didn't care as I'd formed an alcohol-induced friendship with another group at the bar who'd been ordering bottles of Prosecco all night to celebrate…something. I couldn't remember exactly what, but they'd been kind enough to share their bubbles with me.

All I knew was that I was glad I'd stayed out. Layla had been right to talk me into it as I'd let my hair down for the first time in ages and had actually had some fun for a change. So much better than sitting at home on my own with only Mr Jones and a bottle of wine for company. Although, thinking of Jonesy, I really should get back home and feed him.

"Layla, come on." I pulled her, protesting, from Nathan's arms. "She'll ring you," I called behind us as we left the bar in a flurry of coats, scarves, and inebriated goodbye kisses. We wound our way, arm in arm, down towards the taxi rank, each of us leaning heavily against the other as we sang our own mismatched lyrics to the last song that had been on in the bar before we left. Normally, there'd be a queue of waiting taxis at this time of night, but for some reason the street was devoid of any cars.

"Bugger." Layla folded her arms around herself, her breath pluming in the cold night air. "Maybe we should just call a taxi company and wait back in the bar for it to arrive."

"Nice try," I told her as I spotted a taxi rounding the corner and heading towards us.

We bundled into the back, instructing the driver to take us first to my address and then to Layla's before collapsing back on the worn seats to giggle about the events of the evening. God, it felt so good, warm in the glow of a new burgeoning friendship. I realised, not for the first time, how much I missed doing things like this with Helen since she'd been gone.

Helen. Another day had passed by without speaking to her. I'd do it tomorrow, I told myself for the umpteenth time. Guilt at the possibility that I was not being as good a friend as I could be loitered at the back of my mind, trying to gain entry, but I shoved it away quickly, not letting it take root. I wanted to continue bathing in the good vibes of the evening I'd had. It was Helen's fault if we were growing apart, anyway. She was the one who'd moved away.

Upon arriving at my house, the driver put on the interior light of the car so that I could rummage in my bag for some money to cover my part of the journey.

"Here." I thrust a tenner into Layla's hand, before diving back into the bag to find my keys.

Layla leant her head back against the seat, closing her eyes while I rummaged, placing items on her lap for her to hold. "Jesus, El, maybe you should get a smaller bag," she joked, opening her eyes once again as I placed an umbrella, followed by a packet of tissues, and then a bottle of water in her hands. "I mean, who are you? Mary Poppins?" She laughed.

I would have laughed too if it wasn't for the dawning realisation that I couldn't find my keys. Starting to worry, I tipped my bag upside down on the seat between us, watching all the items that were left inside cascade onto the ripped leather. Purse, pens, sweets, lip salve, tampons, all landing in a jumbled heap. I then thrust my hand back inside the bag to do a final sweep just in case my keys had got caught in the lining. They hadn't.

"Oh, shit." I looked at Layla, panic setting in.

"What?"

"Everything alright, love?" The taxi driver had obviously sensed my angst, too.

"I can't find my keys!"

"Are they in your pocket?"

I knew they weren't, but I patted them anyway. "No." This was all I needed.

"Did you leave your bag unattended in the bar?" Layla was sitting upright now, her full attention on me.

"No, I…well, maybe a bit." What an idiot. I needed to take better care of things, pay more attention. I'd left my bag sitting on the sofa next to Layla and Nathan while I talked to my new friends at the bar. But they wouldn't have noticed if a UFO had landed next to them, let alone someone stealing from me. What if someone had taken my keys from my bag? What if Saul...?

No, that was just crazy thinking. Yes, I was drunk, but I would have noticed if he was at the bar, wouldn't I? And why would he be following me anyway? Surely, he'd have better things to do with his time.

But the figure across the road, the feeling of being watched the other night…I couldn't shake the unease that it had instilled in me.

"I don't suppose you've got a spare set of keys under a plant pot?" Layla asked, oblivious to the path that my thoughts were taking.

"No. Nor with the neighbours." The only spare set we had were in that giant mess of a bowl in the hallway. Damn it. "Oh God, Layla, I don't know what to do. I don't know where they…"

And then the awful realisation dawned on me.

"Oh, crap."

THIRTY-TWO

"What?" Layla still clutched some of the contents of my bag.

"I know where they are."

She looked at me, the unspoken question in her eyes.

"I'm such a bloody idiot."

"Well, let me be the judge of that." She smiled.

"I gave them to your brother."

"Eh?"

"The keys. My car keys. I didn't take them off the key-ring with all the others on it. I just gave him the whole lot. Oh, God!" Tears filled my eyes, half from relief and half because I couldn't believe I'd been so bloody careless. What must Layla think of me? A complete disaster, just pinballing from one ridiculous scenario to another. I was just a bloody mess. A drunk mess. Tears started tracking down my face for the second time that day as I just gave in to it.

I don't know what I expected from Layla. Maybe a hug, or some soothing words but what I didn't expect was to hear her burst into laughter. The noise startled me out of my self-pity.

"You muppet!"

I looked at her, startled, as she continued to laugh.

"But what am I going to do?"

"Oh, Ellie." She wiped the tears of mirth from her eyes and started handing the contents of my bag back to me. "Pack up all this rubbish back into your Mary Poppins bag. You can come to my place and crash there."

I was filled with a sense of relief that everything seemed so easily solved, and not the total nightmare that I'd imagined. "I *am* a muppet, aren't I?"

"Yup." Layla carried on handing me items, now singing the theme tune to *The Muppet Show*. I couldn't swear to it, but I was pretty sure the taxi driver might have nodded his head, too.

Layla lived on the second floor of a block of flats just outside of town, but in the opposite direction to my house. It was nice inside, if a little messy, but as I collapsed onto the bright blue sofa which was liberally dressed with mustard-coloured cushions. I immediately felt at home. The lounge was decorated the same way that Layla decorated herself. Bright and cheerful. I loved it.

"Coffee?" she offered, as she wandered over to the doorway which I assumed led to the kitchen.

"That'd be great."

I heard her filling the kettle and instructing her Alexa to play some chilled-out music, which filtered through a speaker underneath the TV. I didn't recognise the song, but it sounded bluesy, relaxing. I let my head fall back and closed my eyes for a moment, listening to the music and the clattering around in the kitchen. It was comforting and very nice to not be alone for a change.

I took the proffered mug from Layla, the smell of rich coffee filling the room on her arrival, and she sat next to me on the sofa, curling her long legs underneath herself and placing a cushion on her lap where she then rested her coffee cup.

"Thanks," I told her. "For this," I nodded at the coffee, "and for this." I looked around the room. "Letting me stay. It's really kind of you."

"It's nothing. I'm pretty sure you'd do the same." She smiled and sipped her drink.

I followed suit, taking a big mouthful, which sent fiery heat racing down my throat and made me splutter. "Jesus, Layla, what the hell is in this?"

Her eyes crinkled up. "Just a drop or two of whiskey. It's for the shock."

So much for my not drinking anymore. I was off to a flying start with the cocktails, then the Prosecco, and now whiskey. God, I was rubbish. Perhaps I should try to take some more responsibility for my life instead of just going along with things all the time. I sighed. Tomorrow, though. I couldn't say no now, not after all my new friend had done for me today. It'd just be rude.

"You can stay in my flat mate's room tonight. I'm sure he wouldn't mind helping a damsel in distress."

"I take it he isn't in there, then?" I heard a small slur in my voice as I spoke and hoped that Layla hadn't noticed. She seemed to be able to hold her drink much better than me. But then I didn't seem to be able to do anything too well lately, did I?

"Er no, don't worry. He's flight crew so he's hardly ever here, to be honest. I think he's somewhere over the Caribbean right now. Lucky sod."

I smiled with some effort as the whiskey worked its magic on the muscles of my body. "That'd be great. Thanks so much."

"You wait there and I'll just check that his room's respectable and make sure there's some clean sheets."

Layla pushed herself up, and after placing my half-drunk coffee down, I again let my head loll against the back of the sofa. I couldn't keep my eyes open any longer. The events of the night before, the keying of my car today, and all the drinks I'd had were conspiring to make my body shut down and get some rest, even though I tried to fight it. I tried to lift my head back up and crank open an eyelid as it seemed rude to just pass out on Layla's sofa while she was being so kind, but I just couldn't do it. I let the lights go out.

The next thing I knew, I was lying down on the sofa with my head propped up with a pillow, and a duvet pulled over me. The room was lit only by a soft glowing lamp and the music had finished playing.

My head swam as I tried to get my bearings. "Wha?" I couldn't even get the words out, I was so tired.

"Hey, sleepyhead." Layla came into the room from the kitchen, with what looked like a washing-up bowl in her hand. "You passed out on the sofa and I couldn't move you, so I thought it'd just be easier to settle you in here."

"Wha?" I tried again.

"Shh. Just try and get some sleep. There's a glass of water on the coffee table, and, well, here's a washing-up bowl just in case you need to puke. Try and aim that way, as I'm kinda fond of my sofa." She winked at me. "Hope you sleep well."

She turned half away from me, rolling up her sleeves as she went, and I noticed she'd changed out of her smart, brightly coloured work clothes into a pair of grey tracksuit bottoms and a black hoodie. It was strange seeing her stripped of colour, and as she left the room and my eyes became heavy once again, it was like watching a shadow disappear.

THIRTY-THREE

The first thought I had upon waking was that I didn't want to be awake. My head hurt, and my mouth felt as if something had crawled inside it and died. I reached over to the coffee table where a glass of water sat, and my stomach roiled at the sight of the washing-up bowl by the side of the couch. I hadn't thrown up, but I still wasn't out of the woods yet.

"How're you feeling?" Layla bustled through the doorway from the kitchen, resplendent in a cerise pink silk blouse and navy trousers.

The colour of the shirt made me want to grab a pair of sunglasses, and I closed my eyes and groaned.

"That good huh?"

I drew my legs in and squinted at her as she perched on the edge of the sofa, her perfume invasive. "I've felt better." My voice was croaky, and I cleared my throat before speaking again. "So much for just having a couple of drinks."

Layla laughed. "Yeah, sorry about that. My fault."

I winced at the noise, not able to understand how the hell she was so bright-eyed and bushy tailed this morning, while I must resemble something that lived in a swamp. "How're you so perky?" I asked.

"I dunno. Annoying, isn't it? Maybe I just didn't drink as much as you. You were certainly throwing a lot of Prosecco back with those people at the bar. Who were they, anyway?"

"God, I don't even know." I shook my head, wincing at the pain the movement caused. I hadn't wanted to be a third wheel with Layla and Nathan, but instead of standing my ground and insisting that I was going to leave, I'd let myself become drawn into another group. I cast around for someone to blame. Layla had wanted me to stay, so I had. But did she really force me into it? I couldn't think straight right now.

"Come on, why don't you throw a sickie today? I can drop you home and we can swing past the garage on the way to pick up your keys."

God, the keys! I'd forgotten the actual reason why I'd even ended up at Layla's. "I don't know. I've got so much work to do. Maybe I'll feel better after a shower." I tried to push myself up, a feeling of vertigo immediately making the room spin around my head. I felt Layla's hands, firm on my shoulder for which I was thankful as, without them, I would have surely been spun from the roundabout that I seemed to have boarded.

"I'm not being funny, Ellie, but if you go in to work like this, I'm not too sure you'll be getting any thanks for it. In fact, the only thing you'll probably get is your P45."

I put my head in my hands, elbows resting on my knees. I could've cried if I had the energy.

"Right. It's decided." I looked up to see Layla putting on her coat and scarf, the bright colours clashing loudly with the pink of her blouse and making my brain ache. "I'm taking you home, and I'll cover for you at work. You can just go straight to bed and I'll check up on you later. I'm not taking no for an answer."

As I entered the house, stepping over several envelopes that had been delivered the day before, I noticed that the building had a different kind of feel to it. I couldn't quite put my finger on what wasn't right, but it just felt somewhat unfamiliar. There was a different quality to the air, not a scent of something new, necessarily, but something other than just me. It was almost like the feeling that you get upon entering a holiday rental not long after the last guests have vacated it.

As I put my keys that I'd been re-acquainted with on the hall table, Mr Jones came padding out from the lounge, pausing to stretch mid-way before winding himself around my ankles and miaowing his displeasure at being left without a meal for so long.

"I'm sorry, baby."

I lifted him and buried my face in his soft fur, again getting that scent that I couldn't place from his fluffy coat. Just briefly, and then it was gone, like a half-formed memory. I stood with him in my arms for a moment, letting the rumble of his purring seep into me, calming me. Stupid idiot, I chastised myself. You're imagining things. Not surprising, really, with everything that had happened lately, all on top of yet another killer hangover. I would use today to recuperate. Have some rest, eat properly, speak to Helen, and have an early night. Then everything would be better.

"Let's go and make a cup of tea shall we, Jonesy?"

I carried him into the kitchen, where he squirmed out of my arms, jumping down to patrol in front of the cupboard where his food was kept.

"OK, OK, let me at least put the kettle on first." I tried to pacify him as I carried it over to the sink to fill it up, noticing two used tea bags sat in its depths, their tannin hopefully only a temporary stain on the white porcelain. I picked up the used bags, pissed off that they had been left in the sink and realising that there was no one to blame but myself this time. Stepping on the foot pedal of the bin, I was immediately confronted by my blue and white checked tea towel wrapped into a small parcel. Spots of dark red had blossomed through the open weave of the cotton, and realisation dawned of what was inside the macabre wrapping.

The mouse. Of course. I'd left it in the bin yesterday morning as I'd rushed as usual to get to work on time. No wonder the teabags were in the sink, as I wouldn't have wanted to face the little blood-stained package for a second time. I certainly couldn't blame myself for that.

I was amazed that Mr Jones hadn't tried to get into the bin to find his unwitting victim, especially without having had a full belly yesterday. I threw the teabags in the bin, and with my stomach churning, pulled out the sack of rubbish and tied the top, holding my breath. Better to deal with it now when I already felt awful.

I flicked the kettle on and lifted the bin bag over to the back door, resting it on the doormat while I turned the key, but it didn't move. Usually, the key would click over easily as I turned it a full circle to the left, but it didn't budge a single millimetre. I let go of the bag so that I could use my dominant hand to turn the key again. It still wouldn't move. My heart seemed to come to a stop before kickstarting again, thudding loudly in my ears. No, surely not. Surely, I hadn't been so careless…

Gingerly, I placed my hand on the doorhandle and pressed down, the mechanisms clicking as it moved fully without stopping. The door was unlocked.

THIRTY-FOUR

Had I really gone out and left my house unlocked? Open to just anyone to be able to walk in? Yes, I'd been under pressure, but I'd never ever done anything as stupid as that. Well, so long as you discounted my involvement with Saul.

I tentatively made my way around the whole house to check that everything was as it should be, and thankfully nothing seemed particularly out of place. There were no damaged locks or broken windows, and nothing of value seemed to be missing, other than my necklace, of course, but that had disappeared way before I'd gone waltzing off leaving the back door open for all and sundry to come in.

As I wandered around the house, checking under beds and behind curtains, loathe to accept that I was a complete idiot, the only other explanation that I could come up with as to why the back door was open led regretfully to Layla's brother, Taff. I'd happily handed over my keys to him at the garage, stupidly including my house keys. I didn't know him from Adam, and for all I knew he could have a side-line in breaking and entering. Hell, I didn't even know Layla that well when I thought about it. She'd only been at the firm for a few months, and we'd only really become friendly over the last few days.

My mind sped down paths which displayed massive No Entry signs, all of which I blatantly ignored. What if she'd set the whole thing up? Keyed my car herself when she went out to get us lunch, then suggested we take it round to her brother's garage. It was her idea that we went out for a drink, too. She could have seen that I'd left my house keys on the keyring, and then stopped me from going home when I wanted to, avoiding me catching her brother in the act. But why?

My exhausted mind flailed around, putting two and two together and having no choice but to add them up to four. She'd been wearing a black hoody at her flat last night, so unlike her usual style that it had stuck in my mind, more so than all the bright, memorable items of clothing that she usually wore. I'd seen the person who'd keyed my car. They too were wearing a black hoody. Commonplace, I know, but…

But again, why? What purpose would it serve Layla? Nothing in the house was out of the ordinary that I could tell, and nothing had been taken. If she had set the whole thing up, there had to be a reason. Why would someone break in and not take or break anything? What other purpose was there? Could they have left something, instead?

I retraced my steps around the house, but this time with more purpose. The kitchen, lounge, dining room, and downstairs toilet were all completely normal. The hallway and stairs were as they should be, as were the spare room, bathroom, and finally mine and Alex's bedroom and en suite. Nothing out of the ordinary. I just couldn't get my head around it, and it was positively buzzing with possibilities, each more outlandish than the last.

Perhaps I just needed to hold my hands up and admit that I'd been forgetful. It was just one of those things…a fluke. I had to stop placing the blame elsewhere, particularly when Layla had been nothing but good to me. I was being an idiot.

Sighing deeply, I fed Mr Jones, finished making my cup of tea, and collected up the post and my mobile. I took it all out to the back garden, heading for the bench which leaned against the facing fence. I felt the scuffed wooden seat with my hand, pleased that it wasn't too damp to sit on. I had to count myself lucky. Be grateful that no harm had come from my house being left open all day and night.

It was still too chilly to be sitting outside this early in the morning in April, really. It might technically be Spring, but the thin layer of frost that glistened on the grass said otherwise. Eventually, the sun would work its way around the garden, but right now it was only gracing half of the bench where I sat, outside of the shadow of the house, and the patch of ground over by the shed, which was Mr Jones' sunbathing spot of choice. As if summoned by my thought, he emerged from the back door, parading his way along the garden path as if it were a catwalk before stretching out in front of the shed door. He'd forgiven me now that he had a full belly again.

I sipped my tea, keeping both my hands wrapped around the body of the mug, not wanting to lose any warmth from it. My stomach had stopped churning now, and I allowed myself a moment to close my eyes, holding my face up to the sun to feel what little warmth it was willing to share. My mind was slowing, calming. I had made a mistake, that was all. Nothing sinister.

Another sip of tea, then I placed my mug on the seat next to me so I could open the post. There were only three envelopes. The first was an update from my car insurance company saying that I needed to renew my policy. They'd take the hassle out of my hands if I wanted and just go ahead unless they heard from me. I knew it meant that the payment would go up, so made a note to ring around for some quotes.

Next was a Visa card bill. Nothing surprising there. I hoped that the third and final envelope would contain a cheque with which I could pay off the other two.

I ripped open a corner of the final unmarked envelope, addressed to both myself and Alex this time, then slid my finger along the top, opening a jagged edge, and retrieved a one-page letter. *CRYOGEN* announced the headed paper. I wasn't immediately concerned. We often received reminders from the cryopreservation company where we had frozen and stored Alex's sperm after his accident. This was bound to be some dumbed-down scientific blurb about how they were updating their systems, therefore giving them the right to charge us more money.

I started skimming through the letter, one hand resting over the top of my mug of tea, the steam heating my fingers.

Dear Mr and Mrs Thompson,

Unfortunately, your annual fee has still not been paid despite numerous reminders. Therefore, we regretfully inform you that unless the full payment is made within 14 days, we shall assume that you no longer require our services, and your sample will be destroyed with immediate effect.

What? What the hell was this? It must be some kind of administration error, either at their end or with the bank. I certainly hadn't seen any reminders, and I felt affronted at the tone of the letter, and the insinuation that we'd purposely not paid.

Taking my phone from my pocket, I opened the banking app. I knew that my own account was looking OK. It was a little depleted bearing in mind all the usual direct debits had been paid, but OK nonetheless. I clicked on our joint account to see what shape it was in and didn't even need to scroll down before I could see how overdrawn it was.

My mouth fell open as the negative figure assimilated itself in my head. How was that possible? How on earth could we be overdrawn, not by just a few pounds, but a few *thousand* pounds? Alex earned a decent wage, and I could see that my own money had transferred across to the joint account each month. I desperately tried to work out what was going on. Perhaps Alex's wages hadn't come through yet? Maybe there'd been some big payment that he'd had to make and forgotten to tell me. There was undoubtedly a simple explanation.

I scrolled down through the account's recent activity, but nothing stood out. There were utility bill payments, pet insurance, food bills, all the usual stuff. The last mortgage payment had been made, and the next one was due imminently, which was worrying. I'd been right in thinking that Alex's latest payment from his account hadn't yet come through, but it was only late by a couple of days which wasn't unusual bearing in mind he'd been away at the convention. I knew he'd sort it out as soon as he got back. It would be fine. It would all be fine. It had to be. It was only just after nine in the morning and already the day felt like it couldn't get any worse.

Suddenly needing to hear my husband's voice more than anything, I closed the banking app and rang him straight away, hearing the ring tone faintly echoing in my ear as I waited for him to answer. As the phone continued to ring, my legs jiggled up and down, partially from the cold, but now combined with my nervous energy.

I wasn't surprised when there was no answer. It was the way things were with us now, and even though I hated it, I had become accustomed to it.

"Alex, its me." I paused in my message, not knowing what to say, which emotion to harness and send down the airwaves to him, and eventually cast them all aside. "Please call me." I hung up, letting out a sigh, and reached for my tea, finding it was now cold in its neglect. Just like me.

My eyes travelled across to Mr Jones, who was totally oblivious of the goings on as he luxuriated in his fur coat, stretched out in the suntrap in front of the shed. I watched his soft belly rising and falling as he dozed, the movement almost hypnotic. I should take a leaf out of his book and take a nap. Things always felt better after a good sleep, and it was something I'd been lacking in lately bearing in mind the recent events. However, I wasn't sure I was ready for sleep yet as my mind zipped here and there, a captive, trying to find its way out of a cleverly constructed maze.

What I needed was a task - a mindless, mindful task to harness my thoughts and calm them down. As I watched Mr Jones in his slumber by the shed, I remembered that I had planned to go in there and find the superglue to fix my shattered vase. Perfect. It would be like putting a jigsaw together, each piece falling into place, fixing something broken and making it whole again.

Pushing myself up from the bench, I headed back inside to get the spare set of keys from the bowl in the hallway. We'd only ever had the one key for the shed, and instead of doing the sensible thing and getting another one cut, we just left it on the ring of spares so either of us could just grab it when we needed to.

I left the back door open behind me, wanting to air the house a bit. I still felt a little displaced as I walked through the hall. Even though I'd checked the place thoroughly, I couldn't shake the strange feeling as if certain items had been moved minutely. A millimetre to the right here, a centimetre to the left there. Stupid, I knew. I was just imagining things.

I rummaged around in the bowl, not immediately seeing the key fob, which was a little metal house shape. A gift which had come with our new set of keys from the estate agents when we bought our house, their name emblazoned across the front. Exasperated, I picked up the bowl and carried it through to the kitchen, where I tipped the contents out onto the worktop, swirling them around with my fingers before placing each item back in the bowl one by one. The keys were nowhere to be seen.

THIRTY-FIVE

So much for embarking on a mindful, calming exercise. My brain was now in complete overdrive. Of course, there was always the possibility that Alex had picked them up and taken them away with him, or moved them somewhere else by mistake. But why would he? He had his own set and he had taken them with him when he left for the convention.

I had my own set too, which was now thankfully back in my possession after last night's ordeal. So where were the spare keys?

Replacing the bowl in its rightful place, and trying to keep a calm head, I checked through all the pockets of the coats hung on the rack by the front door, finding nothing but old tissues, used train tickets, and lint. This was ridiculous. They had to be somewhere.

Alex must have moved them, that's all there was to it. I'd mention it to him when he got home and he'd say, 'Oh yeah, I forgot to tell you I'd moved them, or lost them, or dropped them down a drain.' I'd then roll my eyes and say 'You could have told me. I've been going nuts trying to find them.' That was exactly what was going to happen. He wouldn't say that they were still in the bowl because that would mean someone else had taken them.

But what if they had?

If someone else *had* taken them, maybe that was why it felt as if another person had been inside the house while I'd been away. Could that person have used my keys to gain entry through the back door so as not to alert any of the neighbours to their presence? Could they then have helped themselves to their own, personal set of keys from the bowl so they could come and go at will?

No, that was stupid. Why would anyone go to all that bother just to steal another set of keys? It would be pointless. And bearing in mind my only suspect was Layla's brother, Taff, it begged the question of why on earth he'd do something like that. From what I could gather, he seemed like a decent bloke with a decent job. He didn't know me and didn't care about me. He was just a good bloke doing a favour for his sister's friend.

No, no. I wasn't thinking clearly. It had to be coincidental.

But how?

No one else had been inside the house for weeks other than me and Alex. I couldn't remember the last time we'd had any friends over, and why would they move anything around anyway? No, there was no one. No one…other than…

My breath caught on the same hook as the thought that had tried its best to swim past unnoticed. Someone *had* been in the house, someone who had invited himself just over the threshold to take advantage of a drunk, foolish woman who'd allowed him to try and kiss away her loneliness.

Just one person, who'd been inside the hallway, within arm's reach, a hair's breadth of that bowl of oddities. One person, a parasite looking to attach itself to a new host and having his narcissistic objectives eventually denied as his prey came to her senses.

Saul.

I hesitated before dialling the number. It had been a while now since we'd spoken and I really couldn't be sure what the reaction was going to be when we spoke after all those ignored messages, but I had to do it. My first port of call in any emergency, other than Alex…Helen.

At first, I didn't think she would answer at all as the phone rang and rang. I could picture her, eyeing the screen of her phone through her black-rimmed glasses. Frowning at my image and wanting to ignore my call, before finally giving in and answering with a curt greeting.

"Hels, it's me," I said quickly before she could lay into me for not returning her calls. "I know I've been rubbish lately, and I'm sorry. Really, I am. But there's just been so much going on, and I don't know what to do." I paused, waiting for her to ask what was up, but she stayed quiet, her silence throwing me off kilter. "I…Hels? Are you there?"

A sigh. "I'm here."

"OK, thank God. I thought I'd lost you for a minute. It's just, oh Helen, so much has happened. Saul wouldn't take no for an answer, and I think he's been hanging around the house trying to freak me out. Work is a nightmare and my car…I haven't even told you about it getting keyed yet, have I? And then Layla took me out last night and when I got home—"

"Ellie, let me just stop you there for a minute."

"Sorry. I know I'm going on, and I haven't called you back before now—"

"It's been a week. A whole week that I've been trying to get hold of you."

"I know, but—"

"Stop it, Ellie. Just stop it."

I did as she said, the authority in her words shocking me into silence.

"I've been going out of my mind worrying about you after our last conversation, and you haven't even had the decency to let me know you're OK. I can't believe how selfish you're being."

I was shocked that this was how she felt. It hadn't even crossed my mind, which in itself suggested that her words may perhaps have an element of truth to them. I held my breath, waiting for her to continue.

"Honestly, sometimes it's as though everything has to revolve around you! Don't you think I have stuff going on, too? You know, like a wedding? My wedding. I told you that me and Christine were getting our parents together last weekend, which was a massive deal, but instead of ringing me to ask how it went, I got you calling me at God knows what time the night before, pissed out of your head when you realised you'd got into a situation you didn't want to be in.

"And guess what? I listened, like a friend. And I called you the next day and pretty much every day since to see if everything was OK and you haven't even bothered to call me back. Don't you think I've been worried about you?"

"I'm sorry, I—"

"Are you though? I'm not sure you are. You didn't care about Alex's feelings when you were playing around with that smarmy bastard, did you? And you haven't cared about mine much either."

"That's not true. I do care, its just—"

"Oh, for God's sake, stop making excuses. All you ever do is ring me when there's something wrong, or something going on in *your* life. Don't you think it's about time you took some responsibility for your own shit?"

I was speechless as Helen fell quiet and the line buzzed in my ear. I waited for her to continue before realising the line had gone dead.

In all the years I'd known Helen, she'd never lost her temper with me like that. I'd seen her lose it with other people and watched them cower in front of her as she unleashed her fiery anger, and often felt grateful that I wasn't on the receiving end. Now I was, and it was brutal.

I wanted to feel offended, angry that she'd even contemplated having those thoughts about me, her best friend. But, try as I might, I couldn't summon the indignance.

She was right. I'd allowed myself to become so wrapped up in myself and my miserable issues that nothing else had even mattered. I had no excuses.

I immediately pressed her name on my phone, wanting to speak to her so we could clear the air but instead of ringing it went straight through to voicemail. Now both my husband *and* my best friend seemed to be avoiding my calls. Before the self-pity could kick in, I left a quick message, apologising to Helen and shamefully agreeing with everything that she'd said. Then, before her kick up the arse ran out, I immediately Googled locksmiths, clicking on the number of a local firm who, when I got through, said they could be with me shortly. At least with the locks changed I would be able to sleep tonight, safe in the knowledge that no one would be able to get in the house.

There was one last contact that I knew I had to make before my newfound resolve ran out. Bolstered by pro-activity, I found his name in my phone and fired off a quick message, my fingers shaking as I typed.

Just leave me alone Saul. I'm having all the locks on the house changed and if you ever turn up here again, I'm going to call the police and tell them that you're stalking me.

The message whooshed off to its recipient and I stared at the screen, imagining the expression on his face darkening as he read my message. Envisioning his fury. Just as I was about to switch off my phone, those three little dots burst into life alongside the words 'Saul is typing'.

THIRTY-SIX

I knew that I should turn my phone off and put it out of the way where I couldn't see it. I should delete Saul's messages without reading them and then block his number before he had the chance to send anymore. But I couldn't. I was drawn in like an addicted viewer binge-watching my favourite show. As much as I'd been emboldened by Helen giving it to me straight, it seemed that I was still the usual weak Ellie Thompson underneath.

I read his message, not quite taking in the words properly the first time, and having to re-read them a second time, and then a third.

You crazy bitch. If you even think about doing that, I'll call your husband and tell him you've been sleeping with me.

My whole body went cold as fear caressed me with its icy fingers. It didn't matter that it was a lie, as it would just be my word against his, and while the old Alex would never have questioned my love for him, I wasn't so sure that the same could be said now. Besides, the feeling of guilt was already there. I may not have slept with him, but I'd wanted to, hadn't I? I'd let him kiss me and worm his way into my emotions, shunting Alex to one side. It would all have to come out if he said anything, and I wasn't sure the fragile relationship that I had with Alex right now could handle it. I messaged back, my words belying my fear.

You can't bully me. He'd never believe a word you said.

I waited for him to reply, eyes glued to the screen, waiting for the dots to appear.

There was nothing.

Usually, he'd be firing back messages quicker than I could formulate thoughts in my head, but now nothing. It was unnerving, making me wonder what else he could be contemplating. I messaged again, wanting to incite a response.

I meant what I said Saul. If you continue to harass me, I won't think twice about going to the police. Your threats don't scare me.

I waited again.

Nothing.

I found it disturbing that he didn't reply, bearing in mind how verbose he normally was. What was he doing? Why wasn't he responding? Where was the normal barrage of messages?

My index finger lingered over the phone's keypad. In some perverse way, I felt stood up.

You don't have his number anyway, I typed, tempted to put a laughing emoji at the end of the sentence, but holding myself back.

Still nothing. Fine, I'd just leave it there. I'd said what I had to, and his empty threat wasn't going to deter me from doing what I needed to do. I put my phone face down on the kitchen worktop. The locksmith would hopefully be here soon and then I could go and have a lie down for a bit, safe in the knowledge that no one could get in the house.

Ping.

My phone.

I grabbed it, proving only to myself that I was on tenterhooks, despite my protestations otherwise.

There was a message. From Saul.

Are you sure?

THIRTY-SEVEN

I hadn't been able to relax after receiving Saul's message. I'd tried to tell myself that there was no way that he could have Alex's number, but I knew that was both stupid and pointless. He could have got hold of it easily from my phone for starters, let alone managed to find it another way. If he wanted to tell Alex, he would do it. There was no doubt in my mind.

I paced up and down the kitchen and tried calling Helen again, getting no answer. I couldn't blame her. I really couldn't. Like she'd said, she was planning her wedding and wanted to share those magical steps with her nearest and dearest without any other dramas bringing her down, much the same as I had wanted to do when it had been my turn. It killed me to admit it, but I'd been sorely lacking as a friend, putting my own needs first with my stupid flirtation with Saul. If only I'd realised what an idiot I was being at the time instead of setting off this bloody awful chain reaction of events. I hoped it wasn't too late to make everything better.

I left another message for my friend, apologising and asking her to call me. Despite my selfish actions, I knew Helen well and realised that she'd need a bit of time to cool off before she'd talk to me again. I just hoped it wouldn't be too long.

I leaned on the kitchen worktop under the window and noted that the sun had finally made its way around to sit proudly in the sky, unsheathing most of the back garden from its morning shade. The earlier frosted blades of grass now looked dewy in the light. Spring was negotiating its way back, even though winter was still fighting to keep its hold. Mr Jones was still lying outside, and, unaware of my gaze, he rolled over, basking in the sunlight like a small furry whale, his claws giving a half-hearted scratch at the wooden slats of the shed, his own personal giant scratching post. What a nice life it must be to have nothing to worry about other than sleeping and eating. Perhaps I could come back as a cat in my next life.

The front doorbell startled me out of my reverie, and I made my way to the hallway, making sure to check through the peephole before answering the door. A man dressed in a navy shirt with the words Lock n' Key embroidered in white on his left pocket peered back at me. I opened the door and he held out his hand, introducing himself as Terry as though I'd just turned up at *his* house as opposed to the other way around.

"Mrs…?" He looked from me to his clipboard.

"Thompson." I saved him the trouble of finding my name. "Just call me Ellie. It's fine." It wasn't fine though, was it? I should let him call me Mrs Thompson, make a point that I was a married woman whose husband was very much in evidence. Why did I always have to be so bloody friendly with everyone? I'd proved already that that was a stupid thing to do.

Terry bundled himself through the doorway, naturally ducking as he did so, obviously used to adjusting for his height. He bent to put his toolkit on the hallway floor, and I backed away towards the stairs. I couldn't help but feel uncomfortable having a man that I didn't know in the house, but what choice did I have?

"Right then, it's the front and the back doors then is it, love?"

"Yes, please."

"No worries. It'll be done in a jiffy. Any chance of a cuppa?" He squatted down and opened his tool kit. My eyes rested briefly on his shoulders and I noticed a light dusting of dandruff. I wondered if he ever wished that his uniform was a paler colour so it didn't show up so much. Stupid, the things you think about sometimes.

The latch of the kit now open, he started probing around inside with his long fingers. Good hands for piano playing, maybe, but they creeped me out a bit.

"You alright, love?" He'd paused in his rummaging and looked up at me, perhaps feeling my gaze on him.

God, I was tired. My mind was latching on to negatives and running away with them. "Tea. Yeah, of course. How'd you take it?"

From the direction of the kitchen, I could hear my phone ringing, and I started backing away, hoping that it was Helen calling to tell me all was forgiven.

"White with three sugars please, love."

I gave Terry the thumbs up and left the hallway.

Alex's face was lit up on the screen of my phone as I entered the kitchen, and I rushed over and grabbed it. Something made me pause before answering, though. What if Saul had carried out his threat? What if Alex had just got off the phone with him after listening to all his lies about me? I paced up and down, holding the phone in my hand as if it were a bomb about to explode. It was so unlike him to call me, especially bearing in mind our lack of communication since he'd left, which had been minimal. I had to decide quickly before he rang off. I'd called him and left a message and that was why he was calling me back, surely? I argued that he hadn't returned my calls any other time. Oh God, I had to decide before—

It stopped ringing.

Oh, no. I dialled straight back. I had to speak to him. I was desperate to speak to him even though he was due back home on Monday. I just wanted to hear his voice, to gauge whether Saul had spoken to him, to know that everything was still going to be OK.

He answered and momentarily I was lost for words.

"Ellie?" He sounded really quiet.

"Alex." Could he hear the trepidation in my voice? "Is everything OK?"

A pause, almost like a time delay. "I'm fine. I'm just returning your call."

I could barely hear him. "Can you speak up? It sounds like you're whispering."

"I said I'm fine. Just busy. It's hard to talk as there's so many people around."

Always a private person, I knew he hated speaking on his mobile when other people could overhear. He was still speaking quietly, his words muffled, no doubt by his hand cupped over the mouthpiece. I'd seen him do it in public before.

"What did you want? Your message this morning sounded…" His words were lost in his hushed tones.

I wanted to tell him everything. Right then and there. I wanted to tell him all about how stupid I'd been and why, and how Saul had taken advantage of me at my lowest ebb. I wanted to blurt out the truth that I was now being stalked by this man who had become obsessed with me, that he'd keyed my car and I was now having to have the locks changed because of it all. I wanted him to hold me in his arms and soothe me and say everything was going to be alright. That's what I wanted to do.

But I couldn't. If there was one thing the phone call with Helen had taught me was that I had to be more aware of what other people were going through. I knew Alex was under a lot of pressure at work and unable to get away. If I blurted all this out over the phone now, then he would feel that he had to come home straight away, which wasn't fair. He was already stressed out and miserable, and what would it solve by heaping more weight onto his shoulders? No, it could wait until he got home. That way, we could sit down and talk things through properly, openly. Together.

"Nothing. I just wanted to—"

"How's that tea coming along love?"

Bloody Terry. I'd forgotten he was even there.

"Who's that?" Alex's tone had changed. No louder, but it had a sharper edge.

Oh God, now what? Did I lie? If I was honest with him, it'd bring up even more questions. I decided to go with the truth anyway. "It's a locksmith. I'm having the locks changed."

Alex's voice maintained its sharpness. "Why?" Just one word, spoken quietly still, and laced with hesitation…suspicion.

"I…" It was no good, I had to lie now. "I lost my keys. I went out last night with Layla and lost them. I'm such an idiot. I had to stay at her place as I couldn't get in..." I wittered on, glad that he couldn't see me, shamefaced in my half-truths.

"Who the hell is Layla?" Alex spoke so softly I could barely hear him.

A small nub of vexation flared briefly. If he'd spent more time with me, more time at home, more time actively participating in our relationship, then he'd know who Layla was. I wanted to say all of that to him, but I forced myself to swallow the words down and doused the flame of anger before it could take hold. "She's a friend, from work."

"Oh, right."

We both fell silent.

"Well, I'd better go. I have to get back to work."

I thought of our depleted bank account, and the letter from the Cryopreservation company, and opened my mouth to bring it up, but not knowing quite how to phrase things.

"Ellie? If there's nothing else, I really need to go."

"Sure." I resigned myself to holding off. "I'll see you on Monday, and I'll leave the new keys with next door in case you get home before me."

"Thanks."

I couldn't just leave it like this, such a formal end to our exchange. I took a deep breath. "I love you, Alex."

"What? You're breaking up. What did you say?" His words were barely audible from across the miles of our air-wave connectivity. Such a fragile thing, easily broken.

"I said I—"

The line went dead.

I sighed, placing my phone down gently and flicking on the kettle before Terry chased me up again.

While I was gutted that he hadn't heard me tell him that I loved him, I was still glad that I'd been able to hear his voice, even if it was in sotto voce.

I listened as the hot water started to bubble in the kettle, which competed with Terry's off-key singing with his own lyrics to "Wonderwall". He could belt it out in full voice for all I cared so long as he got my locks changed quickly and I could feel safe in my own home again.

I spooned sugar into a mug, feeling a little more encouraged after Alex's call. The more I thought about it, the emptier Saul's threat now sounded to my ears. There was no way he was going to call Alex, and even if he did, the likelihood of Alex actually answering his phone while he was at work was practically zero.

And while I hadn't brought up the pressing money issues, it was for the best that we hadn't got into it over the phone. I decided that I was 100% happy with my decision to hold off until he was home again. It could all keep until Monday.

THIRTY-EIGHT

The bus journey to work hadn't been too bad, despite having to sit next to a young woman who spent the whole trip loudly facetiming her friend, Chyna. She'd been dolled up as though she was on her way to an audition for Love Island, but from what I could ascertain, her name was Hayley, and she was actually on her way to university. I think she would have preferred the former, though, as the two friends complained about their coursework and made jokes about one of their classmates, Bethany. A first-class loser, by all accounts. They made me glad I was no longer part of that world. Not that my current one was much better. Hopefully, though, that was all about to change.

I hopped off the bus at the closest stop to my office, grateful that I'd remembered to bring my umbrella with me to avoid a soaking from a sudden downpour. I made it through the glass doors to the reception area ten minutes before I actually needed to be there, and I couldn't remember the last time that had been the case. This day was going well so far, and I told myself that it was the start of things to come.

I put my wet umbrella alongside several others in the stand near the reception doors and waved at Layla who sat in her usual spot behind the big wooden desk which dominated the dimly lit area. The ambient glow from the reception lighting bounced off the golden lettering of the company logo behind the desk.

Instead of waving back as she would normally do, she held up her hand, palm facing me, silently asking me to wait while her current caller continued to chatter through her headphones. I could hear the muted ringing of another line on the switchboard, and Layla rolled her eyes at the inconvenience.

"I have to go in," I mouthed at her. "I don't want to be late."

I started to walk past and she stood up, still holding out her hand, and now covering her mouthpiece with her other hand.

"No. Wait. I need to tell you something first," she whispered, before addressing her caller in her normal voice. "Just one moment, I'll put you through."

I stood impatiently while she redirected the call.

The phone started ringing again.

"Look, you're busy Layla. We can catch up in a bit. You explained to Dickhead that I was ill yesterday, right?"

"I did, yeah. It's not that, it's—"

"Are you going to answer that?" My boss had materialised in the doorway through to the main office and he glared at Layla, before turning his miserable gaze on me. "Would you like to come with me please, Ms Thompson?

It wasn't a question, but I answered anyway, dread seeping into my response. "Sure."

Dickinson turned on his heel and strode off towards his office, leaving me to follow him after a panicked look at Layla who had done as instructed and answered the incessant ringing of the phone. I raised my eyebrows at her, my face a question mark, and she shook her head in return, mouthing "Sorry, I tried to warn you." She turned her attention to the next caller, and I followed in the wake of my boss, still wearing my coat and with my bag hanging heavily on my shoulder.

He was already positioned behind his desk when I got there, and I hovered nervously on the threshold of the room.

"Come in and shut the door behind you, please."

I did as instructed and waited to be offered a seat. He gestured to the two chairs on the other side of the desk and, unbuttoning my coat, I sat down on one, waiting for him to lay into me for not calling in sick through the proper channels yesterday.

I hated the fact that I could still be made to feel like a school child, summoned to the headmaster's office for a minor misdemeanour. It was ridiculous, but I couldn't help it. Taking a deep breath and trying to take some semblance of control, I thought I'd try to pre-empt my telling off by getting my excuse in first.

"I'm sorry I didn't call in sick yesterday, Mr Dickinson, but Layla assured me that she would let you know that I was ill. I'm afraid I felt too unwell to ring in."

He looked at me with what I could only assume to be surprise at my audacity for speaking, but the expression lasted only a moment before his features fell back into their usual unpleasant folds. "I didn't call you in here to talk about your attendance record, Ms Thompson." He sniffed. "Although your time keeping *does* leave a lot to be desired lately."

Well, he did have a point there, I supposed. "I know, I'm sorry. It's just that there's been a lot going on in my personal life at the—"

"Yes, you've said. And while you have my sympathy, you also reassured me that it would not affect your work any further."

I bowed my head a little. I had said that. "Um, Mr Dickinson, I know. I didn't think I—"

"Ms Thompson…Eleanore…I entrusted you with more responsibility based on your past work and your assurance that you had everything in hand."

"I know, I…I don't understand what the problem is." I was racking my brains. I'd done everything I was supposed to, hadn't I? The Kelsey-Williams purchase was well underway. The Martinkova purchase was due to complete in three days, and the Mills purchase was still in its early stages. What had I missed? Oh God, what was it?

And then it hit me, like a tonne of bricks a fraction of a second before my boss told me in no uncertain terms of my misdemeanour, his words highlighted by the dawning realisation of what I'd done wrong, or rather what I hadn't done at all.

"As you should be aware, Ms Martinkova is supposed to be completing on her purchase next week and you were supposed to request mortgage monies from her lender."

I looked down at my shoes, noting how dirty the left one was, muddy rainwater having splashed across its toe and pebble-dashed my black tights.

"We received the Notice to Complete from the seller's solicitors, and this seems to have become lost in the pile of work sitting in your in tray. This is inexcusable."

I closed my eyes, squeezing them tightly.

"Do you realise that your behaviour means that our client could potentially not only lose her purchase but also be obliged to forfeit her deposit on the property?"

I felt like I couldn't breathe. I'd screwed up. Badly. I could remember seeing the Notice to Complete when it came in. I could remember holding it in my hands, and then, yes, I'd been distracted by my problems. It proved Helen's point even further. I was so consumed by my own life, my own issues, that I had taken my eye off the ball with everyone else around me. And now it was going to have a massive impact on our client. My actions were going to cost her everything.

I gasped for air, the following breaths now coming fast and shallow, as if my lungs were trying to make up for the lost time when everything had stood still. It was as though no air would reach them, though, and I opened my eyes in a panic, my gaze landing on my boss's face and then veering quickly away from his unsympathetic expression.

Hot in my coat, and panic making me feel somewhat weightless and close to fainting, I tried to slow my breathing and ground myself by gripping the wooden sides of the chair I was sitting in, pressing my fingers onto the smooth varnished surface. I let my gaze travel around the room as my boss continued to talk, and I counted the tangible objects in the office. Desk blotter. Green lamp with gold stand. Parker pen. Buff-coloured files. Each object anchored me a little more to my chair, to the present, to this awful reality that I found myself in.

"I don't know what to say. I'm so sorry."

My boss sniffed again. "I don't think 'sorry' is going to cut it with our client, do you?"

"No." I let go of the chair edges, my hands finding each other, fingers entwining, an image of supplication.

"Now..." He paused for effect. "Fortunately, one of us kept an eye on the ball, and in going through your in tray yesterday while you were *'unwell',"* I could hear the invisible quotations that he put around the word. "I was able to ascertain what was going on and rectify it just in time."

My heart slowed a little with the relief that his words brought. I couldn't care less that he was blowing his own trumpet, I was just thankful that my stupid mistake hadn't caused Ms Martinkova any distress. But where did it leave me? I picked nervously at a hangnail, worrying it back and forth while Mr Dickinson continued.

"Unfortunately, this does now mean that I will be taking away all the extra responsibilities that I gave to you."

Did that mean that I wasn't getting fired? Oh, please God, don't let me get fired, I pleaded silently, pulling at the hangnail. It hurt, but I didn't care. "I understand."

"I hope you do, Eleanore, as I will also be putting you on a written warning. Your performance of late has been undesirable, to say the least. This current situation is a very serious matter and were it not for my quick thinking, we could have been in a lot of trouble."

I nodded. At least he'd started using my first name again now. I didn't care that he was being a dickhead. For once, he was entitled to be.

"I will be keeping a close eye on you going forward."

"Yes, Mr Dickinson."

He sniffed again, before withdrawing a handkerchief from his pocket and shaking it out in front of him. It made me cringe at the thought of what had probably just shaken loose. "Right. Well, there's nothing more to be said, so let's get back to work." He nodded at the doorway and covered his face with the hanky before blowing his nose loudly into it. I was dismissed.

I wasted no time in leaving his office, removing my coat as I went, and avoiding the curious gazes of my colleagues by keeping my eyes focused straight ahead.

I laid my coat on the back of my chair, and threw my bag underneath the desk, noticing a red light flashing on my desk phone, alerting me that there was a voicemail message. Taking a seat, I drew a notepad over and bit the lid off a Bic pen before pressing play. I didn't want to miss anything else of any importance.

The electronic voice kicked in and I held my pen, poised, ready to write down the message.

"You were called today at 9.09am…" The disembodied voice read out the number, and I chewed at my hangnail, eventually pulling it loose with my teeth, releasing the metallic tang of blood in my mouth. The caller cleared their throat before speaking.

"This is a message for Mrs Thompson. It's Jessie from Best Friends Veterinary Practice. I tried ringing your mobile but there was no answer so thought I'd better try this number instead. We, er, we have your cat here. Mr Jones." I tried to swallow but found I had no saliva to do so. "He's OK, so please don't worry, but your neighbour found him lying under the hedge outside the front of his house and brought him in. It looks like he may have eaten something potentially poisonous."

Oh my God, surely Saul wouldn't stoop so low as to hurt my cat. Would he?

THIRTY-NINE

I'd practically run to Layla's brother's garage straight after work to collect my car and I arrived sweaty and breathless, hoping against hope that my car would be ready. All I could think about was getting to Mr Jones, and while the veterinary surgery had assured me that he was OK, I still needed to see him for myself.

Fortunately, the car was good to go, Taff had done a great job of patching up the paintwork and his good-natured demeanour went a long way to quash any residual suspicions that I had about him doing anything untoward with my house keys. While he didn't want to take any payment for the work he'd done, I still thrust £20 into his hands so he could at least buy himself a beer or two by way of a thank you. He'd smiled widely and put the money in the pocket of his grease-streaked overalls before guiding me as I reversed out of the lot to make sure I didn't scratch the paintwork on mine or anyone else's car on the way out.

It's amazing I didn't do any more damage to my car on the drive to the vets as I'm sure I probably racked up a couple of speeding tickets and narrowly avoided clipping the wing mirror of another vehicle as I hurled mine into the surgery car park. I was stupid to drive the way I had, but all

I could think about was my little ball of fluff and how much I needed to see him.

He cut a very sorrowful image, curled up in a little ball, his usual rumbling purr silent as he slept. I stroked his downy fur, trying my hardest not to cry as my lip quivered precariously.

"Please try not to worry," the vet told me, her hand a small, fleeting comfort on my shoulder. "We'll hold on to him here for a couple of days just to keep an eye on him, but he's doing well. He's likely just eaten something he shouldn't have from the garden. There's plenty of daffodils and tulips out now which are pretty toxic to cats, and if he's prone to snoozing in flowerbeds, he may well have ingested something."

"Oh, Jonesy..." My voice wobbled as I continued to stroke him. My eyes were almost full to the brim with unshed tears and one blink would bring them hurtling down my cheeks. The suggestion that it was more plausible that my cat had somehow just ingested something from the garden instead of Saul actively poisoning him to hurt me further allowed the knot of fear that I'd held clenched in my stomach all day to loosen slightly. I couldn't let it unravel completely, though. The man undoubtedly had issues, as surely it could only have been Saul who'd keyed my car, and while I didn't want to believe that even *he* would be so cruel as to hurt my cat, I couldn't be 100% sure that he'd had nothing to do with it. I had to stay on my guard.

The moment I got through my front door and locked it behind me, I gave Helen another call, determined that I wouldn't start the conversation off with news of Mr Jones. The vets had promised he was doing alright, and I desperately needed to build some bridges with my friend. Relieved that she answered my call, I could tell by her voice that she was still pretty fed up, but at least she was speaking to me. For now, that was enough.

"I'm sorry for being such a crap friend."

"It's fine."

"It's not though, is it?" I was ready to shoulder some blame. "I haven't been present for you at all, and I'm so sorry. Really, I am. Please tell me everything that's been going on with you." I kicked off my shoes, lifted my legs onto the sofa, and then tucked the phone between my ear and my shoulder so I could massage my aching feet whilst listening to my friend.

Helen grunted before continuing. "Honestly Ellie, it's fine. I'm over it. So long as we're both there for each other, that's all that matters."

"Well, I promise to be there for you more."

"Good, because otherwise, I'm going to have to put you in the most revolting bridesmaid dress to get my own back."

I couldn't help but laugh. "Please tell me it'll have big puffy sleeves."

"Yes, and it'll be lime green with frills."

"And a bonnet?"

"Totally."

We both burst into laughter, and it felt good to be back talking rubbish with my friend, taking my mind off everything else that was weighing so heavily on it. "I wish you weren't so far away, Hels."

"Yeah, I know. Me too. The things we do for love, eh?"

I stretched my legs out further on the sofa and looked around for Mr Jones, my heart dropping as I remembered he wasn't there for me to hold. "Yeah…love."

There was a momentary silence, and while I wanted to, I wasn't sure I could fill it with talk of weddings. I knew Helen felt it, too.

"So, tell me." She broke the standstill.

"Tell you what?"

"Come on, don't go all quiet on me now. Tell me what's been going on."

"No, no. Honestly, it's fine. It can wait. Tell me more about the wedding." I didn't want to just go bulldozing my way back in, making things all about me.

"Wedding shmedding," Helen pooh-poohed me. "Seriously, tell me. I've told you how I felt, and now it's all good, I promise. What's that slimy bastard Saul been doing?"

"Oh God, what do you want to know?"

"Everything."

It felt so good to get everything off my chest at last. The stalking, my car being keyed by the anonymous person in the hoody, my ridiculous suspicions about Layla and her brother, the house keys going missing, Mr Jones being poisoned, all the trouble I was in at work, and, finally, Saul's threat to tell Alex that I'd been sleeping with him.

For the most part, Helen kept quiet, only interjecting now and again with questions where she needed clarification. "Jesus Ellie, I wish you'd told me all this sooner. Forget my bloody wedding. Now I'm just annoyed that you didn't let me know what was going on. Why didn't you ring me, you idiot?"

"I don't know. I guess I thought I was on top of things."

"I hate to break it to you, but—"

"Yeah, yeah. I know."

"For what it's worth, I think you need to come clean to Alex."

"Yeah, I know." The thought of it was horrifying. I honestly didn't know how he would take it. Any of it.

"Seriously, Ellie."

I sighed.

"What is it?"

"I'm just not sure Alex even wants to be with me anymore. He never wants to talk to me, even when he's at home, let alone when he's away. I honestly think he might have met someone else." I looked over at our framed wedding photo on the mantlepiece, tears pricking at my eyes to see so much love in that couple's eyes. Where had it all gone?

"You know that sounds crazy, don't you?"

"I know you think the sun shines out of his backside, but you haven't seen him lately. He's always moody, never wants to do anything with me. He's changed so much."

"But he adores you."

"Adored. Past tense. I swear to God, Helen, it's like he doesn't even want to be near me. He's away all the bloody time these days and he never answers his phone when I ring him. Whenever I do actually manage to speak to him, he's whispering as if he doesn't want anyone to hear him talking to me."

"But it's just his work, surely?"

"Not late at night, it isn't." I'd had visions of him sneaking off from candlelit suppers for two, making excuses to whoever he was with that it was his boss calling him late.

"Maybe you're just going through a rough patch?"

"You don't say."

The pair of us fell silent again. This time, it was more comfortable, just two friends in a natural pause in conversation. "Look, why don't I come down to see you? I could be with you by tomorrow afternoon."

I could think of nothing that I wanted more than the security of having my no-nonsense best friend by my side for the weekend. "I'd love that," I told her. "But what about Chrissie? Don't you guys have plans?"

"Don't be daft. She won't mind in the slightest. In fact, she'll probably be glad to get some peace and quiet from me banging on about place settings and wedding flowers."

I laughed at the thought of Helen turning into a bridezilla.

"In the meantime, lock all the doors and windows, even the bloody cat flap!"

"OK."

"And Ellie, you need to call the police."

"Alright, alright. I'll do it first thing in the morning."

"Don't leave it until then. Do it now. Promise me, OK?"

FORTY

"So, you've reported everything to the police?" Layla drummed her brightly painted nails on the scarred wood of our table while we waited for Helen to return from the bar with our first round of drinks.

"Yes. I wasn't going to, but Helen talked me into it." I turned my cardboard beermat over and over in my hands, full of nervous energy. It'd be good to have a glass of wine in them to calm me down. "The police were really nice, actually. They took it a lot more seriously than I thought they would."

"Why on earth wouldn't they take it seriously?"

"I guess I thought they'd think I was stupid. That I'd brought things on myself."

"Hey, we've all done daft things. It doesn't mean that just because you flirted with some bloke, he has the right to make your life a misery if you change your mind about being with him."

"That's exactly what I told her." Helen placed a tray with three drinks in front of us, and I wasted no time reaching for my glass of white wine and bringing it to my lips. "It's not even like you were in a proper relationship with him. One kiss and that's all."

"It wasn't just that, though, was it? I suppose I must have led him on." I started fidgeting with the beermat again, ripping little pieces from it and scattering them on the table like ruined confetti.

"Like hell you did. The guy is a total nut job. He told you everything you needed to hear. He *manipulated* you into thinking that you wanted him."

Layla was nodding in agreement with Helen's words. "Amen to that."

"Maybe." I looked down at the mess I'd made on the table and swept the tiny pieces of card into a small pile before taking another long sip of my drink.

"Definitely." Helen gave me a look that brooked no argument. "That aside, he shouldn't be stalking you or threatening you. He broke into your house for God's sake!"

"And he keyed your car," Layla added. "You 100% did the right thing going to the police."

I smiled, bolstered by my friends' support. Helen had arrived that afternoon as she had promised, and it had been her idea to invite Layla along for drinks with us in the evening. She claimed it would be to provide moral support, but I knew she was curious about my new friend and wanted an opportunity to vet her properly.

"Just remember you're *my* best friend," she'd said with a wink, an element of seriousness behind her words despite her jokey tone. "But she can borrow you while I'm away."

Now, as I watched the two of them chatting away as if they'd known each other for ages, I couldn't be happier that they'd met. I was a fool to have even questioned Layla's motives over the last couple of days. An idiot, paranoid after too many strange things happening and way too much alcohol consumption. I pushed my glass away in recognition and picked up another beer mat to fiddle with instead.

"So, what did the police say they were going to do?" Layla turned to me. "Are they going to arrest him?"

"I don't think it's as straightforward as that, unfortunately." I started shredding the second beermat. "I think they're going to question him, but they haven't told me when."

"Well let's hope it's soon." Layla raised her glass of gin and tonic. "Here's to that son of a bitch being arrested!"

Helen's vodka and coke joined it. "Come on, Ellie. Let's toast to that bastard getting what's coming to him."

I lifted my glass of wine, and the three of us clinked glasses, the other two singing out, "Cheers."

I took a small sip of my drink and watched Layla drain her glass in one go while Helen looked on admiringly. I couldn't help but grin.

"Right." Layla pushed herself up from the table. "Just popping to the loo, ladies, and then I'll get another round in on the way back. Same again, Helen?" She nodded. "Ellie, you've hardly touched yours. Drink up."

"I might take it a bit easy tonight." I went back to fiddling with my beermat.

"Hey, so am I!" Layla laughed as she tottered off to the toilet in her five-inch green heels which clashed spectacularly with her orange skirt. I noticed quite a few men in the bar following her progress, and, as I turned back, I saw Helen doing the same.

"What?" she asked, all mock innocence when she saw the expression on my face. "She's cute!"

I poked her arm. "You're getting married, remember!"

"I know." She laughed. "Speaking of weddings, I need to show you some photos of cakes to see what you think. Chrissie really wants something girly with flowers on it, but I was thinking it might be more fun to go with one of those personalised character toppers modelled on the two of us. You know, like two little brides?" Helen called up her Pinterest account on her phone, which she'd created especially for wedding planning and opened the cake section. "See, gorgeous flowers, but a bit boring right?" I watched as she swiped through several floral versions of what was basically the same cake. "Or these? Look." She pointed at the tiny edible figures positioned on the next confectionary creation.

"Could you perhaps have both?" I suggested, taking another small sip of wine, and trying my hardest to remain interested in the line-up of cake paraded in front of me. I hoped Layla would be back soon to take the pressure off me, and I looked up just in time to see the door to the bar open and an all too familiar face come through it. I froze.

I could still hear Helen talking, but it was as though the volume in the room had been turned down. Like I'd been plunged into freezing water and, above me, life carried on as normal, only blurred and muffled.

"Ellie, are you listening?"

I continued to stare straight ahead, transfixed by the figure in front of me as he pulled down the hood which had been partially covering his face and looked around the room, searching for something, someone.

"Ellie? Hello? Am I boring you?"

My throat constricted as his eyes found what they were looking for and locked onto mine.

"Ellie?"

I registered Helen's hand, warm on my arm, as he started walking towards me.

"Ellie? Oh shit. It's him, isn't it?

FORTY-ONE

Before I could say or do anything, Helen was up from her chair and had manoeuvred her body around the table to stand between myself and Saul, who continued to walk towards me. I, too, rose from my seat, aware of it scraping along the wooden floor as it was pushed back. Not once did Saul and I break eye contact, and for a fleeting moment, despite knowing what he was really like, I had the feeling that he was going to walk over and kiss me. I was transported back to that flutter of emotion he'd originally seeded inside me. It made me feel sick.

"What the fuck are you doing here?" Helen threw at Saul as he stopped in front of us. Her stature, though petite, bristled with indignation, and her accusatory words drew a cursory look from a group at a nearby table.

Without changing his expression, Saul slowly drew his eyes from mine and focussed his gaze on Helen. "I'm sorry, we haven't been introduced, have we? I'm Saul, and you must be Helen." He held out his hand. "I've heard so much about you."

My friend ignored his proffered palm, crossing her arms over her chest as if to create a barrier from him. "Well, I've heard plenty about you, too. Unfortunately, none of it is that complementary."

"Shame." He looked back at me, easily dismissing Helen. "Can we talk?"

"She's got nothing to say to you." Helen hadn't budged.

"Is that right?" Saul cocked his head to one side, narrowing his eyes, but still keeping them focussed on me.

I nodded, not trusting my voice to come out without wavering.

"Hmm, that's surprising, bearing in mind the nice little chat I had with the police earlier. Seems like you had plenty to say to them about me."

I couldn't believe that the police had already been in touch with Saul. I'd only spoken to them last night, and while they'd been unbelievably reassuring, I really hadn't expected them to act quite so quickly. It was great that they'd already spoken to him, but it had unfortunately only served to bring him crawling out of the woodwork to track me down, which undoubtedly was not their intended result.

I cleared my throat, trying to pull on every ounce of bravery that I could muster. "I told you that I'd go to the police. It's not like I didn't warn you."

Helen took the cue to step to one side, but she still stood, poised for action. Her eyes flicked between us.

"Oh, yeah, you warned me alright, didn't you. Told me to leave you alone or you'd go to the police. *You* messaged *me* remember?"

"Yeah, I know I did, but that's because you've been hanging around my house, my car."

He laughed out loud at my words. "And why the hell would I want to do that? Don't you think I've got more important things to do than hang around your house waiting for a glimpse of the person who told me to leave her alone?" He gave me that familiar crooked grin of his, only instead of it turning me to jelly, it made me want to wipe it off his face. "I've moved on, Ellie. Why would I want to be involved with someone like you? Someone who wants me one minute and not the next?"

"What about the keys?" I threw back at him, telling myself not to rise to his bait.

"What keys?"

"You took my keys."

"Why the hell would I want your bloody keys?"

"So that you could break in and mess with…" My words petered out as I saw the look of incredulity on his face. Damn, he was a good actor.

"What? What exactly am I being accused of here? The police used the word 'stalking', but I'd like to see them find any proof that I've been anywhere near you since you asked me so nicely to leave you alone."

"But I saw you."

"Are you sure you weren't just imagining things?" He cocked his head to one side, tapping at the side of it with his finger. "Had a bit too much wine to drink, perhaps?"

I wanted to wipe the look of fake pity from his face.

"See, you're thinking about things now, aren't you? Maybe you should've done that before going to the police, you crazy bitch."

It felt as though he'd slapped me, and I stepped back. God, was he right? Was he the innocent party in all this? His measured words were making me doubt myself and I felt foolish suddenly, like maybe I had over-reacted about things, blown them up bigger than they really were.

I had no proof. My car being keyed could be just a coincidence, as could Mr Jones being poisoned. Even so, I'd been sure that someone had been watching me at the house, and the keys had gone missing after Saul came round. But was my mind just playing tricks on me? An overactive imagination fuelled by alcohol, loneliness, and fear. I felt stupid, doubting my reality.

As if bored with baiting me, Saul turned to Helen. "By the way, did you know your good friend here practically threw herself at me? Did she tell you that? She's not as innocent as she makes out, trust me."

Helen puffed herself up to her full height of 5ft-nothing, and responded, her Scottish accent thick with rage. "Trust *you*?" she countered. "I'd be more likely to trust a viper. I know damn well you coerced her."

We were starting to draw more attention from the people around us now, a couple of the other tables and some people that were standing behind Saul at the bar were openly staring at the scene unfolding in front of them, and it made me feel uncomfortable.

Saul smirked. "Coerced? Are you having a laugh? She was messaging me all the time. If anything, I could say *she* was stalking *me*!"

I baulked at his words. Oh God, it was like I'd said to the girls earlier, that the whole mess could be seen as me leading him on. There's no smoke without fire, after all.

"That's rich, bearing in mind you've blatantly followed us here." Helen was not backing down.

Saul let out a bark of laughter. "Prove it."

The pair of them stood stock still, like two gunslingers in the old west, ready to shoot at the merest flinch. The small crowd around us was quiet, waiting to see what happened next. Saul broke the tableau, pushing his hair out of his eyes, and changed tack.

"Anyway, I'm sure her husband would love to know everything that's been going on." His eyes were back on me, boring into mine, the threat obvious.

"He already knows everything," Helen continued to fight my corner, her hands in tight little fists at her sides.

"Is that right?"

"Stick around and you'll find out. He's on his way and he could smash you into next week. Have you seen the size of him?"

Saul rolled his eyes. "Oh, yeah, Ellie mentioned you were his number one fan. Are you sure you bat for the other side? If I were her, I'd be looking in your direction each time my husband went away."

That was too much for Helen, and she leapt forwards, jabbing him in the chest with her finger. "You slimy bastard. Why don't you just piss off and leave Ellie alone."

He batted her hand away, lowering his face to hers so the venom behind his eyes could clearly be seen. "Why don't *you* mind your own fucking business, and if you touch me again, I'll have you done for assault."

Behind him, the bar staff were looking concerned, and one of them raised the bar hatch, the assembled crowd parting for him to get through. "Come on, folks, let's cool things down, shall we?"

"Just what I was saying, mate." Saul tried to get the other man on side. "Why don't you call off your guard dog, Ellie?"

I felt Helen tense up and I grabbed my friend's arm before she could do anything stupid, facing Saul head-on. My thoughts had finally assembled themselves in my head, and I spoke calmly and clearly. "Just get out. I've had all the locks changed on the house so just leave me alone and stop trying to scare me."

The bartender rested his hand on Saul's shoulder. "You heard the lady. I think it's time to leave, sir."

Saul shrugged him off, and without breaking our gaze, he tapped the side of his head with his finger for a second time, his expression dripping contempt. "You're fucking crazy, you know that?"

I swallowed, and with fear lodged in my throat, I forced myself to turn away from him and sit back in my seat at the table. Without even glancing in his direction, I spoke as calmly as I could. "I think you've just proved who the crazy one is, don't you?"

"Don't fucking push me." His words spat out at me, and I saw Helen flinch in my peripheral vision.

"Come on, mate, I've asked nicely. It's time to leave." The bartender spoke up again, and I noticed that another, larger man had now joined him.

"Don't worry, I'm going." Saul had given in to defeat. "Get your hands off me."

I turned in my chair to watch the two bartenders escorting him from the room and as I did so, I noticed the small white lettering on the back of his black hoodie. This time, I was close enough to make out the word written beneath the outlined wings. 'Alpha'. I wanted to run after him and push him out of the door myself for keying my car, but I knew there was no point. I was the only person who'd seen it happen, and if I ran after him now, he'd easily twist things around by saying that I'd attacked him for no reason. Instead, I let the crowd of onlookers close around the retreating threesome to watch their progress to the door just in case it kicked off again. Those near our table continued to look in our direction through shaded eyes.

Helen lowered herself slowly back into her chair, and drained her drink, before placing the empty glass back on the table and exhaling. I could see her hand shaking a little, and I took hold of it with my own. We smiled at each other cautiously.

"Jesus, what a dick." She leant back in her seat, pulling her hand back with her. "Well, I can see why you liked him so much."

The pair of us burst into laughter, loud and hysterical. The kind that starts to slow down and as it does so, hits you with another wave, larger than the first. "I mean, what a charmer!"

Another wave of manic laughter took us over, and no doubt the patrons around us were wondering whether the bar staff had removed the wrong person.

Just as our wild laughter started to finally tame itself, I spotted Layla weaving her way back over from the toilets. She had her mobile phone clutched triumphantly in her manicured fingers and a massive grin on her beautiful face.

"Sorry I was gone so long," she announced on her approach. "Nathan called me! You know the guy from the other night, Ellie? He…wait…what?" Her smile dimmed into uncertainly as she took in the state of us. "Er…did I miss something?"

FORTY-TWO

"Honestly, Layla, you really didn't have to come back to my place as well. You know that Helen's staying with me, so I'll be absolutely fine."

"You mean your guard dog?" Helen giggled from the front of the car.

Layla patted my hand which rested on my lap. "Are you nuts? There is no way I'm abandoning ship. For all we know that arsehole could be hanging around your house right now. Nope, we are going back there mob-handed. Besides…" She winked. "I don't want to miss any more of the action!"

I rolled my eyes, enjoying the warmth of our mutual laughter in the safety of the taxi.

"Actually, she's right." Helen twisted around in her seat to face us. "He was pretty pissed off, so who knows what he's capable of doing next. I know I'm feisty, but I'm more than happy to have Layla as backup. I mean, he could've come back here and broken in. And then what?"

"Jesus! You two aren't exactly filling me with confidence, you know?" I leaned my head back against the grey vinyl headrest and concentrated on my breathing.

Layla squeezed my hand. “Sorry Ellie. We don’t mean to scare you, but we must look at the facts. He sounds like one manipulative son of a b—”

“He is!” Helen interjected. “You could just see it in his eyes. I mean, I don’t scare that easily, but I have to say I was shaking when he left. You saw my hand shaking, didn’t you El?”

I nodded. I had.

After Saul had been escorted off the premises, the lovely bartender who’d interjected had come back to check on us and insisted on buying us a round of drinks, which had been much appreciated.

The other patrons that had previously shown so much interest in us had quickly grown bored of our saga and returned to their own dramas, and Helen and I had recounted the whole ordeal to Layla who had sat open-mouthed, shocked at how much had unfolded while she’d been in the toilet.

“Perhaps we should stay here a little bit longer,” she’d suggested. “You know, just in case he’s hanging around outside.”

Helen and I had both nodded our assent but after one more drink, I couldn’t put off going home any longer. I was exhausted now that my adrenaline had abandoned me.

He hadn’t been waiting outside, thank goodness, but we’d still nosed our way out of the front doors of the bar slowly, keeping an eye out for his car and checking shadowy doorways as we made our way to the taxi rank. It had been a welcome relief to see a row of waiting taxis and to climb inside one.

Now that we were on our way home, though, combined with my friends’ concerns, I was starting to feel anxious again. He’d said not to mess with him, and I’d done that already, by going to the police. I had no idea what he was likely to do next. Not for the first time, I gave myself a mental beating for ever getting involved with someone like him.

What if he *was* at my house? Even though I'd had all the locks changed, there was nothing to stop him from forcing entry. The back garden was pretty secluded, and I doubted my elderly neighbours would hear much of anything over the volume they generally had their TV at.

Horrible thoughts wandered through my head, images of a smashed window with a brick lying in the middle of the kitchen floor; letters full of lies sitting on the doormat ready for Alex to find; Mr Jones convulsing in pain after eating poisoned food thrown into my garden. Oh, God…my mind was running riot with awful possibilities.

Perhaps the girls were thinking along similar lines because we all fell silent as the taxi neared my house. There weren't many streetlights in my part of town, and the dark stretches between each one had never felt so apparent as we drove down my road. I was nervous, even with the company of my two strong friends.

The car pulled up just shy of my house, and the driver put on the interior light, mumbling the fare for our journey. I handed some cash over to him, ignoring my friends' offers to contribute as I felt they were doing more than enough for me already, just by being there.

The driver acknowledged payment with a grunt, and the three of us stepped out of the car into the cloudy night. Wind whipped my hair around my face, and my eyes took time to adjust to the unlit surroundings after the brightly lit interior of the taxi. I saw unfamiliar shapes everywhere, merging into the inky streetscape around us.

Helen linked her arm through mine, and with Layla on my other side, the three of us walked quietly down the street, with no sound other than the rustling of trees and the clack of Layla's heels against the pavement.

It only took a few seconds to reach my house and we paused as one, taking in its silhouette against the night sky. Clouds scudded along, quickly providing us with glimpses of the moon which was trying its best to stay hidden.

Nothing looked immediately out of place on the property's façade, thankfully. Lights glimmered comfortingly from my neighbour's homes on either side, and a dim glow came through the small window in the front door of my own house from the lamp that I'd left on in the hallway. Other than that, the house was dark…quiet…at rest.

"Ready?" Helen asked.

"Yeah, sure…I—" Stopping, I squinted my eyes to narrow my view. I blinked, certain that my mind was playing tricks on me. But I was sure I'd seen something move. "Do you see that?" I pointed towards the house, to my bedroom window, where I'd left the curtains unpulled.

"What?" Layla stepped forward, and I grabbed the back of her coat, holding her steady before she could set off next door's motion sensor which would flood us all in light.

"There, by the top floor window on the left-hand side." I pushed my hair from my eyes, and the wind immediately forced it back.

The three of us stood, stock still, like a miniature representation of the Anthony Gormley statues positioned on Crosby Beach.

"I think it's just the wind," Helen whispered. "See? It's moving the branches of that tree around, that's all."

We stayed motionless, waiting for the wind to die down. Leaves rustled, branches swayed, and an empty plastic bottle rolled its way noisily down the pavement and into the gutter.

Then, just as I was about to admit that my eyes must be playing tricks on me, I saw it again. Difficult to pick out in the darkness, and if it weren't for the minimal light filtering through from the hallway of my house, almost impossible to see. But there it was. Not the branches of a tree waving in the wind, but a figure moving ever so slowly, *inside* the house.

FORTY-THREE

"Jesus Ellie, what are you doing?"

I'd started moving towards the house, but Helen had held on to me, stopping my progress as I had done to Layla only moments before.

"I've had enough of this crap. I refuse to let that man scare me anymore." I pried my friend's fingers from my sleeve. "He will not keep me out of my own home!" For once, instead of feeling scared and vulnerable and just letting things play out around me, hoping someone else would take control, I was filled with anger. How dare Saul come back to my house, taking advantage of the fact that I wasn't in it? It was time I took control of things once and for all.

"Help me talk some sense into her for God's sake," Helen hissed at Layla stepping in front of me.

Layla shrugged and clicked her tongue. "Maybe she's right. Perhaps we should all just go in and take the bastard by surprise."

"What? Are you nuts?" Helen's eyes grew large behind her glasses. "We should call the police!"

"He didn't exactly respond too well to that last time, did he?" Layla responded. "Maybe we could all go in together, outnumber him—"

"For God's sake, Layla, this isn't bloody *Scooby Doo* you know?"

"I know." She pulled a face. "I'm just saying…"

I slipped around Helen while she and Layla went back and forth and walked straight across my small front garden instead of going down the driveway and setting off the neighbours' motion sensor. I didn't want Saul to know I was coming.

"Ellie!" Helen hissed behind me. "This is a bad idea."

I turned and held my finger to my lips, shushing her, and she scowled back at me before turning her attention to Layla who was trying to follow my path, her heels sinking into the earth.

"Where the hell are *you* going?" Helen asked her.

"I'm going with her." Layla pointed at me and continued across the grass until she reached me. "Are you coming?"

Helen's shoulders rose and then fell dramatically in a sigh. "Fine. Let's do this together, but I'm calling the police at the first sign of any trouble." She took her phone from her coat pocket as if to prove her point.

"Deal." I turned around and headed to the gate at the side of the house.

"Wait! Where are you going now?" Helen whispered to me.

"Round the back, of course. The front opens right onto the hallway, and he'll hear us coming in. If I go in through the back door, it'll give us the element of surprise."

Helen pursed her lips, which I took to be regretful agreement, and I quietly opened the latch of the side gate giving us access to the dark passage between mine and the neighbour's house. I could hear their television faintly playing some Saturday night theme tune through their wall before the wind whipped it away from me and replaced it with a banging sound which seemed to come from my back garden. I looked at my friends, and I could tell without us sharing any words that they had heard it, too.

We crept forward, slowly, myself in the front, my left hand keeping hold of the wall of the house, steadying me. Behind me was Layla, and then Helen brought up the rear. All of us close together, strength in our solidity.

The sound came again. Bang. Then a pause as the wind dropped slightly, before kicking back up a gear. Bang, bang.

I stopped at the corner of the house, removing a few strands of hair from my lips which the wind had lodged in my mouth. Slowly, I very carefully edged my head around the brickwork, trying to make as small a target as possible for whatever was there.

The garden, while bathed in darkness, looked as it should. I watched the foliage intently waiting for something to leap out at me, or perhaps I was just putting off actually going into the house.

"Can you see anything?" Layla's lips were near my ear.

"Nothing, I—"

Bang.

Heart in my throat, I jumped back, stepping on Layla's toes and making her wince.

"Oh God, I'm sorry. Are you OK?"

She nodded and lifted her foot giving her toes a quick rub.

I peered back around the side of the house, just as another bang sounded, and this time instead of it raising my heart-rate, the sight of what was causing it made my heart drop so low I could have dragged it on the floor behind me.

The source of the noise was the back door banging against the frame. It was open…again.

FORTY-FOUR

At least this time I knew I wasn't going crazy.

Helen and I had made sure that all the doors were locked before we'd gone out that evening, so whoever was inside had to have a key or the skills to pick locks.

The locks had only been changed two days ago, Alex wasn't home yet, and I'd given the only spare key to Stanley next door that very morning. So, unless my kindly 70-year-old neighbour and his wife had taken up house breaking in their spare time, I could only assume that someone had indeed broken in.

What an absolute bastard Saul was. To try and use reverse psychology on me, to make me think that I was losing my mind, when in fact he was doubtlessly enjoying all this game playing. Trying to scare a woman who was home alone. What kind of sick person did that? I was nauseated that I'd fallen for his tactics, and it fuelled my anger even more. I was not going to let him get away with it.

Beckoning Helen and Layla to follow, I crept forward and slid through the door into the darkness of the kitchen. As I tiptoed further into the room, I could only make out a few objects dimly lit by the lamp in the hallway which valiantly attempted to throw its light into the gloomy kitchen.

My friends followed me in, and Helen pulled the door to behind her with a small click, shutting out the sounds of the wind which was getting stronger and stronger. We all stood facing each other, silent. Waiting. Our eyes flicked from one to another, to the doorway into the hall, and back again to each other.

"I'm going through," I mouthed, pointing towards the hallway, and Helen and Layla looked at each other then back at me, nodding their reluctant consent.

Turning away from them, I took a step over to the counter and pulled a knife from the chopping block, its blade glinting in the light from the hallway. Helen frowned at me, and I mouthed, "Self-defence."

"OK," she mouthed back, shrugging her shoulders while her eyes still begged me to put it back.

I continued forward, rounding the island worktop, and then paused. I could hear footsteps upstairs. I stood still, listening to whoever was up there moving around. Not creeping about, like I was doing in my own home, but moving with purpose from one room to another.

I held my breath, whipping my head back around to my friends who were frozen in place behind me as if we were playing a sick game of 'What's the Time Mr Wolf?'. Breaking the stillness, Helen held out her phone for me to see her dialling 999, the police only a touch of the screen away. Her finger hovered over the green button, ready for me to give her the word.

As one, we crossed the room, pausing again by the threshold into the hallway, where we once again stopped and listened.

Above us came a creak and then a scraping noise which sounded like wood on wood. I had no idea what the noises signalled or even from which room it was coming from. It sounded almost central to all of them as though they were coming from the upstairs landing.

Head cocked to one side, I continued to listen but heard nothing but me and my two friends' breathing for the space of several heartbeats. Then came a thud from above, and a grunt, proving that whoever was up there was definitely male. Like I'd had any doubt.

What was he doing? Going through my drawers? Defacing my clothes? My underwear? Seeing what other personal items he could take? I'd had enough.

A surge of adrenaline coursed through me, and without thinking any further, I stepped out into the dim light of the hallway. I vaguely registered Layla gasping at the suddenness of my movement as I reached stairs, taking them two at a time. I got to the top of the first short flight of stairs quickly and rounded the tight corner ready to take the next flight and face Saul head-on.

As I looked up towards the landing, the shock of what I saw hurled me back against the wall, almost taking me off my feet. The knife that had been so firmly clenched in my fist, fell to the floor, bouncing down the stairs to where my friends stood at the bottom, watching me.

"Helen?" I whispered through a throat constricted by fear. "Call for help. Now!"

FORTY-FIVE

Helen took a step towards me, her expression hidden, the lamp light in the downstairs hall putting her face into shadow.

I held up my hand, stopping her in her tracks and hissed at her, "Call the police and an ambulance…NOW!"

She stepped back, and keyed in the password for her phone, which must have timed out. As much as every fibre in my body screamed at me not to look, I forced my eyes to refocus back on the landing at the top of the stairs.

"Ellie? What's going on?" Layla breathed. I heard her tread on the stairs, but I couldn't speak, scared that any more words would trigger something unbearable. I continued to stare straight ahead to the landing, eyes and limbs paralysed in rictus. A lifetime passed in a snippet of time, and I wondered if this was what drowning felt like.

The gusts of wind had scurried the clouds along so that the moon had been freed from its restraints once more, and now its beautiful light shone through the upstairs window, illuminating the scene on the landing.

A still life.

Still.

Life.

A board placed across the opening of the loft hatch.

A chair placed underneath.

A man stood upon it with his head held low.

A rope uniting him with the board.

Still.

Life.

Layla, getting no response from me, turned just as I had done moments earlier and stood as motionless as if someone had nailed her feet to the floor. “What the fuck? Who’s that?”

I felt my tongue drop where it had been pressed against the dry hollow cave of the roof of my mouth, and although scared to speak, I forced myself to whisper the words laced with disbelief. “It’s my husband.”

As if waking from a daze and realising I was there, Alex lifted his head to look at me. Clutching his hands to his heart, as if to stop it from hurting, he uttered only two words:

“Look away.”

FORTY-SIX

I watched in horror as my husband took a step from the small chair that he'd been standing on. Then, as if propelled by some kind of powerful force, every fibre of my body zinged into action and every cell in my mind started firing with crystal clear knowledge of what I needed to do.

I climbed the second flight of stairs in what felt like a single jump, and as he took his second foot from the cushioned seat of the chair, I reached him, taking his full weight in my arms as he dropped.

The chair had toppled to one side, and I felt Alex's weight pressing down on me, heavier and heavier. I tried to brace myself, legs wide and back straight. His legs kicked and his hands flew to his neck, his body fighting to stay alive, but fighting me at the same time. I could feel him slowly starting to slip through my arms and I called out to Layla who was still frozen in place halfway down the stairs, eyes wide with shock.

"Help me, Layla! Help me, please!"

Thankfully, my words seemed to break the spell that she was under, and she scrabbled up the stairs to me, helping me to support his weight.

"The chair," I sobbed. "We need the chair. Can you reach it?"

Layla extended her leg trying to hook the chair with her foot, but it was just out of reach.

"Shit, no. Can you hold him if I let go?"

"I don't know. Oh God, Layla, I don't think I can. He's too heavy." My husband's tall frame was too much for me to support on my own and I couldn't ask Layla to shoulder that responsibility alone.

Alex had stopped struggling now, which, whilst making it easier to hold him, scared me to death. If he'd stopped moving, did that mean he'd lost his fight? Was it too late? I renewed my efforts to heave him upwards and open his airways.

"Ellie? Layla?" Helen's familiar voice filtered up from downstairs. "I've called the emergency services and they're on their way."

"Oh, thank God! Helen? You have to come upstairs. We need your help."

I heard her footsteps on the stairs as she took to them and registered the look of shock and incredulity which fell on her as she rounded the corner. Not allowing the revelation to freeze her as it had done us, Helen forced her way onwards, shouting, "Tell me what you need me to do."

Sweat pouring down my back, I yelled, "Grab the chair and put it underneath him."

She cast about for a moment before spotting it behind us, righting it, and placing it directly underneath Alex's feet. "It's there," she told us. "It's underneath him."

"Are his feet on it?" I asked.

"They are."

"OK, Layla?"

She nodded, blinking sweat out of her eyes.

"We need to lower him slowly, so his feet take some of his weight, alright?"

She nodded again.

We started to lower him gently, guided by Helen, who was trying to hold his knees straight, stopping them from buckling beneath him.

"Stop," she called. "It's no good. He's out cold and he won't be able to support his weight. We're going to have to cut him down."

She was right, of course. It was all well and good having the chair back underneath him, but it would be of no use if he couldn't support himself. "Right, let me think." We all held our horrific tableaux while I grappled with my thoughts. "OK, Layla, you and I need to lift him again and take his weight. Helen, go into the spare bedroom and pull out the dressing table stool."

Helen waited for us to take the strain and then ran into the bedroom, returning straight away with the stool.

"Now, find the knife. I think I dropped it down the stairs. We need to cut him down."

My friend immediately fled to retrieve the blade and she held it aloft like a warrior as she ran back up the stairs.

"Climb onto the stool and cut the rope. Quick, Helen."

She wasted no time in mounting the stool, knife in hand, and I saw her reach up before it dawned on me that she just wasn't tall enough. She looked at me, her expression frantic. "I don't know what to do. Oh shit. What do I do?"

Without hesitation, I ordered her down and she complied, following my next instructions to swap places with Layla. Of course, Helen wouldn't be able to reach the bloody rope. How stupid I'd been to even think it. Layla, on the other hand, was tall and with her heels on, she had a good few inches on both myself and Helen.

My shoulders were screaming now with the strain of holding Alex up even with Helen's help, but there was no choice. I pulled in my core and held fast, watching Layla as she climbed onto the stool. She reached above Alex's head and relief flooded through me to see her begin to saw backwards and forwards with the knife against the length of rope.

In the distance, I could hear sirens as the knife moved back and forth, back and forth. I prayed that they would get to us soon, but they sounded so far away.

"How's it going, Layla?" I asked, my muscles burning in pain. I could tell Helen was struggling as well as her face twisted with effort.

"It's…I'm getting there. It's really thick."

The sirens were a little louder. Closer. I willed them to hurry up.

"I don't know how much longer I can hold him up," Helen sobbed at my side.

"What are you talking about?" I asked, trying to hide my fear. "You're the strongest person I know. You can do this. *We* can do this. All three of us."

At my words, I felt Helen brace herself, giving a final push.

The knife continued to go back and forth against the rope, but slightly quicker.

The sirens were louder still.

"I think I'm nearly there." Layla's words were laced with disbelief. "Yes, I am." She paused. "Do I keep going? Will you guys be able to hold him?"

I looked at Helen, and while no words passed between us, none were needed. "We're ready."

FORTY-SEVEN

It all happened so quickly.

The small landing, now flooded with light was crowded with uniforms; black and white for the police, and dark green for the paramedics. I'd never been so thankful to see them as they seamlessly stepped in and took over the scene.

Now that I'd been relieved of holding Alex, I found that the last thing I wanted to do was let go of him, and I held tightly onto his hand while the female paramedic spoke to me gently but firmly, ascertaining the situation that she'd been called to.

"OK, Ellie, my name's Kate Williams. Me and my colleague, Vince, are going to do everything we can for Alex. I'm going to ask you to let go of his hand now, so we can do what we need to do for him."

I complied with her wishes, understanding that I needed to give the paramedics space while they worked. Moving out of their way, I watched as they laid Alex on his back, holding his head in alignment and keeping it still. I vaguely felt my friends move to either side of me, a hand on my arm and another around my shoulder, trying to keep me in some kind of alignment, too.

"His breathing's slow. We're going to need a bag."

At Kate's request, Vince produced a piece of kit from the bag which sat on the floor by Alex's head. Kate tipped his jaw upwards, then positioned a clear mask over his mouth and nose before starting to periodically squeeze the apparatus.

I heard a sob, before realising it came from me.

"It's OK, Ellie. He's doing good." Kate twisted her head towards the two police officers who were standing at the top of the stairs looking a little lost. "Perhaps you could take Ellie downstairs while we look after her husband?"

"No!" I cried. "I need to stay with him."

"I understand you're worried, Ellie, but it will be better for Alex if we can have some space to do our job properly." Her brown eyes were tired and kind. "We've got another unit already on the way to help us get him down the stairs, and until they arrive, we need to keep him ventilated. I promise you we will take good care of him."

I nodded mutely and she smiled at me, small creases appearing at the corners of her eyes before she turned back to Alex.

I allowed my friends to escort me to the stairs, and I almost lost my footing on the top one, falling against one of the policemen who caught my elbow, supporting me down to the bottom and into the lounge where I collapsed onto the sofa.

One of the police officers made milky tea for us all and I forced myself to sip at its sugary sweetness, vaguely registering the sound of more sirens and more people entering the house. The urge to run back upstairs to be with Alex was immense, but I wasn't sure my legs would be able to carry me.

My brain couldn't compute what had happened, and my hand automatically went to my throat to twirl my sycamore seed necklace before I remembered that I no longer had it.

My hand dropped, empty, to my lap and Helen scooped it up in hers, squeezing it tightly.

We sat there in silence, Helen and I on the sofa, Layla in the armchair by the fireplace, and one of the police officers stood awkwardly in the doorway. I had no idea where the other one was. I didn't really care.

Eventually, I heard the paramedics manoeuvring Alex down the stairs and I leapt to my feet, squeezing past the police officer into the hallway, in time to see my husband carried down the last few steps on a stretcher, with Kate slightly ahead, still ventilating him, keeping him alive.

They placed him onto a waiting trolley, and I watched as they wheeled it out of the front door towards an ambulance, light spilling from its open doors onto our driveway.

"Can I go with him?" My voice was quiet, tremulous, but loud enough to be heard by Kate who looked up and nodded.

"Of course, you can."

I climbed into the back of the ambulance, twisting to look out at my friends who stood in the driveway.

"You go." Helen reached in to squeeze my hand. "We'll take care of everything here."

Behind her, Layla nodded, a small, sad smile briefly ghosting its way across her face before Vince closed the doors.

I sat next to Alex and rested my hand gently on top of his, loving its familiarity and relieved at its warmth. I never wanted to let go of it again.

FORTY-EIGHT

As I got out of the taxi the next morning, I was relieved to see my front door flung open revealing Helen. She walked up the driveway towards me, her arms open wide, and I practically threw myself into them, allowing her to hold me tight.

Behind her, I saw another figure materialise in the doorway, and as she came forward into the morning light, I recognised Helen's fiancée, Chrissie.

"I hope you don't mind?" Helen asked. "She wanted to come and help."

"Of course, I don't." I held out my hand to Chrissie who stepped forward and took hold of us both.

"Come on, you two, come into the warm," she offered. "I'll put the kettle on."

Tea. It made everything better, didn't it?

I let the two of them lead me into the house and on into the lounge where I curled up on the sofa under a blanket.

"Where's Layla?" I asked Helen as Chrissie made her way to the kitchen.

"She's had to pop home, but she'll be back later to see you."

I nodded and closed my eyes, feeling them dry and scratchy with tiredness against my lids.

"You must be exhausted." Helen sat beside me. From the kitchen I heard the kettle bubbling to life. "How's he doing this morning?"

I opened my eyes and looked at my friend. "He's doing OK. Well…as OK as can be expected, I guess."

I'd been in touch with Helen the night before to let her and Layla know that Alex had come round, and his breathing and heart rate had thankfully been steady throughout the night. As his eyes had eventually focussed on me, they had filled with remorse and he'd pulled the oxygen mask from his face to speak, mouthing the words 'I'm sorry' over and over again while tears ran from his eyes to dampen the thin hospital pillow beneath his head.

"It was awful. Just to see him in so much anguish. And I never knew. How could I not have known how he was feeling?"

She squeezed my leg. "You mustn't blame yourself. You can't do that, or you'll drive yourself crazy."

"But I should have realised. I should have known something was badly wrong." I slammed my fist down on the arm of the sofa. "I feel like I've let him down."

"Don't be silly. How could you have possibly known this was going to happen?"

"I just…I don't know. I tried to talk to him, but he was like a closed book. I just wish…" My words petered out and I put my head into my hands. I felt so ashamed. I'd only been aware of how Alex's behavioural changes had affected my own feelings and my own life without questioning why. "I just wish I'd handled things differently."

"It's OK." Helen moved closer, putting her arm around my shoulders. "Come on, let it all out. Just have a bloody good cry."

"That's the thing." I dropped my hands. "I can't. I literally can't cry. It's like I already used up my quota of tears on all the other crap that's been happening, and now there's nothing left."

"You'll cry when you're ready." Helen rubbed my shoulder, her hand moving in a circular motion. "You're in shock right now. You've dealt with the most horrific experience and the adrenalin is just taking its time to wear off."

"I just feel like there's nothing left in me to give."

"Of course, there is. You just need some rest."

"Yeah. Maybe."

She was right. I desperately needed some sleep. I'd been awake for nearly thirty hours straight and those hours had been filled with enough drama to last me a lifetime, even without the build-up of the preceding weeks.

Chrissie joined us, filling the silence with the rattle of crockery on a tray, and she placed it on the low table in front of us. "Can I do anything else? Fix you some toast, maybe?"

I gave her a half-hearted smile. "No, thanks. I'm not hungry. To be honest, I might just take Helen's advice and take my tea upstairs to bed. Try and get some sleep." I swung my legs off the sofa, reaching for my mug of tea.

"Do you want me to come up with you? Stay with you until you fall asleep?" Helen's eyes were etched with worry.

"No, it's fine." I gave her a weak smile and left them in the lounge, exchanging anxious glances. I trudged up the stairs, grimacing as I turned the corner at the memory of what had confronted me the night before. Thank God Alex was going to be OK, as, otherwise, I'd never feel like I could step foot in this house again. As it was, it was hard enough just to imagine what might have been if we had arrived home any later.

I forced myself to climb the rest of the stairs using the bannister rail as a much-needed support. I was relieved to see that everything that had been left in disarray in the hallway the night before had been put in their rightful places once again. I made my way into the bedroom, noting that either Helen or Chrissie had already closed the curtains, turned on my bedside lamp, and pulled the duvet back ready for me to slip underneath. I put my tea on top of the bedside table and sat heavily on the edge of the bed, feeling what little reserves of energy I had left departing my exhausted body. Laying back, without even undressing, I pulled the duvet over me, and let my eyes close.

———

I woke up only a couple of hours later to the murmur of voices drifting up from the lounge. For a moment, I was seized with panic at the noises coming from downstairs when I should be home alone, but then I remembered that Helen and Chrissie were there. Relieved, I ordered my heartbeat to slow down, and rolled on to my side, trying to reclaim some peace.

The voices below continued. I couldn't make out what they were talking about as only the odd, raised word reached my ears. I lifted my head off the pillow, propping myself up on my elbow to hear better.

"You have to tell her."

"Shh. I know. Just keep your voice down, OK?"

Tell me what? Oh God, what else could there be? I pushed myself up and out of the bed covers, reluctantly leaving my safe cocoon as I padded across the room and back down the stairs.

I pushed the lounge door open to find Helen and Chrissie sitting side by side on the sofa, both now staring mutely at the TV, its volume so low that it may as well not be on at all. They turned in unison to face me.

"What is it you need to tell me?"

Chrissie sprung from her seat and took my arm, guiding me gently over to take a seat on the sofa next to Helen, whose eyes were now avoiding my own.

"You're up. I'm so sorry if we woke you," Chrissie said.

"I heard voices. Heard you talking."

Helen's eyes cast about the room, still not wanting to settle on me. It was unlike my straight-talking friend to not want to come out with something she needed to tell me.

"Helen needs to tell you something." Chrissie moved from my side to her fiancée's, squeezing her shoulder, and Helen looked down at her hand.

"I…oh God."

"What is it? You're scaring me."

She reached into her pocket and pulled out an envelope, and at the same time, Chrissie backed out of the room saying softly 'I'll leave you both to it. If you need me, I'll be in the kitchen."

"Hels? What is it?"

She held the envelope out to me. "It's a letter…from Alex."

My heart plummeted to what felt like the core of the earth as I took the offering in my hands. It had to be, didn't it? A suicide note.

Swallowing hard, I ripped open the envelope. Like pulling off a plaster. The sooner I did it, the sooner it was over.

"Do you want me to leave you alone?" Helen got halfway to her feet, before I grabbed hold of her arm.

"No. Stay with me? Please?"

She sat back down and rested her hand on my leg, the contact giving me the strength to open the pages of the letter. Alex's familiar scrawl met my gaze and I started to read.

As I read, they came. The tears. And I felt like I was drowning.

FORTY-NINE

My darling Ellie,

I don't know how to start this letter other than by saying I'm sorry. I'm so very sorry to do this to you, but I just can't go on like this anymore.

I know right now everything must seem very confusing to you but trust me, it's for the best that I'm gone. You will be able to move on with your life with someone who can give you what you want. What you need.

Yes, I know about *him*. About the man that you've been seeing and while I can't bear the fact that I've lost you to someone else, I can't blame you either, so please don't feel guilty.

I know about the card you hid away and the flowers he sent you. I saw all the messages you'd been sending each other when you left your phone at home that day. I know I shouldn't have breached your privacy, but I just needed to confirm things for myself. And then I saw you with him, kissing him, and it broke my heart.

I know I should be angry, but do you know what the worst thing of all is? I know it's all my fault. I've been a terrible husband. I've let you down. I should have talked to you, but I just couldn't find the words, and now it's too late.

You see, I've got myself into a hole that I just can't get out of, and I only hope that you can forgive me.

OK, here goes.

I lost my job weeks ago. They fired me for incompetence and, as much as I hate to admit it, they were right to do so. I promise you I tried my best, I really did, but I couldn't keep my act together. It seems like an excuse to blame everything on my accident, but I don't know what else to do. I know it looked like I was getting better, and for all intents and purposes I was, but it was in here…in my head, where everything was falling apart.

I couldn't keep on top of things, and I kept screwing up, and then I couldn't face telling you about it because I didn't want you to think I was weak. I couldn't heap even more on top of you after the accident and the knowledge that we could probably never have the family that you'd set your heart on. That *we'd* set our hearts on.

It must sound crazy, but I thought I could get away with not telling you at first. I was sure I'd be able to pick up another job quickly and then everything would be OK, but it just didn't happen, and the days soon stretched into weeks.

God, I feel like such a loser writing this down. I can't believe I've been so stupid, getting up each day and pretending to go to work. Some days, in the beginning, I did go to interviews, but nothing came of any of them, and more and more often I just found myself sitting in the library or riding on the train until it was time to come home again.

When my pre-scheduled work trips and the convention came around, I'd been lying to you for so long that it had become second nature, and I was way too ashamed to tell you the truth. So, I told you that I went away and, each day,

I'd sneak into the house while you were at work. In fact, it made things easier to deal with as it meant I wouldn't have to face you every day.

And even now, I'm such a coward that I can't look you in the eye and tell you all this. I'm a failure, Ellie. I've let you down and I've let us down. I have nothing of worth to give to anyone.

That's why I can't blame you for meeting someone else. I know that I've been absent from you, even when we've been in the same room, and it is the biggest regret of my life because I've lost you. I've lost everything.

I hope you can forgive me, my love. Please know that I love you more than anything in the entire world, which is why I want you to go on and be happy without me.

All my love, always,

Alex

Tears streaming down my face, I handed the letter to Helen to read, watching her eyes travel across the page until she reached the end and silently folded it in half.

"I don't understand." My voice in the quiet of the room seemed excruciatingly loud. "Where was he the whole time he was supposed to be away?"

Helen shook her head as if surfacing from a nightmare, then stood up and held out her hand. "Come with me."

FIFTY

Helen led me through the house to the back door, passing Chrissie in the kitchen who was sitting at the island nursing a cup of tea. She looked up at us and then quickly back down, staring intently at her cup as if trying to read our futures from the tea leaves.

Once in the garden, the cool air bundled around my shoulders and the grey sky pushed down on us as Helen led the way towards the shed. Without a word, she pulled open the door and, releasing my hand, ushered me forward. The inside of the shed was cloaked in gloom, the weak daylight from the doorway only managing to make it so far inside before giving up its effort. My nostrils were filled with the smells of wood shavings and grease, rust and dust, and years-old packaging.

My fingers felt against the rough wood on the inside of the doorframe and were rewarded as they stumbled across the light switch. I flicked it on and saw the familiar wooden shelves crammed with gardening equipment, old buckets, and everything deemed not fit enough to live alongside us in the house.

The work bench was graced with a small kettle, Alex's '*man cave*' mug and other tea-making accoutrements.

Beside them, a bowl, plate, and cutlery nestled together, overlooked by various packages of noodles, cereal bars, bottled water, and a half-eaten packet of Jammy Dodgers. I hadn't realised how much junk Alex had accrued during time spent tinkering on old bikes. I guessed it was hungry work.

Then, in the space of a heartbeat, I saw the rest of it. A narrow put-you-up bed was stretched out low to the floor half-heartedly covered by old, crumpled blankets and pillows that I vaguely remembered going on a supposed one-way journey to the loft ages ago.

At the head of the bed sat Alex's briefcase and his open travel bag, a bottle of vodka peering guiltily out of the top, an unlikely neighbour to his toiletries. A metal hanger gripped the lip of a shelf, dressed in one of his work suits. It hovered listlessly over shoes which had been polished for no purpose.

I stepped forward, my hands going involuntarily to my mouth, for what reason I did not know. To stop myself from speaking, crying out perhaps? To stop others from seeing my distress? Neither was of any importance. It was purely reflexive.

I heard Helen's light tread on the wooden floor behind me, her body stealing a little of the light from the open doorway. She didn't speak. Didn't have to. It was enough to know she was there.

My shin grazed against the low-slung bed, and I crouched down at its edge, gathering the blankets to me, taking in the stale smell of my husband that lingered on them. I noticed that he had tacked a photograph to the horizontal strut of the shelving on one side of the bed. The picture was one that Alex had always kept in his wallet and showed an image of me, the autumn light rich on my smiling face as I held out my left hand to my new fiancé for him to capture the moment on film for us to treasure always.

I reached for the photograph, pulling it free from its pin-tacked home, but lost my tenuous grip on the glossy paper, watching it flutter down to the tatty old pillow that lay at the top of the bed. It was only as it came to rest that I noticed the glimmer of something half-hidden beneath it.

Dropping to my knees, I leaned across and lifted the edge of the photograph to reveal the shimmering gold of my sycamore seed necklace underneath.

FIFTY-ONE

ONE YEAR LATER

I undid the strap on my helmet, relieved to be taking it off after the lengthy cycle ride. It had been so long since we'd ridden to this spot. Not since we'd first become engaged, in fact, so while it was a journey full of ups and down, much like our lives, it felt appropriate that this was the place that we should come to.

As I'd pedalled, I'd thought back over the last twelve months, each rotation of the wheels churning through the memories, and then letting them drift behind, leaving them where they should be…in the past.

Alex had thankfully made a full recovery from his attempt to…I still struggled to say the words out loud, but I made myself form them in my head. His attempt to take his own life. I couldn't run away from things anymore.

After a psychiatric assessment at the hospital, Alex had been diagnosed with clinical depression, which was unsurprising bearing in mind everything that he'd been through. I still kicked myself for not realising sooner. For not knowing my husband well enough to see the signs that his world was falling apart, piece by piece. It broke my heart that instead of being there for him, I had selfishly thought only of my own needs, reading his increasing separation from me as a lack of interest, a loss of love, when really, he was just trying to hide his pain to protect me.

It must have killed him to be sleeping in that shed night after night, only able to come into the house when I went to work. But it explained so much and, while each unfolding envelope of truth revealed such pain, there was relief there too.

Of course, it had been Alex who had taken the spare keys which were the only means of getting into the shed. He'd avoided speaking to me on the phone as much as possible as he had no idea if I'd be within earshot, and only spoke in a whisper when he felt it absolutely necessary to do so.

He was the one who had smashed the vase in a fit of anger after finding the flowers from Saul, and not poor old Mr Jones who had taken the brunt of my upset. Alex's jealousy and disbelief had also made him hide in the shadows across from the house at night to keep an eye on things, which had only made things worse…for both of us.

Alex was also the one who had left the back door open as he'd rushed from the house in a panic when I came home unexpectedly. His admissions had been heartbreaking to hear, but even though the situation was undeniably awful, it was a relief to know I hadn't been losing my mind.

I felt dreadful about everything that had happened, but I couldn't let the guilt take over. My therapist had told me as much numerous times when I'd started to go down that route. Guilt served no purpose. Alex's own counselling had been ongoing ever since that awful night and, while at first, he struggled to talk about things, over time he had started to open up more and more. And now that I was equipped to listen, we found a new, stronger bond between us.

I'd explained to him about Saul, admitting to the temptation that had been manipulatively offered to me whilst I'd been at my lowest ebb. Even though it obviously upset him to talk about it, he'd accepted the reasons behind what I'd done. He'd understood the spiral of both our behaviours impacting upon each other, spreading ever outward like the ripples of once still water disturbed by a cast-away stone.

I'd found out recently that Saul not only had a wife of his own who was very much present, but also a small child, both of whom he'd been willing to put at risk with his behaviour. Another thing for me to feel guilty over. Although, perhaps not, as Layla had told me she'd spotted him out in town on two separate occasions since with different women. I decided that if he didn't feel guilt, I shouldn't shoulder it myself. And, while he may not have been the stalker that I'd thought he was, he was undeniably a manipulative predator, and I'd just been unfortunate enough to fall into his radar at the worst possible time.

I looked over towards Alex who was shaking out a checked blanket underneath a tree, the same one under which we'd sat all that time ago, with hope in our hearts and light in our eyes. He looked tired after the long ride, unused to so much exercise these days. I hadn't been sure that he'd be up for it, but it was a beautiful Spring day and I was glad he'd agreed to come with me.

I unhooked from my bike the picnic bag that I'd filled with goodies at home, having had to coerce Mr Jones to get out of it first, and carried it over to the blanket, batting away Alex's offer of help. It felt good to be looking after someone else again, thinking about their needs instead of my own. I'd vowed to always try to be more aware of others going forwards. If nothing else, what we'd been through had taught me that.

"How're Helen and Chrissie doing?" Alex asked as I started to lay out our picnic underneath the lush canopy of the trees.

I smiled. "They're great. Looking forward to next week."

Alex smiled.

Helen had reached a whole new level of bridezilla that no one could have ever imagined. She'd been hesitant in involving me in things to start with, worried that it would give me extra stress on top of everything at home, but I'd assured her I wanted to help as much as I could, and it felt good to be able to offer her some respite. It had been great to get to know Chrissie more, too. She'd been wonderful in her support over the last year, and I was overjoyed to be able to now classify her as a friend as opposed to just being Helen's partner.

"What about Layla? Is she bringing anyone?"

"Didn't I tell you? She's bringing Nathan, so it looks like they're official at last."

"Great. It'll be good to meet him."

"Yeah. He's nice. I think you'll like him."

I was looking forward to the wedding so much. To have all the people that I cared about in one place to celebrate something so joyous. It was the perfect antidote to everything that had so nearly fallen apart.

I finished laying out the food and pulled out a half-size bottle of bubbles from the depths of the bag.

"Oh wow. What's the occasion?"

"We're celebrating," I told him as I opened it up.

A nearby family group looked over at the noise, a couple of them letting out a cheer, which made me smile. There'd be plenty of Champagne corks popping next weekend at the wedding, too. Noises of happiness and celebration. I'd have to think of a good excuse as to why I wouldn't be drinking, though.

I poured a glass for my husband and handed it to him, reaching back into the bag for my bottle of sparkling water.

Of course, I was desperate to tell my closest friends in the whole world of my amazing news, the miracle that I thought might never happen. But this time, it could patiently wait in line while we celebrated their happiness first.

I chinked glasses with Alex, and as I leaned forward to kiss him, the embers of the afternoon sun glinted against the golden sycamore seed that once more rested against my heart.

There was plenty of time. Around nine months to be precise.

A NOTE TO THE READER

I really hope you enjoyed 'Free Fall'. Everyone says how hard it is to write your second novel, and they aren't wrong. Still, I am tenacious, if nothing else, so here we are. Thanks so much for investing your free time in reading 'Free Fall', unless you've skipped straight to the end to find out the twist, in which case thank you for your support in buying the book anyway.

On a serious note, if you or anyone you know is affected by depression or any other mental health issues, please do reach out for help. Please don't suffer in silence.

I'd love it if you could take the time to leave me a review on Amazon or any other suitable forum. You can find me on Facebook, Twitter and Instagram, as well as my website: www.sherryhostler.com. Sign up to my Readers Club for news of my latest books and other treats here: sherryhostler.com/contact

ACKNOWLEDGMENTS

Wow, so it turns out I had a second book in me, which means I have a whole new load of thank you's to make.

A massive thank you to my brilliant hubby Jon for putting up with me. He continues to be the most wonderful person I know. I don't tell him often as I don't want him to get a big head, but I guess, now it's out there and he will undoubtedly refer to this acknowledgement in all future disagreements.

I can't leave out my bonkers German Shepherd, Barkley who makes me smile every day without fail. He makes sure I go outside for some vitamin D every day, which is much needed as otherwise I lose track of time when I'm lost in my characters' worlds.

Big thanks to my fabulous editor and friend Claire Jenkins who is still waving her red pen around far too freely for my liking. Thanks SO much to Peter Woodliffe-Thomas and Elaine Hunter for proofreading. If you find any spelling mistakes, I'll pass on their phone numbers to you. LOL.

I'd also like to say thank you to Steph Proctor for helping me with my police procedural research, and a whopping great thank you to my good friend Vince Clarke for his advice on paramedic procedures. More thanks go to Jessica Bell for a brilliant cover design, and a mahoosive thanks very much to the wonderful author, Dave Sivers for all his guidance. If you haven't read his books yet they are great, so go and check him out.

Thanks to all my friends, family, and my writing group for all their support. The fact that everyone has kept asking when my next book was going to come out has kept me going. I hope everyone enjoys it as much as the first one. If not, please just tell me you did anyway.

Finally, I would like to thank my muse…wine. I recently discovered a phrase from the illustrious Ernest Hemingway who is quoted to have said “Write drunk. Edit sober.” Wise words Ernest…wise words indeed.

ABOUT THE AUTHOR

Sherry is the author of the psychological thrillers 'Hypnotic' and 'Free Fall'. Before this she spent many years 'living the dream' in various jobs which have given her plenty to write about.

Sherry enjoys a bit of 90's dance music and thinks she does her best writing (and dancing) after a few glasses of Rioja, but this is possibly not the case. She loves her home in the rural southeast of England with her husband and dog, but often hankers for the sunny beaches of Australia where she used to live.

Her award-winning short fiction and non-fiction articles have been featured in Writers Forum, Hertfordshire Life, Vale Life, Dogs Monthly and various Cake magazines.

Keep up with Sherry's book news on sherryhostler.com or connect on:

facebook.com/SherryHostlerWriter
twitter.com/SherryHostler
instagram.com/adropofsherry

Printed in Great Britain
by Amazon

25065679R00158